SANDS OF ARGURUMAL

ARGURMA SALVAGER BOOK 3

S.J. SANDERS

❀ Created with Vellum

_I_ t was strange to think that a human who spent most of her life in crumbling ruins on Earth would feel more at home in space. After leaving the ruins of the _Evandra,_ and the fucked-up planet that served as its resting place, far behind them, Terri no longer saw the little ship as a prison. No, now she was an active member of the ship's two-man crew. Veral had taught her how to work many of the systems, and she participated in salvage assignments as well.

She knew that he still filtered out what he considered to be more hazardous assignments—no going to the firepits of Delthon Minor to locate a vein of delthon ore used in the construction of many high-class starships, for instance—but that didn't hurt her feelings any. Terri considered it a process of baby steps. At least he trusted her to leave the ship.

As gratifying as it was, she understood that some of that newfound confidence was due to the extra protection that the gymotakin symbiont provided. She personally appreciated the hell out of it, so as far as she was concerned, it made sense that Veral felt more comfortable with her out and about in the dangerous universe. The bio-tech was a nasty bit of machinery, after all. Yet she also knew, by his own admission, that he had since come to see just how capable she was.

Not that it stymied his overprotective nature, but his demonstration of trust had gone a long way in making a true home for the two of them on the ship they had renamed *The Wanderer*. Even Veral had agreed it was a good choice, since they spent considerable time wandering and taking on odd jobs. There had only been one dark spot in the recent months, one that she was now staring directly in the face as she lay in the medbay bed, trying to control her racing pulse. Her mate hovered over her at her side as he supervised the bed's scanner running over her.

Something was wrong.

Although Veral wasn't the most expressive male, he had a particularly pensive look on his face, dark mandibles clicking softly as he read her scans on the datapad in his hand. Shit. That just confirmed what she already knew... Her pregnancy was advancing abnormally fast.

Even with her human genetics taken into account, all of her scans until that point had indicated she would have a gestation period close to that of an average Argurma female, meaning she shouldn't have started to show for another year and a half. With a three-year gestation, Argurma offspring didn't begin to grow rapidly until the last four months of gestation.

She could tell just from looking at herself that something was wrong. Seemingly overnight, her belly had visibly grown. It currently resembled a melon, a year and a half before schedule. She bit her lip as she looked down at her exposed belly, the soft tunic pulled up over it.

Everything was okay. It had to be. But she couldn't help but feel a niggle of worry as she watched her mate.

At first, Veral hadn't been too concerned, assuming that they just needed to make adjustments for human physiological differences. He patiently applied cooling cream over the tight, itchy skin of her growing abdomen daily without comment. Now, however, the dark coils of his vibrissae rustled around his dark gray face with sharp rattling sounds that alarmed her as she slipped out of the medbed and joined him where he stood a short distance away.

Absently, she scratched lightly at the bio-tech symbiont imbedded in her forearm as she watched him.

"How bad is it?" she asked cautiously.

One brilliant cybernetic blue eye turned toward her. He took a deep breath and the thin, tentacle-like vibrissae settled once more around his muscular shoulders. With one finger, he projected a hologram from the surface of the datapad. A tiny smile tugged at the corner of Terri's mouth as she looked at the compact fetus curled up on itself. A little leg kicked, sending a burst of bubbles through her abdomen.

Resting a hand over her belly, she grinned at the tickling sensation and her mate's expression softened, his lips ticking up at the corners. It was fleeting, but sent warmth through her at their shared moment before his expression once again turned solemn as he returned his attention to the hologram.

"The fetus is growing at a rapid rate. At its current growth, I calculate gestation to be concluded within one hundred and fifty standard rotations. Roughly four lunars," he clarified with a disconcerted click of his mandibles. "Everything else is normal for an Argurma fetus, but the speed is alarming, possibly due to interference from the gymotakin symbiont."

His brows drew lower as he enlarged the projection and worked at taking measurements, turning the hologram to make notes at various displayed angles.

"I was not prepared to return to Argurumal so soon, but we may have no choice now. I was prepared to deliver our offspring here in the medbay, but with the interference of the symbiont and the growth surge, it would be prudent to have access to a skilled

3

Argurma medic who is more intimately familiar with our species' physiology," he muttered.

At her distressed look, he vibrated his mandibles in a reassuring purr. "Do not be concerned, anastha. The scans are showing that our offspring is healthy and otherwise developing normally. We are merely taking necessary precautions. They would have a better way of calculating the offspring's development and whether or not the symbiont will be an issue during or after birth, or how it might be affecting our offspring's development in ways this scanner's limited capabilities cannot detect. It is still too much of an unknown factor, and we appear to be running out of time."

"Considering that they wanted to experiment on me, I'm not sure how thrilled I am over this idea," she returned. "Can't we just go to a nearby space station and have a medic take a look?"

He shook his head. The shorter lengths, that were slowly regrowing from the damage sustained months ago from their tangle with pirates, whipped expressively with the movement.

"I have no intention of making our presence widely known," he stated flatly. "The Argurma are the only species who utilize cybernetic bio-tech. Although the symbiont is far superior and unlike anything we have designed, an Argurma doctor would be able to analyze the nanos that you acquired from our mating and any changes that may be occurring due to the symbiont. There is also the matter that it would draw too much attention to us. There is too much risk of information about our offspring getting to the council. The wisest course would be to attend a medic on Argurumal who would be both knowledgeable and trustworthy."

"Okay," Terri muttered doubtfully. "I'm assuming you know a place where we can lie low?"

He clicked his mandibles in agreement. "I do. My family line has holdings at a far outpost. It will keep our location known only to a trusted few. The medic that serves my line and those of my mother's house will be discreet out of loyalty alone."

"And you can trust them?"

His brow quirked slightly in the smallest gesture of surprise. "Of course. Medics are solely loyal to their maternal line. The medic who serves my mother's line was her cousin. The record-keepers who come when they receive alert of a birth are another matter," he growled. "By that time, we will be far from Argurumal."

Terri swallowed back a lump of fear as he continued to take measurements and make notes on the datapad. He was right. There was probably nothing to worry about. Other than growing quickly, their baby was healthy, and he was certain that they would be someplace safe while they got assistance. If he was confident about it, then she should be too.

Pushing back her worry, she used the opportunity to get a closer look at her baby. Her heart melted at her first real look at her baby. Vibrissae curled against its neck, its tiny features perfect. To her surprise, although the fetus was dominantly Argurma, she could see a little of herself in the shape of its smooth brow, nose, and delicately curved lips. The tiny buds of its mandibles were only just visible at its jaw.

At her side, Veral grunted. From the corner of her eye, she watched as he tapped a few character keys at the bottom of the screen and stilled.

"What is it?" Terri asked as she turned to face him, her heart jumping anxiously. "Is there something wrong?"

"A complication," he said slowly. "The fetus has developed to the stage in which Argurma sex is determinable. According to the scans, it is a female... Our offspring is the heir to my mother's house." His brow drew lower in contemplation.

"Well, that's good, right? That should give her some sort of protections... right?" Terri hazarded.

He cocked his head. "Perhaps. However, I am uncertain how this will affect our reception by my mother's kin. Since her death, my mother's second sister has doubtlessly been directing our holdings. A daughter of my blood would be the head of the household once she came of age. It could stir disagreement among my mother-kin."

"Which means what exactly?" she asked. "Why would they care if she inherits your mother's house?"

A raspy chuff left him. "Not her house in the manner you are thinking. My mother's household refers to our line's domestic complex, in which my mother's home was the fore wing overlooking the great gates. Unlike the Argurma in the cities, those who live farther out in the deserts keep to our ancestral ways. The entire complex and all of our produce will belong to our offspring by law, as it was my mother's before her, despite her sentencing."

The reminder of his mother's termination drew a heavy silence between them. Although he would not admit it, she knew that Veral struggled to deal with that loss. Although he claimed more than once to barely have any memory of his mother, she knew that he still hurt, and she felt that pain for him. Like Veral, his mother had been considered malfunctioning due to her programming's inability to suppress her emotions. Terri regretted that she would never meet her, for it was clear that he had loved her dearly, regardless of how much or little he remembered.

"It's possible that your family will be happy for our daughter's arrival," she murmured. "They might see it as gaining some small part of her back."

The corner of his mouth lifted, and he curled his large arms around her and pulled her against him. Despite her belly being large enough to be inconveniently in the way, she was able to comfortably rest her cheek against his chest. His voice rumbled through her ear as he spoke.

"Word among my mother's kin has suggested that the

malfunction is prevalent and hidden quite well among us. From what I understand, they never would have discovered her if she had not become enraged when I was separated from her for my first implants upon my adolescence." His lips tightened. "It displeases me that the implants block so many of my memories from my youth. I do not remember the sound of her voice or the image of her face. I just have impressions that come at times."

Terri wrapped her arms tightly around him, wanting more than anything to be able to take away his pain.

"Maybe returning there will help you remember."

His mandibles vibrated in a low, buzzing purr. "Do not concern yourself over it, anastha. Although I dislike my lack of memory, I do not suffer from it. It is far more important that we focus on our offspring."

She let out a discontent huff and he chuffed and pressed his mouth against the top of her head, his mandibles sliding through her hair. She allowed herself to lean into him until he gently pulled away.

"Go eat. With our offspring's accelerated growth, you will require extra nutrition," he instructed as he strode toward the medical bay's exit.

"Okay, and what are you going to be doing?"

"I will be on the flight deck inputting our route into the navigation systems for Argurumal. You can join me there once you are finished. And do not forget to eat a portion of axna fruit."

She scowled at his back, but it did not go unseen. Veral chuffed as slipped out the door. Despite herself, an amused smile danced on her lips as she followed him out the door.

Before turning down the small hall that would lead her to the ship's galley, Terri paused to admire the way the shiny blue cloth of his tunic clung to the heavy musculature of his body as he made his way down the corridor. Although he was sexy as hell in his skin-tight, flexible body armor, the sight of him in the simple tunics and robes of his homeworld that he took to wearing aboard the ship—now that he no longer seemed to feel that he needed to be armed to the teeth at all hours—never failed to take her breath away.

A gurgle from her stomach put her in motion just as he rounded a corner and led her the rest of the way to the galley. She didn't try to hold back her delighted smile. Although she had gone hungry often for much of her life, food was one thing she absolutely refused to go without and Veral spoiled her by providing all the best supplies for the replicator to sate her appetite and most of her cravings. A lack of food was the one thing that could ruin her mood, especially with her passenger snuggled within her womb.

She patted her belly as she programmed the replicator for her favorite dishes and grinned when Krono slipped inside when the first fragrant steam drifted up from the food. The dorashnal, what could only be described as a giant alien dog with black scales and his own mane of vibrissae, grinned up at her. She chuckled and tossed a bit of meat to him which he expertly snapped out of the air.

"Come on then, Krono. I've got plenty to share," she said as she carried her bowls over to the table bolted against one wall.

Krono ducked beneath the table and tucked himself against her legs, his enormous body warming her feet and calves as she slipped him chunks of food. She could practically hear Veral scolding her for sharing her food with the beast, which just made her grin broaden. He didn't approve of anything but raw meats for his friend, but it was so hard to say no to the shameless beggar. Right on cue, Krono put his large head on her lap and whined.

"I am such a sucker," she laughed, and she handed him another bite of meat. "This is our secret."

Despite Krono's "help," Terri packed away a fair amount of food before her stomach was satisfied and she headed to the flight deck. Although it was no doubt several days or perhaps weeks until they arrived on Argurumal, she wanted to see to the plotted course for herself. She was still nervous about approaching the planet after the Argurma warriors had attempted to capture her on Earth, but she couldn't deny an insatiable curiosity about Veral's home and family.

Besides, he was certain that they would be perfectly safe.

2

---

*V*eral pulled up the star chart, his lips thinning. He had hoped to delay returning to Argurumal... permanently. Taking his pregnant mate to his homeworld was the last thing he wanted. He had preferred not to return with his offspring at all, but with the youngling not yet born it added new complications. Although he was certain that Terri would protect herself and their unborn offspring ferociously, he also knew that her current heavily burdened state made her more vulnerable than before.

His fingers twitched against the armrests of his chair as he settled himself and mentally sent up the command to bring up the star charts for Argurumal and his current position on the view screen. Immediately the view of space blanked out as the charts layered each other. The last chart that opened up showed *The Wanderer's* position in the star system through which they currently traveled.

His vibrissae twitched as he shifted the charts around, looking for the quickest but least obvious route to his homeworld. Fortunately, most of the planetary security was on the desert flats, the side of the planet where the majority of the Argurma population lived in the tall cities built around and over the large ground water wells. Few bothered to scan the great dunes on the other side of the planet. It was a harder life out there, dotted with various outposts and family complexes that traded amongst themselves. Although the warriors from the great dunes were regarded as the strongest and hardiest among their species, it was no secret that few among the council worried about attack in that inhospitable landscape. An alien, even an unprepared Argurma from the cities, would find it difficult to survive in such an environment.

He frowned in consideration. He would need to keep close watch over Terri to make sure that the intense dry heat of the desert did not sicken her. Although she came from a desert environment, it was not as dry, nor was the gravity as heavy as it was on Argurumal. Despite her strength, cleverness, and resourcefulness, he was worried about his small mate. The planet would not be kind to her, and, despite his assurances, the odds were not in favor of his mother-kin being pleased with him bringing home an alien female.

Especially not one bearing an offspring of only half Argurma blood.

Tension radiated down his spine as he plotted out their course. As much as he preferred not to seek out advice on the matter, he opened a line to Kaylar. The male's mother currently sat at the head of the household. If anyone had any insight as to how his mother's sister might receive his mate and offspring, it would be him.

This better be good, Veral. You interrupt my hunt, Kaylar's brusque voice snapped through their connection.

Veral paused in surprise. He had given his cousin such convoluted coordinates to Earth, tracing the most haphazard route that he could come up with, that he had not truly believed the male would find his way there before turning his attention to something more profitable.

My apologies, cousin. Your hunt? he inquired cautiously.

The male's amusement came through so clearly that he could visualize Kaylar's sharp grin.

Clever of you to attempt to hide this planet from me. I imagine it is due to some softness you have developed when it comes to your mate that you wished to protect her people. It is admirable, but a waste of effort. What was it that you were truly attempting to do with this?

To delay you until you lost interest, Veral retorted honestly.

There was a stunned silence and then a chuffing laughter that filled their shared mental pathway. More than that, there was an edge of excitement that indicated that the male was on the trail of the one he pursued.

Clever indeed. Perhaps that would have been true once, but things change. This was worth the wait, and with all my assignments cleared, I have had nothing but time to unravel the tangled trail you gave me. Now tell me, to what purpose do you contact me now if not to inquire on the fruits of my hunt?

Does your mother, Featha, still head the household?

Another weighty silence fell before his cousin begrudgingly answered.

She does, but I have no immediate knowledge of anything going on within the household. She and I have not spoken in many revolutions.

That surprised Veral. Of all his mother-kin, Kaylar was the male who was entrusted in a way that Veral had never been due to his mother's misfortune, with upkeeping the welfare and honor of their line. Although Argurma offspring had their pasts erased, upon the finalization of their implants, they were reintroduced into their extended family units to provide them with guidance and tutelage even if the parents had chosen not to rear their offspring when they were younger. To guide a juvenile Argurma was considered the responsibility of the entire family, and those who had not yet met their offspring established lineage bonds with them, which determined inheritance.

As his mother's heir, Veral had not been forbidden from the Monushava complex of his mother's line. Yet no one had made a secret that there were concerns he would draw scrutiny onto their line rather than being the son of an unfortunate isolated case. It was one of the reasons that Veral had not felt duty-bound to remain on Argurumal, hiding his malfunctions like the rest of his line did. His absence had made it safer for everyone. So Featha took up the head of the line, and Kaylar was entrusted to guard it.

This turn of events, however, was not one that Veral had ever calculated for.

For what reason?

Another mirthless chuff filled their connection as well as a general dismissive feeling.

My mother did not like that I refused to mate. She did not find my reasoning satisfactory because I did not wish to bring a female to our complex whom we would all have to keep pretense around. I was not amenable to her objection over my refusal. It has been five revolutions, twenty-three rotations, four hours, and three minutes since I was last in communication with her. For what purpose do you wish to know?

There may be a medical emergency with my mate, Terri. Something unexpected has occurred, causing our offspring to develop unnaturally fast. I will need to seek the opinion of our line's medic.

And you are worried that she will not be welcoming, Kaylar reasoned.

Among other things, Veral agreed. He hesitated for only a moment as he debated with himself on how much to tell. *Terri carries a female of the line.*

Tension flooded the pathway, and a sort of shocked stillness that Veral could appreciate. When Kaylar spoke again, his mental voice was halting as if he were attempting to find the correct response.

This is surprising... Are you aware of the reason that the council wishes to have Earth females?

For some experiments. Terri mentioned something about breeding, but there is a high probability in her moment of duress that she misheard. Our kind doesn't breed with others.

She is correct, in a manner of speaking, his cousin admitted slowly. *They want to dissect and study the effects that breeding and bonding with one of our males has on their physiology... not only on the females but on any offspring conceived. They have been unable to find the cause of the malfunctions within our own species and are hoping that observing the alien females might give them further insights to where inhibitors can be placed without doing significant damage. To our knowledge, we have had no other instances of mating bonds between an Argurma and another species, much less offspring bred, and so the council sees this as a profitable opportunity.*

Veral's claws extended from his fingertips and dug into the metal of the armrest with a metallic screech as a tremor of rage ran through him. His cousin's silence was understanding even though the male was currently in pursuit to fulfill the whims of the council.

And yet you hunt for them, he bit out.

I do what the council demands. We both know the risks of going up against them. You have gotten away with your unlicensed departure from Argurumal, but I cannot risk their further disapproval on our line. It does not bring me pleasure, but I will do my duty.

Releasing the armrest, Veral dropped his head into his palm and rubbed the sensitive spot just above his orbital sockets. The bone was thinner there, unprotected by the thick bone that covered his brow. Unfortunately, it brought him little relief from the tension that clawed through him.

And you have no problem hunting and caging a female knowing that you hand her over to death? he asked, unable to avoid pricking at his cousin's reasoning.

The feeling of forced nonchalance came through so strongly that Veral was disturbed by it. Kaylar was being dishonest but would not admit it even if Veral confronted him with it.

I cannot show any feeling toward it. You know that. Our programming is for obedience. I will be immediately labeled as malfunctioning if I do not control myself and keep some distance. As you should have done. You would not now be in this situation if you had.

Veral thought of his mate, who was likely eating at that very moment in the galley, and their offspring whom he had seen so clearly on the hologram. He was protective of both of his females and would not give them up for anything, not even if he had known then what he would be facing now.

I regret nothing.

Good, since you have little choice on the matter now. As for your mate, it is not wise to take Terri there, but I understand your reasoning. Do not be concerned about my mother. Despite my arguments with her, I know that our line will keep Terri and her young safe. A female of the line will be celebrated, even if they need time to become accustomed to the idea of the offspring being half-alien. But they will help even if it is to upset the efforts of the council. Many of the females believe that our malfunctions are natural and will resent the council's experiments to eradicate it.

Veral bowed his head, comforted by his cousin's observations as he finalized his course.

My thanks, cousin. He hesitated but tentatively offered his advice. *When you find your prey, I ask that you not be too hurried to bring her back to the council. Really see the female and think hard about what your decision will mean.*

A sigh drifted through their connection, accompanying a reluctant agreement.

It will change nothing, cousin, but I shall keep your advice in mind.

Of course, he replied just before the connection between them closed. His lips twisted in a smirk as he considered just what his cousin may be in for when face to face with a human female, trying to reason with her rather than just hunting a nameless prey.

Soft footsteps drew his attention to the entrance of the flight deck, and his mandibles vibrated with pleasure at the sight of his mate on deck, Krono lazily striding at her side. She grinned as she slid into the chair beside his command station and leaned forward to press her lips against his jaw in affection. As she drew back, a soft sound escaped her, her eyes riveted to the viewing screen.

"Is that our trajectory?"

"It is," he agreed. He moved his hand, drawing up an image of the orbital path around Argurumal. The red planet gleamed like a gem broken with black lines of hard, jutting stone of their mountain ranges. "And this is our destination."

"Amazing," she whispered. "And all of that is sand?"

"Everything red. The black striations are mountains." He drew up one section of a sprawling red desert near a wide mountain range on the southern continent of the side of the planet hit most frequently with the storms that shaped the great dunes. "This is where the Monushava complex is located. The household of my line," he clarified.

Terri leaned forward and folded her hands together before pressing them to her lips as the screen drew closer until she could clearly see the wind-whipped sands stirring as lightning broke out over the deserts. A shiver ran over her. She swallowed and gave him a weak smile.

"I guess that is home."

"Home," he said slowly, tasting the unfamiliar word on his tongue.

He was uncertain how he felt about it. It did not feel like anything he recognized as home. *The Wanderer* was his home. Even before Terri had come and made it into a true home for them, it had been his sanctuary. He did not associate any such feelings with the complex that he had not seen since his adolescence and his mother's death. He shook his head slowly and met his mate's eyes.

"No, anastha. It is merely a place that we are going as necessity demands. This is our home, not that place."

She gave him a doubtful look, but he chose to disregard it as he drew up her hand to his lips and pressed his mouth against the delicate skin of her knuckles. He did not care about his mother's line hidden away in the complex. They had made no effort nor any indication that they wanted him. Not like his Terri. All he cared about was his mate.

wo weeks was all the time that it took to arrive on Argurumal. The ship dropped down over a vast desert on the opposite side of the planet from most of the major cities that had formed around supplies of natural ground water. The darkness of the desert at night as they skimmed over the sand reminded her a lot of home, except the desert floor wasn't hard and compact but rather a rolling landscape of red sands that she could clearly see from *The Wanderer's* front exploration lights.

Terri stared as the complex slowly came into view. It looked like a small walled-off village except that it was one large, winding house rather than numerous tiny houses. The tops of the tall walls were barely visible behind the enormous, gated wall that surrounded the property. The black stones of the structure and wall were nearly identical in composition, each swirled with red sediments, giving the place an almost magical look. Terri wondered if the blocks were cut and hauled down from the mountains piece by piece. They certainly didn't look anything like the synthetic structures they had seen in their travels. They didn't even look like the old brick buildings she'd seen on Earth. She wondered how much of that was fact and how much was illusion.

A society as advanced as the Argurma wouldn't be living in stone buildings.

She turned to look up at Veral seated at her side. He stared out ahead at the landscape, his expression closed, not revealing a hint of what was going on internally.

She leaned toward him. "A penny for your thoughts," she murmured.

His eyes snapped up to her, narrowing at the corners slightly as they did whenever he was trying to work out something that he did not understand.

"I'm interested to hear what you're thinking of right now," she clarified with a smile. "A penny is a coin that was used on Earth a long time before I was born. Like offering a credit to hear whatever's on your mind."

A soft, amused snort left him. "A strange sort of bribery to reference," he remarked. "If you merely mean that you wish to know my thoughts, then say what you mean, anastha."

"Fair enough," she chuckled. "So, what are you thinking?"

A slow hiss escaped him. "I am thinking that it has been a great many revolutions since I have been here. We have little choice but to come here, but I am uncertain of how my mother-kin will greet you. I will be displeased if they disrespect you."

"Ah," she sighed. "Yeah, I admit I am a bit nervous. How huge and rugged everything is doesn't exactly put me at ease either. It looks like it's inhabited by a whole bunch of warriors who are going to come swarming out at us without a moment's notice."

"Astute observation. The Great Dunes people are comprised of many strong families. The greatest warriors of Argurumal can be found within the provinces of this side of the planet."

"From where I'm standing, that doesn't surprise me any. I guess I just expected your home to be a bit more... I don't know... technological," she murmured.

S.J. SANDERS

Veral chuffed at her side, his vibrissae sliding with his amusement. "It has an intentional design. The outer wall is stone. It protects and insulates us from the harsh desert. It is meant to be simple and durable. You will see that the protected interior is fashioned for our technological needs."

She gave the stone gates a skeptical glance as the ship moved off to the side and slowly began to descend into what she assumed was a large docking structure attached to the side of the wall. She frowned. Nothing there looked like it belonged to any species who soared through the stars in superior starships. Instead, everything she had seen looked like it was better suited to keep out some sort of monstrous beast. Veral chuffed again as the complex disappeared from sight, behind the thick stone wall that now surrounded *The Wanderer*. He had no doubt noted her expression and had been entertained by it. If he was, he didn't otherwise comment as he gently took her arm and led her from the flight deck through their ship. She was grateful for the support when the impact of the planet's gravity hit her fully as the ship powered down. A soft groan of dismay eked out, but she didn't complain. It was a little bit more difficult to move quickly or with ease, but it wasn't *that* bad.

Exiting the port, she glanced up to see a large dark metal shield slide silently shut above them, enclosing their ship in the docking area. The complete darkness of the docking bay made her freeze until several interior lights suddenly snapped on, casting pale illumination. Veral's own eyes glowed in the dim lighting, letting her know without a doubt that he could see perfectly well. Still, she was comforted by some range of visibility available. Curling her fingers tighter around his, she stared at her surroundings in awe, Krono a noticeable presence as he trotted at their heels, until they finally came to another gate at the end of the corridor.

At first, she wondered if they were going to have to bang on the door or do something to get someone's attention, but to Terri's surprise, the gate swung open with a heavy whoosh of displaced air and sand as it parted to reveal a beautiful stone courtyard lit up with electric lanterns filled with pulsing energy, casting a soft pinkish glow over their surroundings.

Enormous dull orange and puce potted plants filled the perimeter of the courtyard, intersected by plants of softer pinks and lavenders that clustered in the shade of the larger plants. In the middle of the courtyard was a shaded foundation in which she could make out the ripple of water from the cascading drops that descended from a cubic figure in the center. In such a dry world, that rippling water called to her, but a gentle tug from Veral brought her back to reality as he led her further in the courtyard. From where she was, she could just barely see a doorway peeking out between the dense fronds. That was clearly their destination, given the direct path Veral set toward it.

The doors parted, and a large female stepped out. About as tall as Veral and with similar features, she was wrapped in a crimson robe with a simple belt just under her breasts. Glowing blue cybernetic eyes turned to Terri and stopped, widening slightly at the corners. A hiss left the female, and she strode forward, mandibles spread wide with aggression as she grabbed a handful of Veral's longer vibrissae.

Terri's mouth dropped open, in equal measure horror and insult. She knew damn well what it did to Veral whenever she grabbed them, and for this female to her put her hands where they didn't belong made her furious. Thankfully, Veral didn't seem to be enjoying it. He snarled at the female, his own vibrissae widening in response. Terri didn't wait around to see what happened next. She stepped forward, her back rigid as she closed in near the female. With cords of reinforcement from her symbiont lacing over her hand, she reached forward and closed her fingers around the wrist of the Argurma's offending limb.

"Release him," Terri demanded.

The stranger's eyes narrowed on her, but she barely had time to react when the female released Veral's hair and whipped around in a smooth motion, her hand snapping toward Terri as a long, thin metallic cord shot out from the Argurma's wristband. A squeak of alarm escaped Terri as she attempted to evade, but the cord snapped around her wrist, the whip-like metal twining around her wrist seconds before she was jerked forward off her feet. Her symbiont tried to react, but the metal whip was wrapped too tightly around it and blocked the tendrils that attempted to escape to defend her.

Terri met the female's triumphant gaze, her lips parting with surprise.

Krono snarled loudly, throwing himself protectively in front of Terri, but Veral's roar startled them both as her mate leaped forward, barreling into the other female with enough power that it stunned the female. Her whip slacked and fell from around Terri's wrist seconds before he sent the Argurma flying through the air. Krono huddled in front of her, providing comfort even as she cringed at the overly loud crack of the alien's body impacting a tree.

They weren't getting off to the best of starts.

To her surprise, a low chuff rose from the tree as the female pushed herself slowly to her feet, her vibrissae stirring in the manner that Veral's did when he was pleased with something.

"Enough, Navesha," Veral growled as a wide, closed-lipped smile stretched across the female's face as she retracted her whip back into her wristlet.

"Very well, I will concede victory to you. It seems that mating has made you a formidable opponent, in any case." She turned a curious look to Terri before her eyes returned to Veral. "It is interesting that, though rumors have proven true that you had mated with a strange alien, nothing spoke of her ferocity. Well chosen,"

Navesha chuffed, her hand slapping the red dust from her robe-covered thighs.

An unamused growl left Veral as he moved to Terri's side, his eyes anxiously running over her. Krono dropped back, taking a guard position at their side as Veral tucked into his side.

"The last you saw me, Navesha, I was barely an adult, just graduated from my training programs. That was many revolutions ago," he rumbled irritably. "All the same, I did not expect to be accosted by you."

The female shrugged unrepentantly. "The situation merited a test once I saw for my own eyes that you had indeed taken up with a primitive. Featha is displeased that you sought a mate outside of our customs. She would have looked the other way for any other male, but you are the heir of the line. Mating and breeding an alien is a great insult to her. She had hoped that once you gained control of your volatile emotions and returned that she could help you arrange a proper mating."

"It was clear that I was not welcome here," he growled.

Navesha shook her head. "The household would not have been safe when you were younger and lacking control. Your mother would have trained you herself during your juvenile years had her malfunction status not made her suspect, and you too by extension, by the council. But Featha was unhappy that you left the planet. It was always her intent that eventually you would return to continue the line with a worthy female. She spoke of it often in the past."

"And I have," Veral hissed. "Terri carries my young. This is why I have returned. I need to speak to Featha at once."

"An heir?" Navesha said slowly, her brow ridges rising. "You mean…" At Veral's nod, her expression tightened. "Featha is not going to like this," she growled. "I will be honest with you: none of the females of your mother-kin's line will." She let out a slow breath, her vibrissae puffing out around her head slightly. "How-

S.J. SANDERS

ever, your… mate… is safe here. I will swear to ensure it. But you will still have to face Featha's displeasure. Your meeting should be interesting," she said as she broke into another soft chuff of laughter.

With a whirl of red robes, she strode away from them, heading toward the door with precise steps. As they followed the female, Terri glanced around curiously, searching for the familiar, shadowy form of dorashnal. Shouldn't she have one? Didn't everyone? She searched her memory, trying to recall whether Veral had ever mentioned it as he led her inside the cool interior.

The door slid closed behind her, and Terri suddenly wished they were back in space and as far as possible from everything on Argurumal. Licking her lips, she tried to ignore the sinking feeling in her stomach as she allowed Veral to pull her along after Navesha's retreating figure as they walked through the corridor to a destination that Terri wasn't the least bit eager to reach.

4

*V*eral narrowed his eyes at Navesha's back and hissed. He had anticipated just this problem arising, but he did not know how to appraise his cousin's offer. What did she have to gain from it? There were no bonds between them outside of their common ties to their line. Logically, it would not be enough to protect Terri against the other females should they prove hostile toward his mate. There was no reason for her to act in a way that could jeopardize her own standing among their mother-kin. She had to want something.

Terri glanced over at him curiously and leaned in.

"What's wrong?" she whispered.

He grunted in reply as he kept his attention trained on his cousin, watching for any sign of deceit. He did not wish to share his concerns with her. Terri was under enough stress and he did not wish to add to it. He knew just from her expression that she would not let it go. At least his mate was no longer offering credits in exchange for his thoughts.

It had disturbed him that his mate would offer to pay for something that he would happily give her freely even if she had not intended him to take it literally. She never had to do more than ask. He was pleased to share everything with his mate and offer it to her. Offering a barter between mates was an extreme insult… one he had ignored knowing that she was of a different species. Regardless, it had still pained him more than he would have expected. It was his responsibility to provide for his mate and their young, for him to give for her comfort. Not for her to give to him.

He met her eyes, looked over meaningfully at Navesha briefly before he met Terri's gaze again and shook his head. He would tell her, but not until they were alone. Terri thinned lips back at him unhappily but remained silent as she walked at his side.

"It is late," Navesha said over her shoulder from where she paced ahead of them. "I was overseeing my station for the first half-night duties when your ship's AI alerted me to your arrival. I was surprised by your sudden appearance, but even more so that your vibrissae appear butchered. You appear significantly damaged compared to the regal bearing you once bore. I am certain that if it were not for your genetic identification markers, none of us would have recognized you, not even Featha."

"When will we be meeting with her?" Veral asked, his eyes skimming over halls that he had hadn't lain eyes on in many revolutions. It had been a long time, but not so long that he couldn't recognize that this was not the route to the gathering room.

Navesha gave him a knowing look and inclined her head. "Not until morning. Since Featha and the others will sleep for several hours yet, you will be permitted to stay in your private chambers for the night until the head mother is available to meet with you." She opened a door to his chambers and gestured to it. "I will return for you in the morning when she is ready to see you. As these apartments are yours, with this entire wing once belonging to your mother, no one will object to your residence here. You should be undisturbed here until I arrive."

"Thank you," Terri murmured, eyes roving curiously around the rooms that made up his private chambers.

Krono immediately peeled from his mate's side, dropping onto the comfortable mat just in front of the sleeping platform. A heavy sigh huffed from the dorashnal as he watched over them. Navesha shook her head at him but made no effort to follow them in. Instead, she remained just outside of the door until they were inside. Only then did her head drop in a curt nod just before the door silently slid shut.

Veral's breath hissed out of him at length, and he lifted his hand and placed his palm on the keypad beside the door. Although it felt absurd to lock his chambers against his mother-kin, he was not going to take any risks with Terri and their offspring. At his touch, he connected with the systems of his chambers so that, with a single thought sent into the panel, he locked it, ensuring no one else could open it, before he turned to see to his mate. She stood among the muted silver and black of his bedroom decor as the single mark of brightness in all his surroundings. One of her eyebrows arched as she surveyed the rest of the room, and she made a small sound at the back of her throat.

"Your people certainly do like a dark decor," Terri observed.

He nodded his head. "It is simple and efficient."

Terri gave him a puzzled look. "*The Wanderer* has a lot of metal, but it's nowhere near as dark and dismal as this."

His ear twitched and turned slightly toward her as he considered her words. There was a difference between the two. He could not deny that. But the simple comforts that he added to his starship since mating were little compared to what was available on his home world. He had noted that his mate had a penchant for picking brighter colors, but she did not understand just how much the complex contained the most desirable comfort and tranquility.

"A starship is designed to be utilitarian. It is not the same as the household of one's line," he said. His vibrissae flared and flattened anxiously. Despite the fact that they were not staying, he wanted his mate to see the beauty and strength of his line. He wanted her to smile, not grimace as she was currently doing. His mandibles snapped as he drew in a sharp breath of what he hated to admit was injured pride.

"It is not dismal," he continued, a disgruntled growl escaping him on the last word. "Not the most luxurious on Argurumal, but it is a worthy complex for our line, equal to any other successful line who dwells upon the Great Dunes." He gestured to the dark walls. "The complex is made of the finest black stone, enhanced only by the metal tech adjoining it to fulfill our needs. You may not see it now, but the darker fabrics are meant to compliment the walls without being too distracting or disruptive to the mind, while keeping our interior residence as dark and cool as possible."

His mate glanced around slowly, her expression blank as she further took in her surroundings. When she met his eyes again, he noted the effort she expended to force a genial smile.

"I see," she murmured but he shook his head in immediately denial.

She couldn't truly know until she experienced the relentless brutality of Argurumal for herself.

"No, you do not." Veral tipped his head and sighed. "You have not seen Argurumal during the day, so until you do, you cannot understand. The brightness of our sun and the intense heat of it will make you long for and appreciate the darkness within our walls. But you should be pleased to know that there are always the shadowed gardens of the courtyard when you seek something a bit brighter," he amended, winning a small smile from her.

"Oh, okay," she murmured as she stepped over to him, her hands sliding up his chest on their path to curl around the base of his neck. "I suppose you make a good point. I just need time to get used to it."

He brushed the tip of his nose against her hair, his eyes half-closing blissfully as his mandibles slid through her hair, delivering a fresh burst of her perfume over his scent receptors. He kissed the top of her head and allowed his mandibles to vibrate in a soft purr.

"We will not be here long. Just be patient, anastha, and we will be back to our starship soon."

Terri silently nodded, though her expression became slightly more pinched. She took a deep breath and offered him a more genuine smile that eased a tightness within him that had gone unnoticed.

"I'll be fine," she said softly, her palm stroking the base of his neck, toying with the vibrissae as they curled around her fingers and clung to her. "Like you said, we are safe here. It's just an adjustment. No reason to talk about leaving when we just got here." She swallowed. "It seems to me that you have some unresolved things to see to with your family. We have to be here anyway, so we will kill two birds with one stone."

His brow dipped. Although he did not know what exactly she spoke of, he was able to infer her meaning well enough. She was encouraging him to make the most maximum use of their time there. Although he had not wished to deal with the matter of his inheritance and had been content to leave it in his mother-kin's care, he knew that he would not be able to avoid it long.

Terri was right. Better to deal with the unresolved matters within his line in light of Navesha's words.

Vibrissae twisting lightly around him, he growled unhappily but pressed his lips against the top of her head.

"I will attempt to resolve our daughter's place within our line quickly," he murmured as his hand skimmed down over Terri's belly to flatten against the swell of his offspring snug within her mother's womb.

He could feel his mate's shiver of apprehension and could taste fear rising only to be squashed beneath her control.

"They won't hurt her… right?" she murmured.

"They will not," he assured her. "Her presence is inconvenient to them because of her origins alone. My mother's sister is most unhappy that I have mated outside of our species—something that no one else has dared to go against the council and do. But they will see your strength, and it will be as I said on your home planet: you will win much admiration. Our daughter can only be accepted as one of the line."

Terri tucked her head against him and sighed. "I wish I could be so confident of that."

"You will see, anastha," he purred.

She squinted up at him. "Navesha made it sound like there was a mate already all picked out for you."

Veral chuffed. "A true mating as we possess is uncontestable and unchangeable. Before you, any female my aunt would have chosen for me, I would have to have been injected with the hormones to trick my body into beginning a bonding process. This is no longer a concern."

Terri bit her lip with an uncertainty that he hated to see on his mate's face. "Are you sure? They… they couldn't attempt to force you to mate with another by doing that, could they?"

He stilled as he felt the symbiont stir against the back of his neck. It was responding to her distress. He began to vibrate his mandibles again in a low purr, seeking to ease his mate and hopefully retract the metal slithering against the back of his neck.

"No," he rumbled through the purr of his mandibles. "Once a mating is done, it cannot be overridden or reset with another female. Featha will be displeased for a time, but she will come to find peace with it."

It twisted with a slight scratch of barbs that suddenly covered it for only a few seconds as Terri trembled against him before she finally sagged against him. The moment she relaxed, the barbs disappeared, and the metal slipped back into the symbiont on Terri's forearm.

"Okay, I can do this," she murmured against his skin.

He nodded his head from where it was rested against the top of hers. "You will be magnificent, anastha. And after we meet with the head of the line, we will have the medic brought to see you directly. Then, as soon as possible, we will leave."

A soft sigh slipped free from her. "Okay," she said. "I hope it will be that easy."

Veral threaded his fingers through her hair. Lifting his head, he looked down at her as his fingers curling to gently knot the strands within his fist. Terri stilled against him, but at his gentle tug she dropped her head back to meet his eyes.

"Nothing is easy, anastha, least of all on Argurumal. But we will conquer and be triumphant against everything. There is no other way."

Her lips twisted into a smile a moment before he dropped his mouth down to claim them with his kiss. Terri melted against him, and he slid his hands down beneath her rump to lift her up high against him. He carried her over to the sleeping platform and set her carefully upon it. Desire and love swept over him as he stared down at his mate. It held him in place until she sat up and reached for him to draw him down onto the surface with her.

5

erri sighed with pleasure, her back arching as Veral's rough hands pushed her tunic up. It didn't take him more than a couple of minutes to divest both of them of their clothes. She felt the rush of cool air brush her skin with the absence of his body's heat, but she didn't even have time to object before he was once more stretched out against her.

His palms cupped her breasts eagerly and she mumbled soft encouragement as he gently gripped them, his thumbs flicking over her nipples. They were extra sensitive lately, and the action sent a tongue of lightning shooting straight down to her belly. There was a light, erotic scratch of his claws as he toyed with her breasts. He did not retract them until his hands swept lower to caress her belly lovingly for a moment before diving between her thighs.

Veral parted her legs, and one hand remained gripping one thigh as his other hand cupped her mound. Two fingers slicked down, grazing her clit as they parted her folds and pushed within her. His thumb circled her clit, sending tiny shocks of pleasure through her as he slowly began to thrust his fingers in and out of her, preparing her in a way that only a male who was now very familiar with her body knew how to do.

Her breath came out in tiny gasps as she struggled to remain in control of herself. She had no idea how close anyone else was to them and certainly didn't want to wake anyone. Considering that she had to face his relatives in the morning, she didn't want to stand in front of everyone knowing that they had heard her crying out in a passionate moment. She certainly wasn't quiet during sex. They both knew that.

Hence the reason why currently Veral's eyes were narrowed on her, a low growl rumbling from him.

"You will not hold back and hide from me," he hissed.

A shiver ran through her, her belly clenching in reaction.

"I'm not," she shot back. "I'm trying to hold onto a bit of dignity and not wake anyone."

Something hot flared in the glow of his eyes and his face set into hard determination.

"There is no shame in this. Let them wake. Let them hear and know I am well bonded."

He dropped his head, his mandibles opened at an angle so that they rested against her inner thighs as his mouth attacked her sex aggressively. His two long black tongues flicked against her slit as they caressed and dove within her. Her hips bucked against his mouth, a low cry ripping from her throat.

A pleased snarl vibrated against her sex as he increased his frenzied pace, his tapered tongues dancing over her. They twined together to plunge deep within her, twisting and flaring as they stroked within her channel until one tongue slipped out to circle her clit. The rough surface gave it enough traction to tug at her clit with every slide over the small bead of flesh.

The sensation of his tongues rapidly moving against her folds and burying into her cunt were ceaseless until they finally succeeded at detonating her orgasm. A loud cry left her as her back arched and thighs pressed tight around his head. The action increased the pressure of his mandibles against her inner thighs even as his vibrissae shifted against her skin. It fed her orgasm as he continued to lap at her sex. Her body twitched with the waves of pleasure that swept over her as it gradually subsided. He took one last lingering lick before he pulled back with an expression of intense need, making his face aggressively harsh.

Terri spread her legs wider, welcoming her mate as he slid up her body, his hips nestling in their cradle. He pressed forward, scales sliding erotically against her inner thighs as his civix emerged. The gentle slap of it as it came into contact with her sopping entrance sent tingles through her. His tip angled just right to make contact and burrowed deep in a hard, relentless plunge to her core, the tubes running down the length of his cock secreting lubrication, easing his way.

Her fingers clenched around the bony spines jutting out from his shoulders, and for a moment she forgot to breathe as his cock moved within her, pressing deep, sliding against sensitive spots within her. As attentive as he had always been, there seemed to be a particular urgency as he claimed her this time. Although careful of her belly, he claimed her thoroughly with every hard thrust, his mandibles clicking and vibrating in a deep, rattling purr. With his intensity and focus, the cybernetics on the side of his face, neck, and pectorals glowed brighter as he quivered against her, his muscles tightening.

"Anastha," he gritted out, lips curling back from his sharp teeth and longer fangs.

Terri didn't have the ability to answer. She was caught up in the magnetic pull between their bodies as if push and pull of their joining created a vortex, dragging every bit of her into it with the build of their passion. Her breath heaved in her lungs as raspy pants for air escaped Veral. One of his hands slid around her hip, gripping her solidly in place as he rutted her, his body arching possessively over her in a manner that seemed to punctuate his every thrust. The sound of shredding fabric where his opposite hand was planted against the bed spoke of his spiking frenzy. That could only be his claws digging into the bedding on the platform, and yet the hand that gripped her didn't even prick her with the slightest threat of them.

It was fucking hot as hell that he was so caught in the moment that he destroyed their bed, while keeping his strength tempered in his every touch.

Terri wrapped her legs around his hips, her pelvis tilting and her bottom lifting to meet his every thrust as she moaned, loud and needy.

Wasn't she supposed to be trying to be quiet? She couldn't remember why now. All she knew was that she was surrounded by pleasure—infused with it. She lifted one hand to bury it in his vibrissae which in turn wrapped tightly around her wrist, holding her tight to him instinctually. Her skin quivered in ecstasy as his hips snapped and drove against her, and that tremor drew deeper within her, tightening within her core. She felt his cock swell within her and the slight pleasure-pain of its hooked head lodging into place as he ground against her with a primal growl.

Another orgasm whipped through her at the contact, cries bursting out of her as she was swamped with white hot ecstasy. With a few more grinding thrusts, Veral followed, his own roar of completion filling the room.

His pelvis was still locked against hers, his lips and mandibles brushing over her face. He crooned some sort of primal, wordless love song as he often did when they were together in their private quarters, coming down from their vigorous lovemaking. Terri sighed and nuzzled her nose against his collar bone—damn his massive size—as she rode out the little orgasmic tremors that continued to ripple through her body. She was half drowsy and relaxed against him when a light by the door flashed angrily and was followed by a loud curse.

Seconds later, it was Veral growling as the door slid open and another male strode in. The stranger came to a complete stop before them, eyes wide as he took in their joined state. Veral gathered the bedding to tuck it around Terri, covering her nudity and swollen belly thoroughly with the fabric. His vibrissae rustled, hissing with the rapid rattling. Even the stunted vibrissae flailed with his anger. The male stepped back a pace with an uncertain expression on his face.

"You have five seconds to tell me the meaning of this intrusion before I incapacitate you, mother-kin," Veral snarled, his voice low and lethal.

The danger was not lost upon the stranger because he quickly nodded his head. "Peace, mother-kin. Forgive me. I heard screams that I was sure was some battle and so I used my authority to override the locks. I am Dreth, son of Featha."

The young male dropped his head respectfully, his eyes turned away. There seemed something so young and uncertain about him that Terri felt an upwelling of sympathy for him. She glanced over at her mate.

"Veral, perhaps we should hear him out. This was clearly an accident. I told you I would wake someone."

Her mate grunted sourly but nodded as he shifted their positions so that he could sit up and face his relative while keeping her on his lap due to their currently locked together state.

"As you can see, we are well, so leave us," he hissed impatiently.

The other male balked but nodded, and he set his shoulders as if steeling himself but didn't otherwise move. Veral's frown deepened into a glower.

"Why are you still here?" he snapped.

Dreth held his ground as he rapidly spoke.

"I know I have no right to ask this, but I heard of your return and wanted to speak before you meet with my mother. I request a favor," he said.

Terri bit back a groan and dropped her cheek against her mate's chest.

Fucking perfect.

---

6

*V*eral narrowed his eyes on his cousin, his processors filing away the male's image and identity. He had not known that Featha birthed a second son. Kaylar had not made mention of a younger brother. This male was young, no older than fifty revolutions, if he was not mistaken. He had been born long after Veral had left Argurumal. He did not understand why the male would come to him if he needed assistance since they were veritable strangers.

"I do not know how I may help you," he replied. "I have not been to Argurumal in many revolutions and have no sway here."

"That is where you are wrong, cousin," Dreth corrected. "You are still head of our line. Mother has been holding it in proxy, but everyone knows that, should you return, the authority would revert back to you. When this happens, I ask that you close any arrangements that my mother may make for me and declare me ganshar, unmateable."

Veral gasped, causing his civix to move just enough within Terri that she squeaked, and even he was forced to hold back a moan in reaction to the pleasurable tug. Instead, he focused completely on the male in front of him.

"To be declared ganshar is no trivial matter," Veral warned quietly. "You will not be able to be around or take a mate from any female on Argurumal. It is reserved usually by only the worst and most violent members of our society. Why do you wish such a punishment?"

The male's somewhat smaller mandible clicked in agitation, his vibrissae puffing up and moving erratically.

"Ever since Kaylar pledged his service to get offplanet, my mother has been quick to see me mated."

"Males and females are encouraged to mate young. It is our way," Veral reminded him.

"Yes, so I am aware. I do not object to a mate. I know it is necessary. I just cannot endure another mate trial. I am only just now seeing thirty revolutions and have had no less than six of them."

Veral's eyes widened ever so slightly, betraying his surprise. Six mate trials at the age of thirty? That was unheard of! The age of mating among young Argurma typically began at thirty-five revolutions, when their bodies completed the maturations processes and their cybernetic systems settled. Dreth spread his hands wide in acknowledgment.

"Six times I have endured being locked in a room with a female under contract in hopes that her pheromones will start the bonding process in me, and each time it has failed. The medic has reported to Featha that she must discontinue them, but she is desperate to continue her line, enough so that she has made arrangements to give me a hormone injection to artificially start the mate bonding. I know she desired that I sire a daughter of the line. If I did and you failed to, it would put our direct line permanently as the head of the mother-line of the household complex."

Veral frowned at the idea of a young male being injected with the hormone. It was more often than not used as a last resort and never on a male so young. Terri's hair tickled his face as she turned her head to look over at Dreth.

"Why not just refuse?" she asked.

Veral chuffed at his mate and tightened his embrace in a show of affection. Naturally, his independent female would think the matter to be that easy.

Dreth gave a baffled shake of his head, his vibrissae snapping around him. "Impossible," he rebutted quietly. "After the cybernetic implants are completed, we are turned over to our mothers for training and placement within our line's households. My programming will not allow me to dismiss my mother's governance. If it could, then sending newly enhanced males and females to their mothers would be reckless. We have no bonds and no memory of our lines if we were even raised among them—which I was not. I still have my identification numbers from where I was reared. Our programming conditions us to be obedient and loyal to our mothers. Only the family head has more authority."

He inclined his head toward Veral.

"She would have no option but to listen to his orders."

Veral growled quietly to himself. "I did not wish to come here to stir conflict with your mother or any of the mother-kin of our line. What you ask could bring Featha's displeasure against me."

"But she would yield," Dreth argued, his voice never rising over the soft volume in which they conversed despite the fierce tension in his expression.

Veral inclined his head in agreement. The younger male was right on that score. Featha would not argue for her offspring.

"I do not like this. I have my own mate to think of. My own offspring to consider," Veral growled unhappily.

"So it is true. You have succeeded in breeding your mate. I assure you that I do not contest your offspring's right to the head of our line. I do not wish for it. I would prefer to leave Argurumal as you and Kaylar have done."

"Why leave?" Terri asked, voicing the question that rose to Veral's mind.

Dreth hesitated, his expression uncharacteristically vulnerable and expressive in his unguarded moment for an Argurma. "It is unwise for me to remain. My malfunctions are more severe than anyone, but the medic knows. He keeps my confidence at my request, but I am prone to great lapses in control of my emotions. Enough that I must lock myself in my chambers until I regain enough control to be able to be among kin."

"It is a crime for an Argurma to have malfunctions, but our line overlooks this tendency within our mother-kin with the provision that we control them so that the council does not find out," Veral explained to Terri who was listening to their exchange wide-eyed. "This prompted my departure, because I knew that they expected I would malfunction to the degree of my mother and be unable to control it."

Dreth nodded. "My mother condemns Harahna's suicide as a lapse from her greater malfunctions that made her unable to control her grief. She claims that Harahna disgraced our line and house. She would say this of me if she knew, and any mate I have would report me if she discovered it. I need the freedom and safety of retreat from Argurumal. If you declare me ganshar, my mother will not object if I decide to leave."

"I will not speak untruths. I will say that you desire this... but... I will support your decision and make the decree," Veral reluctantly agreed. "If your mother peacefully gives me control, that is. I cannot promise that she will not attempt to withdraw the ganshar status when we eventually depart and prevent you from leaving the planet."

The younger male's expression hardened. "Then it is an adequate reason for me to leave the planet when you do."

Veral gave a low, rattling growl. He sympathized with his cousin but worried that making such a decision might make his aunt a greater adversary. His decision would effectively terminate her attempts to extend her own direct line and any efforts to keep her claws into the honorable seat of the head of the line.

"I give an oath to remain by your mate's side and assist in protecting her," Dreth offered as he correctly surmised Veral's misgivings. "I can do little directly against my mother, but I can be of assistance against any threat. The Great Dunes of Argurumal forge many alliances out of such necessities."

Veral grunted in agreement. They would likely be on the planet surface for a half month at least, if not longer. There was a sixty percent chance that the medic would wish to supervise the remaining period of gestation and delivery. Not only because theirs was the first Argurma interspecies offspring, but also the first to deal with unknown tech.

He cast a disgruntled look toward the symbiont but the soft touch of fingers in his vibrissae helped settle him. Terri rested against his chest, breath fanning his neck as she spoke.

"It wouldn't hurt to have more help. We help him—he helps us. It's a good trade," she murmured in a barely audible voice pitched for his ears alone. "I think I would feel better knowing that we have someone undeniably in our corner—someone, unlike Navesha, who has something to lose as well—if you think you can trust him."

It was not in Veral's—or any Argurma's—nature to be trusting. An Argurma by design was a solitary creature who owed no allegiance to anyone accept the council. They followed the minimal directive programming that was implemented to establish order within the households and condition them to following the strict hierarchy within their society, but that made most of their kind unlikely to otherwise form close relationships. After so many revolutions of looking in from the outside, Veral could clearly see that it was intentional.

With the loss of the memory of early emotional bonds established in their youth, it proved difficult to forge such bonds as adults. This was part of the purpose of the memory wipe. The programmed allegiance to their maternal households kept interbreeding low and order among citizens while maintaining a level of isolation that kept their people from unifying in any way. Not as he had seen among the humans and other species. Among any of them, they might have easily claimed trust of their kin. But it was not so easy a matter for him.

Narrowing his eyes on the male, he considered Dreth.

His cousin, to all appearances, was earnest and possessed a subtle air of anticipation around him that was quite unlike the calculated attitude of most Argurma. That alone was a point in his favor when it came to the truth of his words. He had no doubt that Dreth could be formidable. The younger male was nearly as tall as Veral and thick with muscle that came from years of battling the harshness of the Great Dunes and the mastery of the sand serpents. To have six lines agree to mate-trials meant that he was considered worthy by neighboring households over the dunes. Winning such approval was accomplished by demonstrations of strength and ferocity that would earn admiration and prove himself desirable for siring strong offspring. He would be a good ally to have to protect Terri.

These things together did not mean that Dreth was not sent to get close to Veral, but the request to be made ganshar was not an idle thing to play with. Even if Featha attempted to reverse it in Veral's absence, being declared such had a long-reaching consequence. It would be difficult to secure a mating contract with another esteemed household.

In the end, that was what swayed Veral that he could trust the male with Terri.

Shifting his mate closer to him on his lap so that she rested belly-to-belly against him as his civix finally slipped free from her hot, wet channel, he glowered at his cousin forebodingly.

"Agreed," he growled. "Now leave."

Dreth nodded curtly, his vibrissae puffing out around his head. "The hour to stand before the household will come soon. You and your mate will require rest. Featha is not one to face without optimally functioning processors."

Veral inclined his head, holding back his mirth as the younger male spun around regally and stalked from the room. Gone was the unsure male now that he had secured Veral's agreement. When the door slid shut behind him, Veral allowed his lips to quirk as Terri laughed in his arms.

"I think you have an admirer," she observed as she leaned back and met his eyes.

Veral glanced down at his mate without comprehension. "I do not follow your meaning."

Terri snickered and tipped her head toward the door. "The moment he earned your agreement, he fluffed up in front of you. You do that whenever you want to seem impressive. I doubt he would be interested in impressing you if he didn't admire you," she teased.

Veral had noted the action but dismissed it as foolish dominating behavior from a male not yet old enough to know better. He would not have come to the same conclusions as his mate. He did not recall if he made such gestures when he was a young male, although he did recall following males around whom he wished to learn from and observing them obsessively.

He huffed in annoyance.

"He will *not* follow me around," he growled. "I will make certain of it. His duty is to guard you only."

Terri chuckled and brushed her fingertips over his brow, up to the edge of the small horns that rested just below the bony plating that framed his fore-vibrissae. The tissue beneath the plating was incredibly sensitive, and the light pressure from her fingers made him sigh in pleasure and lean into her touch. He indulged for several minutes but withdrew to see to it that they were wiped clean with a damp cloth and settled comfortably in bed. Once he had her in his arms again, he rested his jaw on top of her head, his hands stroking her arms and back until he felt his mate relax and eventually succumb to slumber.

Although he joined her, he remained partially alert. He did not bother to reset the locks if there was any chance of anyone else being able to hack the system. Instead, as he rested, he monitored his surroundings for any intrusion. Although there was a chance that his aunt would welcome him without contest, it was not significant enough for him to surrender his safeguards. Especially not with the new information presented to him. Featha appeared to be determined to keep control of the household, and that did not bode well. From what Navesha said, his aunt had been working to turn the household against his choice of mate, no doubt with the goal of striking his direct line from that of the household. What more might she do if that failed?

More than anything, Veral desired to take his family and leave.

$\mathcal{T}$he gathering room of the household was massive. With the long, cushioned benches and chairs around a central hearth she might have compared it to a living room on Earth, except it had the size and grandeur of a castle from a fairytale. An Argurma with dark charcoal scales on her body and vibrissae sat in a large throne-like chair before the rest of the household, her face set in ruthless lines as Terri neared at Veral's side.

Every Argurma assembled in the room ranged from black to dark gray, each with the same glowing cybernetic scarring on their bodies, though there seemed to be some variety in where it appeared. Like Veral, much of it was facial, no doubt due to the implants in their brains and skulls, right down to their glowing eyes.

Terri's eyes ran over the crowd until they rested on Dreth's stoic face from where he stood just off to the side of the throne. Standing at attention a short distance from him was Navesha, a sort of mechanical spear at her side which she gripped with one large hand. This wasn't the casual, mocking female from the night before. Instead, every muscle was stiff with tension.

It was a bit much for a family reunion.

She glanced warily at her mate, but Veral's eyes were locked on his aunt with a sort of a predatory stillness about him despite his long stride. He didn't stop until he came just several feet shy of where she sat. She fought back a proud smile as she observed just how regal and strong her mate looked. Spine straight, he had abandoned his tunic and pants for the black leather armor of a warrior, giving him an air of deadly power as he faced them.

Terri wore the same attire, her flexible armor clinging to her like a second skin, although it emphasized her swollen belly. It had seemed strange at the time when he insisted that they wear it, but now she was glad for the extra protection, and the fact that they had Dreth, and possibly Navesha, in their corner—even though she could easily believe otherwise with the blank, cold way they now regarded her and Veral.

It didn't mean anything.

Her skin prickled as Featha leaned forward on her throne, elbows braced on the armrests as she clasped her hands in front of her. The female's eyes were penetrating as they narrowed on Terri —more specifically on her rounded belly—before they pierced Veral with a look of distinct disapproval.

"Now that I see with my own eyes that you have mated and bred an offworlder...I ask you why you have come and brought that… *primitive beast* here?"

Terri's head whipped back with shock at the chilling vehemence in Featha's voice.

"Do not address my mate without respect," Veral hissed, his vibrissae rattling violently enough that the older female stilled, her eyes widening as her sole indication of her surprise. "I expected my mother-kin to greet my mate as continuer of my line when we arrived… not this insult."

Painted red lips peeled back from Featha's sharp teeth, her vibrissae puffing around her dominantly. "You insult us by mating her. You should have returned home to be matched by your mother-kin when you felt ready to mate. I would have secured a profitable contract for you, instead of being disgraced by a female who brings nothing with her addition to our house."

"You say that, and yet rumor tells me that you have made every effort to set your youngest to inherit in my stead," Veral replied sharply. "Even mating him prior to age of maturity. Do the members of the mother-line know this, or has all they heard been your talk of my mate and offspring... my female offspring, a daughter of the line."

A heavy silence fell, and Terri wasn't sure who everyone was staring at more: her or the horror that broke through the cold indifference that Featha wore until that point. The female had half-stood at the announcement but slowly let herself fall into her throne as the family murmured around them.

Featha's throat worked and her claws, which had sprung from her fingertips, dug into the armrests. Her head dropped, and something like misery crossed the female's face.

"A half-breed is not worthy of our line," she choked out. A shudder of what Terri assumed was disgust ran through her. "You are correct in your surmise. I had hoped that your shame would keep your taint away from the household, unmated and without claim to the head seat. When I heard from Kaylar that you mated an offworlder, I foresaw this probability. I hid nothing speaking my concerns—each is valid—but I have been hastening to mate Dreth in hopes that the household would uphold his pure progeny instead of a half-breed offspring of a deformed castoff," she added, her gaze zeroing in on his damaged vibrissae.

Veral nodded stiffly. "That comes to an end now. The seat is mine." His eyes narrowed. "Remove yourself, mother-kin."

His aunt's jaw tightened, but her face was otherwise inscrutable once more as she regally rose. Her voice trembled only slightly as she spoke, doubtlessly with restrained fury.

"Monushava line initiate transference of lineage authority from Featha'monushava'katala to Veral'monushava'skahalur. Code 67369."

Eyes flashed brightly at the transference, and Featha stepped away with dignity from the throne to stand at its right. Terri wondered if that had any meaning, but she wasn't given a chance to think much about it. Veral lightly took her arm and he strode up to it. He released her long enough to seat himself before drawing her into his lap. Terri flushed at the way everyone stared at his proprietorial action. Several of the females exchanged looks that made her even more uncomfortable. Even Navesha's eyes widened, and somehow her demeanor seemed to stiffen even more.

A sharp dragging sound at her right caught her attention, and she smiled in thanks to Dreth as he slid a heavy stone chair beside the throne. The male's vibrissae puffed and flattened with mild discomfort as he dropped his head in a jerky nod and stepped back once more to his place.

∼

*V*eral scowled at the chair. He understood why Dreth brought it and was thankful that the male thought to provide it, but it rankled that he would have to release her from his protective embrace. Although Terri had the symbiont, her control of it was still imperfect. Even with it, she was smaller and more delicate than even the smallest adult among his mother-kin.

He debated tightening his arms around her and refusing to let go, but his eyes slid over to his family, and the shock and censure on their faces made him reconsider. Even Navesha was scrutinizing his action.

He bristled. He knew that they were looking on his mate now

as if she were weak... less than them. This would not help their efforts.

With an irritated rattle-click of his mandibles, he reluctantly allowed Terri to slide out of his lap and take a seat at his side. A hiss from Dreth's vibrissae signaled his watchful guard and Veral relaxed. Nothing was going to happen to his mate. Drawing in a deep breath, Veral settled back in the throne and narrowed his eyes on his mother-kin as he drummed his claws on the armrest. He glanced at his cousin, meeting the younger male's hopeful gaze.

"My first address as head of household is this," he growled, "Dreth'monushava'kavath, approach." The male strode over to stand before Veral. Head held high, the male regarded him with a mask of solemnity from where he stood. Veral resisted the urge to smile at the front the male so effectively put up. "Dreth'-monushava'kavath, initiate Monushava line programming code 894, authorization Veral'monushava'skahalur." The male's eyes brightened, indicating the programming was now open. "At your request, and my agreement for the violations of the laws of major-ity, I place upon you the ganshar." He ignored the gasps that filled the room and Featha's shriek of denial as he continued to speak. "You will take no mate from this planet, and you will not sire any young on any Argurma female," he pronounced. "Confirm."

There was more to the sentencing, but Veral stopped there. He would not influence his mother-kin's programming to condemn the male to a life without a mate—even if he had to seek it with another species. Dreth paused. His cousin knew that there should have been more but did not argue. Instead, he inclined his head respectfully.

"Confirmed," Dreth rasped, his eyes brightening a fraction more before returning to their normal brilliance.

He turned to return to his place, but his mother snapped a hand around his forearm, her vibrissae rattling angrily.

"Why do you dishonor me this way?" she snarled.

Dreth glared back at Featha, eyes lit with anger as he wrenched free from her hold.

"Because I refuse to be your tool to control the Monushava line. It was the only way to be free of your attempts to mate me… and your plan to accomplish it. I do not wish a forced, unnatural mating and now I do not have to suffer one," he snarled.

"Idiot child!" she shrieked. "Now you will have nothing at all. No inheritance, no mate, and no young."

"I will have peace!" he bellowed back.

His breath heaved in and out for a moment as he worked to compose himself before he turned away from his mother to bow his head to Veral once more.

"I have concluded my necessary disruption," he said coolly.

Veral inclined his head and turned his head away to look down at his mate fondly as she gave him a wide grin and lifted her thumb in her human manner of encouragement. He resisted the urge to vibrate his mandibles as he used the moment to give Dreth the opportunity to walk away with his dignity intact as he returned to his position. Once he was certain that his cousin was no longer the center of attention, he glanced back out among his mother-kin. There was a watchfulness and uncertainty as they met his gaze from where they stood and were seated.

"I understand that this is a new challenge—a new change for our line," he said with a clear, even voice. "An interspecies offspring was unheard of among our kind until now, and for this reason we have come. Only among my mother-kin did I feel that there was a worthy sanctuary and medic for the arrival of our young."

That had their attention. A rolling rattle of vibrissae rose with the murmur of approval from among the males and females of the Monushava line.

"This is not without danger. Our household must be prepared

to deflect interest away from our complex at this time until we can secure her safety."

"You speak of going against the laws of the council, Veral," another female said quietly.

It had been many revolutions, but he knew the female before him by her voice and familiar, unchanged face. Like of all their race who lived for hundreds of years in youth before a rapid decline when the nanos wore out, she was as beautiful as he remembered and as strong as any of his cousins. Despite that, there was a peculiar gentleness to her that was odd for their species, but it had been that quality that made her the only one of his mother-kin who had assisted his mother when he had first returned and had been confused. Her mellow voice had soothed him then, and he was grateful now to see her amid the chaos of change occurring around him. He recognized his grandmother's sister with a deep, respectful bow of his head.

"Anahal, you are correct," he acknowledged. "The law of the council does not serve us. It strips us of our identity and returns us to our mother lines broken, only to wait to see our own offspring stolen. If the council permitted me to keep Terri, they would implement the same procedures that would remove everything unique from my mate. That is if they did not carry out their current plans to dissect her in an attempt to learn ways to remove what bonds we have kept—our mating bonds. My offspring would be destroyed in their experiments," he added, directing these words to Featha, whose eyes widened as a look of fleeting horror passed over her face.

Good. Her horror would protect his young. Featha was conniving, but she was not a monster. Kaylar was correct on that matter. Despite her distaste for the situation, she would protect an innocent daughter of the line. He could see that in the sudden rigid set of her shoulders as she took on the weight of responsibility. There was still a significant probability that she would adjust. He would work toward those odds.

"We allow the council to restrict who we mate with. We do not know what opportunities we have missed. There may be many species who would further strengthen and grow our line," he added.

The males and females among his kin again exchanged looks, communicating among their private lines.

"I will stand by you, mother-kin," Navesha said loudly as she pushed her way up to his side. Her lip curled back in a sneer as she looked over the rest of their people. "Does anyone else stand with us against the cruelty and crippling laws of the council?"

Navesha's support, as a female of the line possessing great standing, proved crucial. Although it was unreasonable to suspect that it was unanimous, his mother-kin promised to guard their secret. The corners of Veral's lips tipped up as he watched his mother-kin edge toward his mate with mixed expressions of curiosity and incredulity. When the medic finally pushed his way through to squint with interest down at Terri, a tension within Veral's systems eased. His mate and offspring would be safe… for now.

erri's eyes widened when a large male—slightly shorter than Veral but broad with muscle—approached, his flared vibrissae making him appear even larger. His entire body screamed barely leashed violence, and Terri tensed warily in reaction. In contrast to Veral's dark silver, he was a starless black hue that seemed to almost suck away any light near him, his glowing eyes like flames set in his face. She was certain that he was going to attack and prepared herself, her symbiont flaring hot as it prepared to unleash itself if required.

Veral stood, seemingly unconcerned about the giant striding toward him. She wished she could share that confidence. She wasn't able to keep herself from jumping when the male's arm swung out only to grip Veral's shoulder spine in a friendly gesture, a deep chuff leaving him. His eyes rolled toward her only for a moment before returning to her mate.

"Veral'skahalur," he drawled in a deep voice. "The chatter through the communication lines is correct—you survived and returned to us. I expected you to be dead or barely clinging to life if you returned. You look much the same, but I see that revolutions in space have hardened you. It did you some good, then."

Her mate grunted and clasped the other male in turn, his eyes narrowing and rising at the corners with an ease that came from evident familiarity.

"Larth'evanshal. I did not expect to see you alive if I returned. I assumed that you would be ranked to an elite warrior and perish on some battlefield for the council. And you are larger."

The male in question chuffed again, not denying it.

"You are accurate, in part," he agreed. "I signed up for one rotation, earned my warrior marks and these upgrades you note, and afterward declined further rotations. I returned to our territory to protect the house and the line. And yet, of the two of us, you are the one who returned with a mate. I never would have expected an honor-bound male, one who would rather flee into exile than draw unfavorable attention to his line, to break council law and mate outside of our species."

"We are both surprised then," Veral replied, amusement in his expression. "I did not receive communication that you had become head of the Ahanvala Guard. I would not have expected you to obtain any position that requires cool calculation. You were always too eager to fight than to use your processor sensibly," he chuffed. "You would have been among the first I would expect to flaunt the council and mate where you like."

"You provide a compelling incentive to do so," Larth said, his eyes fastening this time on Terri with interest.

She held an amused snort. He was judging that by what, exactly? Her winning personality as she stood there and literally said nothing? The way she rounded out like an inflatable rescue device?

Although it wasn't possible for her to share a private communication line with Veral without having implants put in, she was certain that he knew exactly what she was thinking because he chuffed and slanted her a knowing look.

"My mate is very compelling in many ways," he agreed with a low, lustful rumble.

Heat flared through her, desire flushing her skin. At that moment, she couldn't say for sure who was compelling whom.

Larth's smile widened into an Argurma grin, showing the tips of his fangs.

"I look forward to hearing more of her species, then," he rumbled, and Terri immediately felt for whatever woman he might manage to snare if he got to Earth.

She had a feeling Larth was the persistent sort. Although that did seem to be an Argurma trait to varying degrees. Dreth might be at the shyer end of the scale—and given his determination, that was saying something—but Larth was noticeably at the other end... as was the male approaching from the side wearing a blue robe. He was hard to miss. Though muscular as any of the Argurma, he had a leaner frame as opposed to the bulk the males and even several females seemed to prefer. He had been hovering close for the last several minutes but hadn't made any move to approach until now.

Veral drew back slightly, making room for the newcomer, and inclined his head.

"Medic," he greeted the stranger, his expression as cold as the glaciers on Xalkilon. He really wasn't keen on people he didn't know. In fact, his brow was dropping into a scowl. "You are not Garalth," he observed icily.

"No. I am Medic Tarik," the male corrected. "Garalth was my father. He now rests with our ancestors, drinking sweet water in the cool realm of Ehanel."

Veral's expression didn't lighten nor did he so much as twitch. Terri prodded him with her elbow. He glanced over at her before returning his attention to Tarik and grunting.

"Garalth was a good male. His loss is a loss to the line," he acknowledged. For about five seconds he was a sympathetic, feeling male, and just as quickly he shut it down. "You received my scans?"

The blue-robed male gave a pleased smile, his vibrissae puffing out with pride as he gave an abbreviated nod.

"Thank you. Yes, Ahanvala. My systems are currently updating with the biological specs you sent me for the human species. I will then begin to go over the data you have provided. I am eager to begin on this assignment."

His eyes strayed to her in an assessing manner... and lingered far beyond what even she felt was comfortable or polite. Unsurprisingly, Veral took exception to it and growled territorially. Vibrissae rustling in surprise, the medic's eyes snapped away from her back to her mate. His mandibles tucked close and tight to his cheeks, his vibrissae twining together in an expression of embarrassment.

"The human is fascinating," he said abruptly. "I did not intend to exceed boundaries of politeness. I will not repeat that error..."

"Do you have experience, Medic Tarik, in assisting females in birthing?" Veral asked suddenly.

Tarik paused in surprise but soon found his voice. "Yes. Actually, I have assisted the birth of numerous offspring before I returned here."

Veral grunted. "Very well. Keep in mind, Tarik, that you will treat my mate with exceptional care regardless of your experience."

"Yes. Of course," he replied.

"Veral naturally worries for his fragile mate. A reasonable reaction for one tied to a weaker species, I assume," a cool feminine voice broke in.

Bristling, Terri turned to confront the speaker only to see Featha beside them, her expression and tight and possessing the bearing—and fury—of a queen. The corner of the female's mouth slanted upward as she met Terri's eyes.

Unlike the few nobles who Terri had come across in her travels with Veral, there was nothing delicate about her, and that was more apparent with the previous Ahanvala looming over her. Featha was as tall as Veral and came close to possessing the same amount of muscle. Terri wondered if she had undergone training as a warrior too. If so, she wouldn't be surprised. The female looked like she wanted to chew Terri up and spit her out but wasn't sure if she wanted to sully herself with the actual chore of doing it.

Terri met her hostile expression with a blank, unconcerned one that had the female's vibrissae twisting through the air in annoyance.

"Nothing survives well on Argurumal except Argurma. Those aliens who serve in our markets do so only because of special habitats constructed for them. How will this human survive? We do not have offworlder habitats here. Like the rest of our planet, there is nothing here but sand and stone. There is a high proba-bility that you will have plenty of opportunities to observe the harm, medic, as I am sure that she will regularly be in your care. Veral will be very occupied just to keep his little alien mate alive," she observed.

"Enough, Featha," Veral rumbled in warning. "I have already warned you about insulting Terri. Why are you still here?"

"It is not an insult if it is fact," the female replied firmly. "You are Ahanvala now, Veral, and I will concede to your decisions just as I am here to give my oath to protect your mate and offspring. Be aware, no matter what oaths are given, they will never belong among us or to this household in any meaningful way."

Veral's eyes narrowed. "Acknowledged. You will, however, be proven wrong. My mate is stronger and more resilient than you assume."

"We will see," Featha murmured before stepping away.

Robes swirling around her legs, she slipped into the crowd,

leaving them staring after her. The oath wasn't unexpected, but Terri wished that she would have had some kind of familial support from that quarter. She should have known that it was too much to hope for that his family would treat her as their own. At the very least, Featha was not going to be in any hurry to, and Terri suspected that her opinion carried considerable weight in the household.

Terri had the feeling that she was going to be avoided like a plague.

"However often you require to see me is acceptable," Tarik offered. "As your mate, Terri's health is a priority, and I will see that she receives the best care. We can begin now. Follow me. I will escort you to the medical unit and we will…"

"No. You will not," Larth interrupted slowly, his deep voice cutting through the medic's chatter. "As the head of the Ahanvala Guard, *I* am the Ahanvala's guard," he continued. "As such I will escort him where he requires to go, or any other guards as I deem necessary. Go back to medical, and I will bring them once they are ready."

Tarik glanced at Veral, but with no objection coming from that quarter, he bobbed his head again and strode away, his spine stiff. Despite the creepy staring, Terri felt bad for him. Of everyone in the household, he seemed the most genuinely concerned about her welfare even if it was out of a fair amount of scientific curiosity.

Larth chuffed after him.

"Tarik is a good male and a good medic. Loyal, too. It is necessary to remind him that there is more to our lives than just his work," he said with another chuff as he gave Terri a smile. "We will get you to medical quarter soon, after the tour. Knowing the layout of the main points of the compound is necessary, and it has been a long time since Veral was here."

As good as his word, he led them from the main room through several large corridors. Weapons room, kitchens, goods storage in case they required anything for their chambers. He even pointed out in passing several assigned wings for various tasks to maintain the household. Although everything was dark and one hallway seemed to blend into another, she was still surprised when Larth stopped outside of a doorway and gestured them inside.

"Medical quarter," he said.

Terri glanced back at him as she started to walk in with Veral, her sudden stop bringing her mate to a halt.

"Aren't you coming?"

Larth smirked down at her. "No need to go into medical if I am not sick. Nanos take care of most things. I will be waiting here when you are finished."

"Okay," she said as she allowed herself to be led inside.

9

*T*he medical quarter of the compound was more than what Terri had expected given what she was used to on *the Wanderer*. It was a true wing, with several sterile rooms designated for the healthcare of the Monushava line. The tranquil blue of the walls was even more unexpected. It was a surprising contrast, given that the dark walls seemed to be standard everywhere she looked—albeit broken up by the panels that tapped into the system controls and large holographic screens that cycled through images that she could only guess were of the family.

Tarik greeted her with mellow smile as she stepped inside, Veral crowding in close behind her. Although he dropped his head in a respectful nod, he slid by Veral, practically brushing him aside and ignoring the threatening growl that rose from her mate as he gestured toward the med-bed.

Although bigger than the one on the ship, this at least was familiar. Terri shot a quick glance at Veral. He glowered at the medic but huffed as he stalked over to the far side of the med-bed where he settled against the wall, close but out of the way of the medic who circled the bed making adjustments in passing. She gave her mate a brave smile in an attempt to comfort them both before she climbed up onto it without comment and stretched out with her hands folded just above her belly.

Tarik leaned over her and ran a handheld device down her body. Veral had done this often enough that she knew that he merely used it to take her vitals. Although he hummed a bit with the rapid vibration of his mandibles, the process was over quickly. He set the device on the small table to her right and placed his hand on a panel on the side of the med-bed. A blue holographic shield popped up above her. In that field, she could see the holographic image of her baby curled within her.

"The scans you gave me were recent?" Tarik asked Veral abruptly.

Her mate nodded. "Yes," he replied gruffly. "They were taken just five rotations ago. At first, I was doing scans daily until it appeared that the gestation was proceeding normally for Argurma breeding. Even with the sudden acceleration in the growth rate of the fetus, nothing else registered as abnormal. Without any way to conclusively interpret what was happening, I decided not to distress Terri with further tests, given my lack of skill in this area."

The medic hummed again as he shifted data around in the hologram.

"She is growing at an astounding rate," Tarik agreed after a moment. "Exceedingly fast. Other than that, you are correct—she appears otherwise normal. Her nanos are already thriving through her bloodstream, although there is a presence of something else that appears to originate from the mother's body."

His lips thinned minutely as he magnified his view of her daughter. Immediately, he moved up and magnified the area of her arm. There she could see the strange, steady internal pulse of her symbiont glowing like a jewel in the hologram. Within the magnification, however, she could see a thin glowing line that seemed to weave into her.

"This is the symbiont you mentioned."

It was a statement rather than a question, but Veral inclined his head again in silent agreement when the medic looked his way.

Tarik's eyes narrowed at the symbiont intently. "It is unlike anything I have seen or anything in the medical databases that I have access to via my processors," he stated flatly. "Our cybernetics amplify the general muscle or muscle group which they are designed to augment, or specific functions of our brains, but this symbiont is connected not only to the female's tissue, but deeply imbedded in her nervous and vascular systems. There is a particularly bright, thick thread here," he observed, tracing a claw over a pulse thread of light. "It is the same line that I see accessing your offspring through the blood exchanged between mother and offspring via the uterine lining. It is tapping directly through your offspring to this…"

He turned the hologram to an angle that hadn't been achieved by their med-bed on their starship and magnified her baby's arm until she was able to see a small glowing jewel that appeared to be growing off of her baby's forearm. It also had a visibly bright thread.

Terri swallowed back her nausea. How had that gotten there, and why? Veral seemed to be of a similar mind because a low, threatening growl rumbled from him as he stared the tiny symbiont growing on their daughter.

"Has that thing infected my offspring?" he hissed.

Tarik tilted his head curiously, not looking away from the holograms. "Not at all. It is replicating itself to pass on its protections to the offspring that it is programmed to protect. It has not infected your offspring but is providing more immediate protection to the developing young. It is no more invasive than our own nanos that our offspring inherit from us to make them stronger, healthier, and longer living. In truth, it is far more advanced than any of our cybernetic modifications that must wait until after maturity to be added in phases beginning in adolescence."

"So it won't hurt her?" Terri asked, desperately needing the clarification to set her mind at ease.

Another mellow smile was directed at her, and the medic shook his head. "There is low probability of that. My calculations indicate that the environment it is creating with the nanos is modifying your offspring, causing a quicker growth. In our species, she already possesses all her organs, and so this is merely a rapid acquiring of mass that would have happened later anyway, but at an accelerated rate accomplishing in weeks what would take lunars. It could be a response to the mingling with the human species' naturally shorter gestation."

A low sigh escaped her mate and his eyes closed wearily, making her heart swell with emotion. Veral did not confess worries, but clearly he had been just as concerned as she was.

"I am pleased to know this," he said at length. "With there being no danger to my mate, I will make plans for imminent departure within the next three days. That should be enough time," he said thoughtfully.

"I did not say that," Tarik replied evenly as he terminated the holographic shield.

The sudden disappearance of the light made Terri blink to adjust her eyes as she slowly sat up in the med-bed. Veral was at her side, his arm spanning around her to assist her out of the bed as he glared once more at the medic.

"Then speak plainly," he growled, his vibrissae whipping.

Tarik didn't look any more flustered by the display than he had throughout the entire exam, his own vibrissae twining in a relaxed state around his shoulders. He met Veral's eyes, and his brow plating rose a little.

"Although the symbiont and the nanos are helping your daughter's and your mate's bodies absorb the stress of the accelerated changes, your female will become more easily tired and need to feed regularly. Large amounts of food are going to be needed for both of them… quality food, not replicated food," Tarik added when Veral bristled indignantly.

Terri didn't blame her mate. He did make sure that she had plenty of food to eat, keeping their replicator stocked, and kept the disgusting axna fruit.

"Replicated food carries all necessary nutrients. It is not inadequate," Veral objected with an annoyed snarl.

Unperturbed, the medic initiated a sanitizer over the med-bed.

"It may contain some of the basic nutrients, but it is inferior to fresh foods obtained here on Argurumal. Also, it would be better for your offspring to have some exposure to our planet's gravity for a period, in my estimation. There is also the fact that females often have difficulty in birthing—we are not beyond risking our females in death from birthing. We still lose some occasionally, even now. I would advise that you allow me to oversee her delivery. I will be able to make the right notations to record her birth for legitimacy purposes in our records and can do so without setting off suspicion. If you want your daughter of the line to have any chance of truly inheriting, she will need records of birth filed."

Veral drew back slowly from where he was standing nearly toe-to-toe with the other male and huffed.

"I do not like this," he grumbled.

Terri wasn't thrilled either, but her overactive imagination kept coming back to the horror of delivering without a medic on their ship, or even being one of the rare casualties of childbirth. The odds would be a lot higher if they were traveling alone on *The Wanderer*. The idea of giving birth in general terrified her. She knew that Veral would do everything he could to help her and wouldn't leave her side, but the idea of having a large family and a trained medic at hand was suddenly *very* appealing.

"Veral, I think we should follow Tarik's advice and stay," she interrupted.

His vibrissae puffed out as his eyes whipped to her.

"Why?" he demanded. "We do not need to hide in fear when we are on *The Wanderer*. We go where we wish, take the work that appeals to us and provides many credits. You like being alone on the starship with me just as much as I do."

"Yeah," Terri hedged. "But this shit scares me, okay? When I thought of my pregnancy, I thought I still had a lot of time before I had to worry about giving birth, but now it's just weeks away and I'm scared. Anything can go wrong out there, and as much as I love it... and love the adventure of just being out there with you... I really want to be here where there are others to help us. Just in case the worst happens," she added.

Her mate eyed her skeptically but let out another, far wearier huff and nodded. Stroking a hand down her cheek and along the curve of her jaw, he leaned forward and settled his plated forehead against hers.

"I worry of these things, too. But I also worry of remaining where our enemies are so close."

"Your mother-kin will help you. We will guard you," Tarik reminded him. "Regardless of the worries and opinions they may possess on your mating and offspring, we understand our duty to each other. I cannot think of anyone who would betray your presence here and not make certain that your mate and daughter are cared for."

Veral grunted. "You speak convincingly. Since when does an Argurma have a quick tongue and persuasive manner like a Vashinakar merchant?"

An amused chuff escaped Tarik, and the corners of his mouth upturned into a smile. "It comes from studying interstellar medicine on one of the galactic space stations before I was called home to take my place as the medic of the Monushava line."

"You could do that?" Terri asked, immediately fascinated.

She didn't think that Argurma left the planet unless sent out for a specific purpose, or if they were running away from it.

The male chuffed again, his smile widening, showing his sharp teeth as his mandibles vibrated in a happy hum.

"There are allowances made by our council to give the intergalactic councils of allied species a sense that we are willing to work cooperatively with others. It is not always necessarily genuine, but it opens experiences for some of our people. My opportunity was terminated when my older sister died with my parents, leaving the role of medic to fall upon me."

"Do you miss it?" she asked curiously as he escorted them to the door.

His smile dropped, tinged with an unmistakable look of regret. "I enjoyed the greater opportunities to see and do more, to experience more than what I would find within the confines of the compound. There is little opportunity to find a mate here since few females desire a medic... one with little station within the household. But I am pleased to be here for this momentous occasion," he added. "I am sending a list of foods that you will wish to avoid during your gestation, as well as those that will be particularly nutritious and pleasing for you. You will find the information waiting for you in your comm."

"Thank you, Tarik," she said warmly.

His vibrissae knotted, but he turned and bowed slightly in deference to Veral as they left the medical quarter.

Her mate nudged her lightly with his arm, his expression unreadable as he looked down at her. "You will take care while we are on this planet. Be observant when away from our chambers, and go nowhere without me, Dreth or Navesha. They were the first to swear their protection when they had no reason to, and so I will trust only them with your safety."

"Right," she agreed solemnly. Glancing up at him hopefully,

she gave him a small smile. "Now can we eat? I'm suddenly starving, and Tarik did say that I will need to eat a lot."

"Not difficult for you, anastha," Veral murmured, his eyes alight with amusement.

"Cracking jokes, my love?" She chuckled. "Come on, feed your mate before I start following my nose to whatever appeals to it."

With an affectionate purr of his mandibles, Veral pulled her beneath his arm and held her tight against his body as he led her through the corridors. She only hoped that it was the way to the kitchens.

*V*eral held in a groan as Terri moaned with pleasure. That coupled with the way she sucked another spoonful of pink mush into her mouth made his civix leap to life within its sheath. His female was going to kill him slowly since there was little to do about his desire with Navesha sprawled in a nearby chair, sharpening her claws on a rough pumice stone imported from the northern volcanic valleys. Due to their conditioning and social norms, it was not considered polite in his society to publicly show affection, much less seduce one's mate in the company of another.

In consequence, he was resigned to suffer with the surge of lust that raged easily at the slightest provocation from his mate. He glared at her, trying to convince his cousin to leave, but the stubborn female merely smirked at him. He felt a growl of frustration climb up his throat and was about to order her to leave when Terri distracted him with another loud moan that sent a fresh wave of heat through him.

"By the gods, it is so good! I can't remember anything tasting so good," Terri declared appreciatively.

"It is versin," Navesha supplied, her smile broadening beyond what was considered good taste so that a hint of teeth peeked out. "It is made from scourra's milk blended with the brain of a corafel with several sweet spices. It is a much enjoyed first meal," she finished approvingly.

Terri paused, her spoon freezing just before her mouth. Veral eyed her with concern. It was difficult to predict at times where his mate's tolerance for unfamiliar foods might end. He did recall her mentioning that she refused to eat bugs, or anything made of a bodily organ. In retrospect, he should have stopped her when she insisted on trying the sweet versin. His eyes narrowed, and his body tensed as her face turned a sickly hue.

"Brains?" Terri mumbled around a mouthful of versin, her face flushing brightly for a moment before all color fled from her cheeks.

Navesha's brow ridge rose, but she pursed her lips and nodded.

Were humans supposed to achieve a pale, slightly greenish hue? He had seen his mate flush reds and pinks and even pale, but he didn't recall seeing her adopt that particular hue before. He glanced at the versin with worry. Perhaps it was an allergic reaction that made her look so terrible.

"Nope," Terri moaned sadly. "I just can't."

Jerking to her feet, his mate speed over to the waste disposal unit and slapped her palm against the lever on its side. The lid slid back quickly, and Terri leaned promptly over to retch into it.

Vibrissae tangling and rattling anxiously, Veral stepped behind his mate, his hand smoothing her back in slow, firm strokes that always seemed to comfort her. Her body trembled with spasms as she continued to empty her stomach of nutrients. He did not dare move until her body stopped shaking and she straightened once more and drew in a deep breath. Swiping her hand over her eyes to wipe away the tears that streaked down her cheeks in the course of her violent expelling, she turned and looked up at him with a weak smile.

"Well, that was awful. So what are our plans for today?"

He cupped her cheek within his large hand, his thumb brushing against her cheekbone lovingly.

"Your only responsibility is to eat and rest. I have things that I must see to."

"Oh, well, that's okay. I don't mind tagging along," she replied with forced cheer, her smile dropping when he shook his head.

"I will be visiting different parts of the compound. It will be tedious and tiring, requiring my attention until late. Your body is already taxed by our offspring. It is better if you rest in our chambers. If you become restless you can take the balcony out to the courtyard gardens, but do not overexert."

She pinched her lips together, and he was certain that she was about to argue, but she surprised him by sighing and giving him a reluctant smile. "I guess a day hanging around our rooms won't kill me," she muttered. She leaned her cheek into his hand, her gaze softening. "You can just make it up to me when you get back."

He stilled, reluctant to upset her further. Veral withdrew his hand and stepped away just long enough to retrieve some water for her. She flashed him a grateful smile as she sipped and cleansed her mouth with the cool water. She spat the mouthful into the waste disposal before taking a grateful swallow of the liquid. When she was finally done with it, he took it back to clean and store the cup before returning.

Standing in front of her once more, he debated how to approach the subject. He settled on dropping his hand to twine his fingers with hers in a demonstration of affection and support that he knew she favored. His mate's brow, however, furrowed with confusion at his small retreat. He hated that what he would say was going to make her unhappy with him, but there would be no dishonesty between them.

"It will not just be one day. I will be spending the better part of the next several rotations shuttling out to various parts of our territories to meet with extended members of our line who care for our herds and oversee various operations. It will be many long rotations that your presence is not necessary for. You would find them tedious, so this will be the most optimal time for you to just rest. There is no reason for you to exhaust yourself."

"I see," Terri replied quietly, her lips thinning with clear displeasure.

"Do not be angry. My oath, as soon as these duties are concluded, we will enjoy some days to ourselves, anastha," he murmured.

She fidgeted a bit. "And I'll stay here the entire time?"

"It will set my mind at ease to know you are here getting the rest and food that your body currently desires."

She dropped her eyes, her jaw tightening. "You aren't going to turn insanely overprotective again, are you? I thought we established that I can take care of myself."

"Which I do not dispute. You are fierce and capable, anastha. Any male would be fortunate to have such a mate at his side, but these circumstances are unusual for both of us. It is advantageous to be cautious."

Navesha snorted from where she sat, and he directed an impatient look to her.

"Did you have a comment to make?" he asked, the light growl in his voice unmistakable.

His cousin shrugged, her smile never leaving her lips. "No. I just did not fully realize until this moment how fragile your mate is. It is interesting to see a male so flustered over his mate's health when Argurma females are strong and have no such need."

He narrowed his eyes, unsure of where she was going with her observation, but she did not make him wait long. She chuffed and leaned forward to prop on one elbow, one free of the thick spikes that a male had at the joint, to regard him levelly.

"I mean no offense, cousin," she said with a relaxed purring vibration of her mandibles. "Now that I see the situation, I will be honored to check on your mate in your absence."

"I would be grateful," he replied formally, and his cousin dropped her head in acknowledgment.

He looked back to his mate, hoping that Navesha's offer would set her at ease with his absence. To his dismay, her face was still pinched as she visibly bristled. His systems took in her elevated heart rate and tension and he nearly hissed with distress. She was not pleased at all and not trying to hide it. He had little doubt that Navesha, if she cared to check, would also mark the response. Not that he cared if it insulted his cousin. He did not like to see his female so agitated when she was usually energetic and enthusiastic. He did not like to see her practically curling into herself with dejection.

A sigh left him. He could not do that to her.

"Very well. If you would prefer to come…"

"No," Terri interrupted with a sharp exhalation of breath. "You are right. I don't like it, but I am more easily tired lately… a little more… *fragile*… than normal, as Navesha implied. I am sure taking a few days to laze about and enjoy the foods will be good for me while I am getting settled and adjusting to all of this… all except the versin," she chuckled.

The smile that accompanied her statement was small but Veral relaxed a little at the genuine warmth that filled it. That was the spark he was accustomed to seeing from his female. Making a pleased rumble, he drew her into his arms, his mandibles threading lightly among her hair as he clutched her close to him.

"Yes, rest well and regain your energy for when I conclude these matters," he whispered into her ear. "Until then, I have a little time before I must leave. Let me see to your nourishment since your stomach rejected what was previously eaten and then I will take you back to our quarters to see you are appropriately bathed and tended to before I depart."

Her soft sigh and the erotic tremble of her body against his was all the answer he required. Pulling her close, he brushed his lips against her brow, trailing them down the bridge of her nose until he could brush them against her soft mouth. Her moan brought another surge of lust reminding him to break off while in front of an audience despite how much his body loathed to.

Drawing back, he turned a curt glance toward Navesha, who watched with unabashed interest. The female lifted one spineless feminine shoulder and winked.

"If you are performing in public, do not expect me to look away. I am the oldest unmated female in our line. I have to enjoy all intimacy secondhand... or firsthand as far as my own appendage goes," she retorted as she lifted her opposite hand and immediately turned her attention to sharpening the claws on that hand.

With a disapproving glare, Veral tucked Terri into his side as he fetched more appropriate food from the cooling unit for his mate and hustled her out of there. He wanted his mate to himself and far away from his cousin's overly bold behavior. His attention was on far more interesting things.

He was barely able to contain his passion before they tumbled through the doorway to their quarters. Mouths locking and hands working at a frenzied pace, their bodies came together with exultant shouts of passion. His entire focus narrowed in on the wet slaps of their bodies together as his civix plowed into her wet heat. Terri's small cries urged him on until he was riding her harder to the point of combustion.

His pelvis slick in the apex of her thighs, Veral growled at his increasing lack of self-control around his female. He knew that it was common among mated pairs to engage each other frequently while the female gestated in order to reaffirm and strengthen their bond. For that reason, he knew that it was not abnormal, even though his body was spasming as he held himself deep within her. Content while locked together, he dragged his jaw against hers, enjoying the way she relaxed bonelessly as his mandibles vibrated in the low purr she enjoyed. It was something he made certain to use frequently in their matings to increase her post coital enjoyment. And he admitted that he found it quite enjoyable as well.

He was starting to understand why so many mated as soon as possible, even if it was with pressure from mother-kin. He thought little of what Navesha said about being unmated until hours later as he dragged a wet sponge over Terri's shoulders.

"Why do you think Navesha isn't mated?" Terri asked, breaking the soothing silence that had fallen in their room outside of the quiet purr of his mandibles and a distant melody that carried through the corridors from someplace within the compound.

He lifted a shoulder and smoothed the sponge around one breast in leisure strokes.

"I do not know. It is possible that a male she bonded with died before they finalized their mating, or that she could not find a suitable male that she was able to bond to her. It happens. If Featha did not consider it important enough to get the artificial hormones, it could be any number of scenarios."

"That's a little sad," Terri said quietly.

He nodded. "It is. That is one reason I say it is important for us to look beyond our own planet to alien races. Our males and females need it, rather than forcing bonds through hormone injections."

Terri turned in the tub and looped her arms around his neck, her blue eyes peering intently into his. "Well, this alien feels very lucky to have found you."

S.J. SANDERS

"As I do with you," he purred.

She bit her lip. "You have to leave soon, don't you?"

"I do," he replied.

A sigh shuddered from her. "All right. Just hurry home, okay?"

"Nothing can keep me from your side," he assured her.

When he left her moments later, dressed in a loose robe as she lay upon their sleeping pallet, tension radiated through him at the impending distance separating them. It was necessary, he reminded himself. Refusing to show weakness and look back, he stepped out of the room, not even faltering in his stride when the door slid shut behind with him a quiet snick.

He would see to his duties and return as soon as possible to his beloved anastha.

---

*T*erri sat on the padded stone chair in the courtyard garden. For four days, she had hardly seen Veral at all. She woke when he slid into bed next to her, but he never attempted to do anything more than twine his arms around her and hold her close. Come morning, he was gone again with Krono before she woke. It was sheer hell, and not even Navesha's random appearances made her feel much better. Dreth made an attempt to be good company when he visited to look in on her, but the distance between her and Veral absorbed all of her attention. Although she tried not to be too much of a downer, the anxiety was starting to get to her.

Her fingers squeezed the fruit in her hand hard enough that they wettened from its juices. Sighing, she set it on the plate beside her, unable to stomach the idea of taking a bite. Veral wouldn't be happy that her appetite recently dropped off, but over the last day it had been difficult to rouse interest in much of anything.

"You know what you need?" Navesha interrupted.

Terri peeled one eye open to look over at her current babysitter. "My mate?"

"Yes, but in this case, incorrect," the female chuffed. "I believe you need a distraction."

Terri sucked her lips in thoughtfully. The other female wasn't wrong. She was so focused on Veral's absence perhaps a distraction would be helpful, though she was too suspicious to fully trust Navesha. She didn't know what it was that struck her as off, and it felt unfair to judge her so harshly when Veral's cousin had done nothing to her.

"Did you have something particular in mind?" she asked cautiously.

"I would not have mentioned it if I did not. I think it would be a good time to spend an afternoon at the market, especially since Featha instructed me to pick up an order for her and gave me permission to take you with me so that you are not 'pining in the courtyard all day.' I have a spare shafna you can use that will protect you from our suns, and we will entertain ourselves with the Ragirsi merchants. They make many credits trading their wares all over Argurumal."

"I don't know," Terri said as she worried at her bottom lip with her teeth. "Veral and Tarik are pretty insistent that I need to rest as much as possible right now."

She didn't want to go do something that would make Veral worry if word got to him somehow—but she was so fucking bored. Navesha's next words did little to help the matter.

"And in consequence be under stimulated and irritable. That is not healthy either. In any case, they are males and do not understand fully that females need a bit of time out to distract ourselves from other pressing concerns. In Argurumal, the weight of the household rests on our shoulders. Veral is gaining some understanding of that responsibility in his current position. It is only reasonable that if Veral is going to distress you by being absent so much then he cannot object."

That was a fair point.

Her companion shrugged her shoulder. "It is your decision. I will travel faster on my own. My malfunction makes me senti-mental in thinking that you may desire to see something more than the walls of the compound."

She stood, her vibrissae sliding behind and coiling with a hint of concern. "Since you prefer to stay and await Veral's return late tonight, I will be on my way."

With a polite incline of her head, Navesha turned and began to stride away, her boots clipping on the hard black stone that cobbled the garden path.

Terri heaved a sigh. She really didn't want to be stuck there. What could a trip to the market hurt? Shoving to her feet, she hurried after the retreating female. Damn the Argurma's long legs, there was no way she was going to catch up.

"Wait!" she shouted.

Navesha turned and grinned as far as the species considered polite to do so with just the edges of her sharp teeth peeking between her lips. She didn't move until Terri caught up to stand by her side. The glowing blue gaze brightened with approval, and Navesha nodded with a hum of her mandibles.

"You have decided... Good. We will go now. Even by flyer, it takes enough time to get to the market, and it never lacks in busi-ness. Even this simple excursion will be lengthy. A good opportu-nity for you to get some new pleasures of our world," the female chuffed once more.

Without wasting any further time on conversation, she set a brisk pace once more, leaving Terri to scramble to keep up with her. This time, however, Navesha moderated her speed enough that she didn't completely leave Terri behind. As long as she trot-ted, Terri was able to keep up well enough.

The Argurma flyer, it turned out, was a compact plane vehicle. It was rather surprising in contrast to the lush gardens and the polished stone of the compound's interior walls. In some ways, it reminded her of *The Wanderer* on an extremely small scale and lacking any personal touches. As tiny as it was it didn't have a personal chamber at all, just four seats in the main cabin, the chair at the fore occupied by Navesha as she piloted the flyer over the sand.

For her part, Terri watched in fascination as they skimmed over the dunes. Since it had been dark when they arrived, Terri had only impressions of the red sands beneath the light of the moons and the artificial light of their starship. In the full glory of the planet's twin suns, the brilliant red sands formed endless waves. Her lips parted in awe as the sands in front of them suddenly trembled and rolled as an enormous beast broke free from them.

Its long neck whipped as it dragged itself through the surface, effortlessly bringing down some sort of winged creature that jerked hard, no doubt squawking in pain in the crushing jaws of the predator. The moment it went limp, its ragged, half-furred, half-feathered wings drooping in death, the creature jerked its head back at an angle, its throat working fiercely as it swallowed down its prey.

It only happened in a manner of a couple of minutes, but Terri watched with equal measures of disgust, fear and awe as it rapidly consumed its meal. Its head snaked around searching its surroundings for another easy meal, but it only lasted for second before the enormous paddle-like legs—or, more accurately, long ridged fingers visible among the thick, flexible tissue that connected them in that form—sifted through the sand, pushing the great bulk of its body forward as its long, wedge-shaped tail propelled it.

It turned its head and looked directly at them, and Terri nearly shouted until the flyer veered sharply away when the animal made a lunge for their ship.

Terri clutched a hand over her racing heart, and she shot a

panicked look at Navesha. The female returned her regard with another sharp grin.

"A Great Enthar. It is a vicious creature that preyed on our people for generations in our early history. We are fortunate that it did not surface beneath us as we flew over. They have been known to bring down flyers and merchant transports."

"Fucking perfect," Terri muttered, ignoring the amused chuffing coming from the other female.

She vaguely recalled Veral mentioning the creatures before when they had first met, but at the time what she had pictured was something graceful in its beauty but ultimately harmless enough. *That* was something straight out of a nightmare. Yes, it had fluid movements, but every part of it screamed lethal predator and was thoroughly aggressive.

"Have you ever been brought down by one?"

Navesha gave her a sidelong glance that bordered on disdain. "No. I am the best pilot in this part of the Great Dunes. My ability to calculate variables and my skill with evasion in flight makes me a difficult catch for them. That does not stop them from attempting to eat me, but they never manage to even taste the wing of the flyer."

It was said so matter-of-factly that Terri didn't think the Argurma was boasting. She spoke plainly, as if it were a commonly known, indisputable thing that needed to be told. After so much time in Veral's company, she couldn't have expected anything less. In fact, that bald statement relieved much of her tension as she allowed herself to sag against her seat.

Although Navesha gave her an amused look every so often, the rest of the trip passed uneventfully. With her companion clearly not interested in talking, Terri amused herself by continuing to watch the rolling patterns made by the sand. It was so unlike the desert that had consumed Phoenix. Here, there wasn't even the slightest bit of green outside the walls of the compound.

She had little doubt that the conditions in the courtyard were carefully kept in order to support life. The dunes lacked any and all kindness. In fact, under the bright light of the midday when it came, she was certain that they looked as if they had been stained with generations of blood.

She wasn't sure how long she stared out at the terrifying beauty of the desert, but when brilliant white structures suddenly pierced the horizon, Terri startled with awe. Unlike the permanent ancestral settlements such as the compound, the rough, whitened buildings were clearly put together from some sort of synthetic material made to reflect the sunlight away as she had seen more than once on her adventures with Veral. They were just as stark as any she had seen before, but in the desert their unnatural appearance disrupted it surroundings so that her eye was pulled continuously back to them as they got closer, no matter where she attempted to look.

Her mouth went dry at the almost forbidding appearance of the buildings as the flyer began to make its approach. Navesha grinned as she brought the flyer down. It hit the sand awkwardly, even with the obvious attempt of someone to level the area to receive visitors. Despite that, there was noticeable give to the sand, which made the landing legs shift hard to the right, sinking one side so that it tipped in an alarming fashion.

Chuffing with what Terri presumed to be undisguised delight, Navesha shoved up to her feet and within seconds had the door sliding abruptly open. Taking a deep breath, the female gestured to the entrance of the buildings with flourish.

"Welcome to the Shanah Market, little human," the female boasted with another sharp grin.

*T*erri blinked with watery eyes and squinted against the bright light as she followed Navesha out of the flyer. The moment was interrupted by a ding, and the female in front of her glanced down with a scowl, muttering as she pulled up a holo-image from her wrist. It definitely seemed to be a list of some sort. It was only up for a moment before she dismissed it and turned to face Terri with a twist of her lips.

"Featha decided that she required a few more things from the market. I regret to say that this is going to take longer than expected," Navesha grumbled. A long sigh escaped her.

"Oh," Terri replied with a slight grimace.

As much as she had enjoyed the prospect for an adventure out in the market, that list had looked a lot longer than what she anticipated. She absently rubbed at her melon of a belly.

"Perhaps I should stay here…"

The Argurma glanced over at her in surprise. "Why would you desire to do that?" Her eyes trailed down to Terri's hand and rested there. "If you are worried about your offspring, do not concern yourself. I will give you an opportunity to rest while I acquire the majority of the items that are clustered within the same square. We will shop a little while I get some of these items nearest to the gates. Afterward, you will rest and eat in the shade, and I will fetch," she added with a chuff.

She was hungry, and the idea of enjoying the market from someplace cool and comfortable did sound nice. She spared a quick look over at Navesha, trying to discern if her companion was up to anything, but the female was once again looking at the list, hissing to herself in annoyance while she waited for Terri's decision.

"I would like to look around," Terri admitted.

Navesha nodded as if she had never had any doubt that her answer would be otherwise. Without glancing away from the list as she busily shifted things around, she began to stride away, leaving Terri to hustle after her. A moment later, she grinned in her peculiar mostly close-lipped manner over her shoulder, the hologram once again dismissed.

"The cities have larger and more impressive markets that host many different vendors from all corners of the cosmos. Everyone is eager to trade their luxuries to Argurumal. Our market here is very small in comparison, but I am certain it is like nothing you have seen."

"I've only seen the markets of the space stations, and they are quite impressive," Terri murmured, her head craning as they passed through a large arched gate, "but this place looks like it can fit three of them within its walls."

"I forget what a primitive species you hail from to be impressed by a space station." Navesha gave a low chuff and shook her head in apparent amusement.

"I take it you don't agree."

The female lifted a shoulder casually. "They are constructed by inferior beings. The variety of species can be fascinating, from what I have seen from instructional vids, but the space station is not a great marvel of technology. Argurma tech built this place to be suitable for the needs of the species who come to sell their wares for our credits. By that alone, it is far superior to the filthy space stations that are barely held together in space."

Terri couldn't argue the point. As they came around a corner, the market stretched out in front of her like a sea of activity. Everywhere she looked she saw shops, many of which had merchants standing out in front attempting to lure in customers. The scent of food filled the air, along with the cacophony of noise from voices shouting over each other, the hum of conversation and a number of exotic alien animals that were perched on arms and shoulders, many of which seemed to be sold from more than one shop.

Navesha nudged her with a smirk, and Terri promptly snapped her mouth shut, heat rising up her neck and into her cheeks. It was bad enough that most Argurma seemed to be of the opinion that other beings were far inferior to their own species; the least she could do was not gape like the primitive that Veral's family seemed to think she was.

"Come along, human," Navesha said with the faintest note of something Terri might have called cheer if it didn't sound almost threatening. "We will begin over there."

Terri trailed after her as the Argurma's large body weaved through the crowd with apparent effortlessness that was lost to Terri. It seemed that the moment the crowd shifted out of the way for Navesha, they closed around her again, making it nearly impossible for Terri to push her way through. Most of them were aliens of different colors and builds of unrecognizable species that she had yet to encounter. She got flashes of horns, webbed frills, scales, those with thick, leathery skin, among many others.

She felt ridiculously relieved that it wasn't a mass of Argurmas. Although there were a large number weaving through the crowd, there were few among those pushing their way past her. Even though they were unlikely to come close to mowing her down due to their sensitive cybernetics, she couldn't help but to be a little intimidated by them.

Growling in frustration, she threw up her hand, allowing several tendrils to escape from her symbiont. They churned in front of her like a protective barrier. Although it didn't spare her from being bumped by careless individuals surrounding her, those in front of her, however, stepped out of her way. Very few were sent off their feet for nearly trampling her in their distracted, hastened state. Terri winced as they stood up and brushed themselves off with pained grimaces.

That had to hurt.

She tensed when the males gave her a peeved look but seemed to reconsider as their eyes fell upon her lashing shield extending out in front of her. Instead, they growled unhappily and departed without conflict. Terri let out the breath she had been holding and faced forward once more.

Where was Navesha?

Alarm shot through her. With muttered curse, Terri pushed her way through to the location where she had last seen the other female. A hard hand suddenly wrapped around her shoulder and turned her around to face a familiar scowling face.

"Navesha," she said with relief as she called back her shielding.

The female's eyes narrowed slightly. "Stay near me. Veral will be displeased if I lose you."

Terri gave a jerky nod of her head. "Sorry, was having trouble pushing through the crowd."

Navesha glanced down with appreciation at her symbiont. "Yes. I thought as much, which is why I returned for you. But this protection you have is like no other."

She tapped one claw against it with interest.

"Yeah, it is pretty handy to have," Terri replied, watchful as an

SANDS OF ARGURUMAL

expression of desire swept over the other female's face. "Worth the buttload of pain, but only one of a kind."

"A pity," Navesha rasped quietly. Eyes lifting to Terri's face, her lips quirked. "Do not look so frightened, human. I have no interest in murdering you for your toy. I am self-serving but not petty."

With a firm pat on Terri's arm, the Argurma turned away to duck into a shop on their left. Terri blew out a relieved breath as she hurried through the doorway after her before she risked getting swept up in the surging crowd once more.

The cooler air inside of the shop was shocking at first after being outside in the intense heat, but it didn't take more than a second for it become wonderfully soothing. If not for the skin protection cream that Veral had provided for her upon their arrival, she was certain she would be sporting vivid sunburns. The intense heat and heavier gravity were both things that she still struggled to adapt to. Half the struggle walking through the market was how much more effort it took just to walk a short distance. Even worse when trying to walk fast. The cool interior, however, was worth the exertion even if she had to wait for her eyes to adjust to dimmer lighting.

Once Terri's eyes adjusted, she was pleased to find it filled with all manner of plants. They filled every inch of the shop with narrow paths carved out going different directions among the rows. Terri bit her lip as she looked for some sign of a pick-up station that were usually conveniently placed in shops within the space stations so that travelers could quickly pick up supplies. That did not seem to be case here.

Terri picked a direction and began to follow it deeper into the shop. Deeper within the vast space, she could hear a trickle of water, but she was completely fixated on the sectioned interior filled with all manner of plants of various sizes, structures, colors, and

87

textures. A vine with bell-shaped mauve leaves trembled lightly around the decorative poles upon which it climbed. Beside it was a tall standing plant with enormous, frilled turquoise leaves that looked softer than feathers. Ruby flowers with many tiny petals bloomed in a long, spiked cluster from the center of the plant. There were orange plants, familiar and unfamiliar shades of green, yellow, and blood red, even some plants that appeared to be a flat gray.

She frowned at that one. She had never seen a gray plant before.

A willowy emerald green alien who appeared astonishingly delicate for the harsh planet giggled from where she stood just off to the side with a watering can.

"You cannot see it, can you?" the alien trilled softly. Terri didn't bother answering since the alien bobbed her head without waiting for a reply. "Yes, yes. I know that look well. Very few species are able to see enough of the color spectrum to see the colors of the Abrinax Cenfola, the heart of dawn flower. Shame. You would not be able to see the dulcet hues of the sunsets on my world for which this flower is named."

The female hummed to herself in a high, buzzing pitch as she watered the plant. Terri eyed the plant skeptically. She had never imagined that there would be something so simple as the color of a plant that she would be unable to see. Curious, she stretched out a hand to touch one of the long, heart-shaped leaves only to have her hand caught by thin fingers tipped with delicate thorn-shaped claws.

"Careful. The sap of the Abrinax causes a terrible reaction for many species with delicate skin." She released Terri's hand and patted it soothingly. "A shame you do not have an exoskeleton like my people do." She sighed as she gestured at her skinny green body. "Worse, you appear more delicate than most. Best to leave it alone."

"I see," Terri murmured, uncertain if she should take offense at being referred to once again in some variation of delicate and weak.

She scowled slightly at the implication, but the alien beside her didn't seem to note it. Or perhaps she didn't register Terri's facial expression as she had a perfectly smooth forehead with the luster not unlike a beetle. On closer examination, tiny joints in the exoskeleton became more visible, creating a peculiar segmentation to her long, thin limbs that should have been stranger to her than it was considering that it was her first time meeting a species with an exoskeleton. Instead, despite the alien's words about Terri's delicacy, it just enhanced the other female's appearance of fragility, one she knew was deceptive given the strength of an exoskeleton.

The lithe alien tipped her head to the side in an insectoid fashion, almond-shaped eyes staring unblinkingly at her. "You see? Do you really? Odd, I did not think you could see it."

"No. I mean that I understand. I will be sure not to touch it," Terri amended. The alien bobbed her head again, and Terri glanced around helplessly. "Actually, I am just looking for my Argurma companion I followed in…"

"A female?"

"Yes…"

The alien's pupils moved as her eyes seemed to complete rotate in their sockets at an odd angle. It was more than little creepy. "Over there around that bend. She is speaking with my sire at the counter." A minuscule flexible joint in the exoskeleton on the bridge of her nose lifted to give the impression of a nose wrinkling in distaste. "A regular client who never ceases to complain how humid we keep the air. Truly unpleasant. We explain to her again and again that Ragirsi cannot survive in that dry heat out there, or even spend prolonged time at the front. Customers must always come in, but this just displeases her more. This is your friend?"

Terri grimaced at the censure in her tone. Why didn't it surprise her that Navesha, even as regular client, wasn't on friendly terms with the merchants?

"More like a relative," she answered.

She would have a difficult time of claiming Navesha as a friend. She was Veral's cousin and one who had promised her aid upon their arrival. That was good enough for Terri to accept the female's presence, but she couldn't deny that the female could be unpleasant at times with her cutting comments and observations. She was belligerent, but at least she was an ally, which made her a bit easier to tolerate.

The Ragirsi beside her sighed. "Oh, yes. Woe to the fates that we cannot choose our family. My sire is gathering her order, so you will have no trouble catching up to your kin."

"Thank you," Terri replied as she hurried off in along the path the female indicated.

Walking along the twisting path between rows of potted plants, Terri finally stepped out in a small alcove that was dominated by a large counter. A very tall green male made an impatient clicking sound as he slid a sealed UV protected bag across the counter to Navesha. The female had her hands braced against the countertop and was leaning her weight on them as she spoke quietly. Not for the first time, Terri wished she had the sort of enhanced hearing that her mate had. Whatever Navesha said seemed to make the male increasingly agitated but he handed over a clear packet with two capsules in it which the female tucked into a pocket with a small smile.

"You have finally arrived," Navesha greeted her as she scooped up the package. "I thought I would need to search for you once more. I am pleased to see that is not the case." She inclined her head toward the merchant. "I will be certain to report on today's service to Featha. I am certain she will reward your shop with future purchases for her little garden, despite its inadequacies. I am not pleased to have to wade through this wet pit only to find a partial order ready."

The male bobbed his head, the tiny joints along his jaw tightening. "The rarer plants take time to acquire, even more so those that will survive Argurumal. Your courtyards are set up with barrier technology, which helps, but her requests take time to fill."

Navesha lifted a hand and tapped on her comm device on her forearm. "I shall relay those exact words and let her decide how to proceed. I have transferred the credits for the dantha olara and the capsules. Perhaps you will remain in her favor to see more credits in the near future," she said with a hard smile.

Tucking the package under one arm, she peered down at Terri with a frown.

"You are leaking water."

Terri glared back at her. "It's called sweat. Humans sweat when we get too warm. It is hot as hell out there, so it's bound to happen."

"It is very inefficient. I hope your offspring doesn't inherit such a trait," Navesha replied with a click of her mandibles.

Gritting her teeth, Terri glared at the female's back as she strode out ahead with an imperious, "Come, human. We do not have time to waste on standing in place."

Giving the Ragirsi an apologetic look, she hurried out back into the sun.

True to her word, Navesha didn't keep her on her feet long. They took a direct path leading deeper into the market, picking up other sealed bundles from various shops. One looked like a perfumery—though she couldn't be certain exactly what was within the glowing vials—other shops held a variety of tech, herbs and spices, as well as butchers with vacuum-sealed cold displays filled with meats and produce stalls. Everything except the tiny packages was sent to be stored on their flyer's cargo hold by for-hire porters who made themselves available at every inter-section.

Finally, they arrived at a large, shaded square filled with fragrant foods being cooked at numerous stalls ringing the area. Terri could see Argurmas and a number of other species seated at tables—some alone, others in pairs or small groups of three to five. Navesha led her to a corner stall, shouting a greeting to an enormous pinkish-gray male standing behind an enormous hot cooking flat. The male's face was wide and angular like someone had carved it out of a boulder and gave him two enormous tusks that sprouted from each side of his jaw. His mouth stretched into a ragged grin.

"Navesha'kanda!" the male barked out with a gruff laugh.

Terri startled at the familiarity of the shortened name, but Navesha chuffed and leaned an elbow at the service counter.

"Gargoluk, I require your special for my mother-kin."

A pair of beady yellow eyes fastened on Terri, and he let out another laugh.

"That is not kin to you... It is a pink little morsel that cannot compare to the sublime strength of an Argurma female."

The female waved aside his comment, her vibrissae puffing out slightly.

Was she... flirting?

"She is a mate to my kin," Navesha clarified with another sound of amusement.

"I was not aware that you mate outside of your species," he replied with obvious interest.

Navesha shrugged. "Nor was I until my cousin brought her home."

The male grunted. "Featha must be beside herself."

"Featha will adapt. She has little choice in the matter."

The male whistled low between his teeth, but Navesha continued speaking uninterrupted.

"I have more errands to see to and the female is not accustomed to our deserts. She will be resting here. Keep an eye on her, see to it that she is unmolested and that her plate and cup remain full, and I will see that you are compensated."

The male gave Terri a thoughtful look but nodded and indicated to a nearby table.

"Seat her there, and I will bring her some food presently."

Navesha grinned at the male again before she took Terri by the arm and seated her at the small square table fixed firmly to the cobbled stone flooring. Although she felt dragged around a bit, Terri didn't complain. Her feet and legs were aching, so she gratefully sank into the chair. To her delight, she had barely seated herself when a large plate full of fragrant noodles with chopped meats and vegetables was set before her with a tall glass of some sort of fruit juice.

"Good. You have food and drink. Now remain here, and I will return in a short time," Navesha instructed.

Taking a cue from Navesha's bad manners, Terri grunted in agreement and snatched up two double-pronged forks. Her eyes followed the female as she walked away and disappeared back in the throng. Her skin crawled slightly at being left alone, but it lasted only a moment before another small plate with a pair of dense rolls was set beside her. Gargoluk gave her a wide grin as he gave her arm a pat hard enough to have knocked her out of her chair if she hadn't braced for it.

"You sit here and eat and do not worry. Gargoluk will kill anyone who tries to harm you." He glanced around with a small grimace, his eyes settling on a number of males and females plying their wares among customers seated at the tables. "Mind them, they will fleece you for all of your credits," he advised gruffly. "Vermin."

With that, he left Terri to her meal. And a delicious meal it was. Everything on her plate was completely foreign to her, but the blend of meats and nutty flavors with a thick, spiced sauce tantalized her tastebuds. She watched the merchants as she ate until her attention became totally absorbed in her food. With one greedy moan and pleased sigh after another, she ate ravenously, slurping the noodles up between bites of the surprisingly light sweetened bread despite its thickness. She barely looked up when a merchant pulled up beside her table until she was surprised by the reedy voice speaking at her elbow.

Glancing down, she met the gaze of a shorter scaled being with a broad fringed head. He couldn't be much taller than her. He grinned down at her and nudged his cart closer. It was filled with a number of exquisite vases, pots and tableware that appeared almost translucent despite being engraved and painted with delicate flowers. He held one particularly beautiful, lidded pot. A bit larger than her hand, delicate orange flowers were carved intricately in a band around it.

"Can I interest a beautiful female in a cosmetic pot? Good for all manner of creams and lotions."

Terri smiled at it with interest.

"It's beautiful," Terri said softly as she took the pot in her hands.

On closer inspection, the pot was even more finely made than she expected and had a surprising weightiness to it. The lid seemed to fit snugly, with no visible gaps that would allow air to seep into it. It was as perfect.

Terri curled her fingers around the small knob at the top, tugging until it released with a pop. A tiny scraping sound came from within it just as she tilted the pot to look inside. Startled, she attempted to shove it back at the seller just as something red hopped out of the pot and launched at her face.

Instinctively, Terri threw her arm up, and thin, metallic tendrils spun out of her symbiont to protect her face, but everything seemed to happen in slow motion. *Too late*, she realized. She hadn't been fast enough. She was distantly aware of her own shriek, but the red creature never landed. A blast sent yellow, goopy innards all over her face, chest, and the plate in front of her.

Gasping for air, she tried desperately not to gag at the foul-smelling remains covering her. Terri swiped uselessly at her face but came away with more of the slimy, sticky substance. She grimaced at the thin yellow ropes clinging to her hands. Slowly, she spread her fingers and shook her hand in attempt to dislodge it.

What the hell is *this?*

A plain gray cloth appeared in front of her face.

"What a surprise to see you here, little human," a familiar cheerful voice said.

Blinking through the slime clinging to her eyelashes, Terri grabbed the dangling cloth and vigorously wiped her face. Once she was sure she had gotten the majority of the guts off her face, she started wiping off her hands. Another cloth was offered, and she gratefully took it and attacked her hands with it. Whatever that creature was, its innards seemed to have a viscous quality to them because every place they touched her skin was red and stinging.

Just great.

Dumping the cloths on her plate of now inedible food, she looked up at the Blaithari, completely failing to conceal her shock at the presence of the tall pirate hovering over her.

"Azan, what are you doing on Argurumal?" Terri asked warily. "And where's Garswal... and your crew for that matter?"

The idea of a crew of Blaithari pirates roaming around sent a ripple of unease through her. As if she didn't have enough to worry about.

The female's smirk broadened into a grin as she dragged a chair over and dropped, sprawling, into it. Unlike the last time she'd seen her, the pirate was wearing finer, fitted clothes and had abandoned her tight topknot for several long braids. She wrinkled her nose at the mess still clinging to Terri's clothes.

"I hate gi'lurth bugs. Deadly if they get ahold of you and unpleasant if you manage to kill them first. But at least you are still alive," she said with a firm slap to Terri's shoulder. "Your little assassin friend didn't get far."

"Assassin?" Terri said, nausea surging up with the thought.

"What else? A gi'lurth bug is not native to this planet and would not have just crawled inside a pot." Azan chuckled.

She lifted one of her six hands and gestured to a scowling Gargoluk. He was storming up to an equally sour-faced guard with the merchant, who had attempted to make a hasty departure, in tow. The male grasped in one of Gargoluk's meaty fists didn't even bother fighting it but allowed himself to be dragged over.

Response time of the guards was impressive. Of the same species as Gargoluk, the male didn't look happy to be there but took the smaller alien with a stern look. Terri wanted to go and question the male, but at the same time, she didn't want to draw attention to herself. Why would the merchant have wanted to hurt her? It was one of many questions that she would have to find a way of getting answers for.

"As for what I am doing here and the location of my crew, we had a surprisingly profitable… let us call it an acquisition… from a system nearby. This was the closest market where we might turn a reasonable profit and far enough away from the main cities to avoid drawing too much attention from Argurma officials. The Great Dunes people are pretty much left to their own devices."

"And Garswal?"

"Waiting on the ship with his… ah, caretaker."

"A caretaker," Terri said slowly. A groan left her. "Please tell me you didn't kidnap someone to nanny the boy."

Azan chuckled. "Ah, we would have been wonderful together. You know me so well. As it happens, we rescued a female who apparently had been heading for the slave market that specializes in rare species. It looks like your mate is not the only one to have stumbled upon your little planet, but given that there was not a whole pen full of them, I imagine they just got lucky with the one and didn't find any others."

"A human," Terri hissed in alarm. "You have a human?"

Azan nodded happily. "She is still… settling in."

Terri blinked at her. "Don't tell me you mean to keep her captive."

"Why not? She is well cared for and a member of my crew, not a slave. It has taken some adjusting for her, but once she realized there was no easy way to return to her planet—a dying planet, from what she says—she is better off with us than she would be alone. Besides, I like her. She's got spirit."

Terri shifted uncomfortably in chair and held back a groan. She couldn't deny that it was likely a safer option for the woman, but it still didn't sit right with her.

"And she's not a slave or in any way forced to stay with you?"

"No." Azan chuckled. "She has half the males on the ship jumping to her demands. She did get separated from us once when she decided to 'escape,' but she decided she preferred our company."

Terri sighed and smiled gratefully at Gargoluk as he indicated for them to follow him to another table nearby. He returned moments later with two plates of food, sitting one in front of each of them.

"On the establishment," he grunted at Azan before stomping back to his kitchen.

Azan dug into the food with delight. Terri watched her for a moment before following suit. They ate in silence for a moment before another thought occurred to her.

"Did you know that Veral and I were here?"

"That is actually a happy coincidence," Azan replied after swallowing a bite of food. "Not to mention fortunate for you. Seems that the gods continue to favor you." Her expression turned contemplative. "If someone is trying to kill you, perhaps I will linger a bit longer. I am quite fond of my human, but I don't like the thought of someone getting to you. Where is your mate, anyway? Last I saw, you two were inseparable, and he didn't tolerate being away from your side for even a moment. He should have been here to kill that male on sight."

Terri frowned down at her food for a moment, the reminder of Veral's absence painful. Azan was right. Before arriving on Argurumal, Veral never would have allowed Terri to be separated from him for days on end.

"He's seeing to some family matters," she muttered.

Azan made a face, and Terri couldn't help but agree with her.

"I never would have imagined that you would have been allowed to come to the market alone," the pirate commented.

"I'm not here alone. I'm with Veral's cousin. She let me stay here to rest and eat while she went to get the rest of the packages she had to pick up."

"And she left you," the female pointed her pronged eating utensil at her, "here alone?"

"Well, she arranged for her friend to watch over me," Terri said, gesturing at the cook once more working over his cooking flat.

Azan hummed skeptically, but Terri was grateful when the pirate changed the subject and turned to regaling her with tales of her recent exploits and latest acquisitions. The tension within her slowly relaxed until a shadow suddenly loomed over them, and Azan snapped her pistols up in four hands, aiming them that the Argurma glaring down at her.

"Who is this?" Navesha growled.

"This is Azan. She's a... friend, I guess you could say. Azan, put those away. This is Navesha, Veral's cousin."

Azan raised a brow at that as she glanced at Terri but slowly lowered her weapons and holstered them. Navesha narrowed her eyes at the Blaithari but, outside of the hiss of her whipping vibrissae, didn't make any other moves. Suspicion crossed her face, but it matched Azan's expression, so Terri considered them equally matched in that.

Terri sighed. "Why don't you sit down, Navesha, instead of standing over us threateningly. Azan isn't going to hurt me."

There was a lengthy pause, but finally the female grunted and dragged a chair over between them. She sat in her chair shooting a glower at Azan, who just grinned smugly. Navesha hissed back but turned her attention to Terri.

"I do not trust this female. Gargoluk told me what happened, and it is too convenient," she growled.

"You mean like your convenient absence?" Azan purred, making the Argurma stiffen with insult.

"Azan," Terri sighed.

The Blaithari waved a hand and chuckled humorlessly. "From an outside perspective, there is plenty to be suspicious about. I am here by chance for a bit of trading, something hardly improbable, but someone attempting to kill Terri the moment she is out of sight of a protector is worthy of suspicion."

"Navesha, is there any way we can talk to that male? He must have been hired by someone."

The female grunted and settled back into her chair. "It will take time. Probably tomorrow at the earliest. The Farhal guards will not let anyone see the merchant until they have processed and thoroughly questioned him. The species is loyal and thus used for casual guard duties no Argurma would desire, but that they follow every letter of the regulations is both beneficial and a hindrance. In this case, the latter. Regardless, Veral wishes to be present when the male is questioned."

Terri rubbed her eyes and groaned. She had hoped to get answers before word finally got around to Veral.

"He knows? Shit. He's not going to be happy."

Navesha grunted again, her mouth tightening as she glared

down at the table. "I commed him the moment I finished speaking with Gargoluk, as was my duty. He is, in fact, very displeased and will doubtlessly murder the male if possible."

Terri winced at 'displeased.' She could imagine that he was, and it was unlikely that his displeasure was solely toward the merchant. He wouldn't be happy that she was endangered while going on an outing that he had no knowledge of. While there was no reason to have suspected she would be in danger, since no one outside of Veral's family was aware they were there, she knew that would do little in the face of his concern for her.

"Just how displeased?"

The female's glowing eyes returned to her, expression flat. "He was not gentle in his assessment of my failure to keep you safe and my misjudgment demonstrated by leaving the compound without Dreth to stand guard." She sighed and waved in Azan's direction. "And I am to bring the alien who assisted you back to the compound. It should be an interesting exchange if you are 'friends,'" she snorted.

Terri glanced over at Azan. She had little doubt, given the mutual dislike between Veral and the pirate, that the reunion would be nothing less than interesting indeed.

*V*eral held his composure as he stared at the male at the other side of the table when, in truth, he wanted to rip the male's head clean off his shoulders. His temper was frayed from days away from his mate interrupted with only brief reunions late in the night. A mated pair was not meant to be separated, but it was not something he could remedy any time soon. Certainly not when his mother-kin watched him with suspicion and hostility.

The males and females who patrolled their territory borders with the herds were not receptive to his presence, nor to news that had preceded him regarding his alien mate and offspring. He had achieved little since he arrived at the eastern border of the territory. Overseeing the supplies and meeting the extended lineages of his line had been rife with tension until it spilled out into the confrontation he was now experiencing with Hitani, the head of the minor eastern household, and her mate, Vand.

The male glared with open hostility at him. Hitani, adorned in finely crafted ropes of chains, stood imperiously at her mate's side with their young gathered around her. Vand glanced over at her, his vibrissae swelling with aggression. Of all those gathered, as the mate of the household head, he naturally stood as the spokesperson against him. Veral could respect that.

However, it was the male's words that drove him to a murderous anger.

The male had charged Veral with endangering their people, and that none of them would submit without cause to acknowledge a male with an alien for a mate and an offspring conceived of an unfortunate breeding that should never have happened.

"We will not risk our mates and young, Veral'monushava'skahalur," his kin growled. "We will not bow to your authority unchallenged. Did you think we would not hear of this bane on our line? All speak of how you dare the anger of the council by mating and bringing an offworld female here. Her presence at your side endangers us. Soon all the territories will hear of her, no matter how we work to contain the secret, because someone will see you together—someone who should not—and word will spread across the deserts until it reaches the council. We will not lie down before the army of the council for your pleasure so you can keep your offworld pet."

A low, angry hiss escapes Veral, his vibrissae snapping with barely contained hostility at the degrading way Terri was referred to. Tension made his muscles expand just enough to make him more imposing as his vibrissae puffed up around him in their lethal dance, the snarl that left his lips full of menace. Hitani stiffened beside her mate and shot him a silent glance, betraying their communication upon their private connection.

He would waste no time for them to form a defensive. He would make his point effectively and succinctly.

Veral's hand snapped out in one quick motion and closed around Vand's thick neck in such a precise manner that he was able to close off his air despite the male's cybernetic enhanced strength. Immediately the male's vibrissae coiled tightly. They pulled and snapped, the sharp tips colliding with the scales on

Veral's hand and wrist, sending pain shooting through him, but he did not let up. His guard, Malraha, lifted her blaster and pointed it at Vand's mate with a stern look of warning as Veral held the male.

Veral slid his eyes over to his guard and bit out a sharp command. "Do not point your weapon at the head of the house, Malraha. She will not attack as she knows that this dispute is one that must be settled."

Malraha blinked her eyes slowly—her only show of surprise —and lowered her weapon as Hitani nodded in gratitude to him. It was on Veral to prove himself to his people, not to wrest control through his guards. The latter was a tactic employed often in the cities but not in the Great Dunes. They had issued insult and would not believe that he could stand against the council if he could not stand against them in protection of his mate. This fight belonged solely to him.

Turning his attention back to Vand, he drew the male in closer, ignoring the sting of the attacking vibrissae in a show of strength and determination. Just behind him, he was aware of Krono pacing, ready to pounce on anyone foolish enough to attempt to intercede.

"You will not insult my mate," he hissed vehemently. "Just as I won't do the insult of killing you in front of yours. I choose to show you mercy as we are all mother-kin. I will protect you even as I protect my dearest, for you are mine as well."

With a growl of disgust, he dropped his kin in the sand and loomed over him as the male wheezed, dragging in large gulps of breath as everyone within the line watched silently from where they stood nearby. Veral growled impatiently and stepped away with the intent on returning to his flyer. If that did not resolve the issue, then he was done here and eager to return to his mate after the comm he received.

"Is this worth the destruction you bring... not only upon us but on your female as well?" the male shouted hoarsely at his retreating back. Veral stopped and looked back at him, watching as the male pushed up from the sand, the red grains falling from his shoulders. "If you valued your mate, you would never have returned to Argurumal to take the seat of our line."

"I had little choice," Veral hissed, addressing not only his opponent but the gathered crowd. "I did not return to take control of the line but found it a matter of necessity. My presence here is solely for my mate. I will protect my mate and young as is right, and I will protect you who are under my care. Do you think I do not understand your concerns? I know that every moment I spend at my mate's side will have a high probability of bringing dangerous attention to her if news of an Argurma-alien mating spreads beyond our borders. There is much risk until it is safe for us to depart. It is something that my processors struggle with, and variables are constantly computed to determine what will bring the least risk. There is no relief from this."

"Then you are foolish," Hitani bit out at her mate's side, her voice resonating with strength and dignity despite the temper behind her glowing eyes as she assisted her mate back to his feet. "A male who is bonded with his mate puts her welfare above all, just as one who leads the line puts the line above themselves. Your selfishness does not accomplish either of these things. There is no protecting her, or us, when all eyes are on you. You should know this, Ahanvala. With mated pairs, where one eyes sees one, they will seek out the other. You wish to protect your mate until you can get her to safety, then you must misdirect with great cunning and make her disappear from all thoughts of any except those closest to your house."

He bristled at the suggestion, but the respected title that fell from the female's lips surprised him. In that one word, she acknowledged on behalf of their minor household his authority of the line and paid him the deepest respect. While others had conceded before him, it was the first time in all the days he spent meeting those of the outlier houses of the line that anyone called him by the honored name. It was for that reason that he constrained himself to a sharp nod in acknowledgment.

"I have recorded your words into my processor," he rumbled and glanced over at the male he had incapacitated. "You have my vow to safeguard the line as is my duty. If you are prepared and willing, we will now go over the data and tour the herds before I must return."

Vand inclined his head respectfully as his mate pressed once more against his side in a show of solidarity and strength. More than anything, Veral wished that he had Terri with him. She was his strength, but at the same time, Hitani's words showed to him the wisdom of his decision.

The rest of the tour continued from there but with far less hostility now that he had gained a measure of respect by besting the foremost among them. It gave him little pleasure in doing so, but with his authority secured, no one else seemed inclined to vehemently oppose him. He knew that it was also due to his acknowledgment of the minor household's speaker. Just as her mate had stood to voice their anger, the female had demonstrated on behalf of that direct line and deferred to him respectfully. His acknowledgment secured him a fragile alliance with the eastern border house.

It was only after many hours that he felt he was able to leave, confident in the house's allegiance to him and now possessing an understanding of the functions of the eastern household and their governance over the line's massive herds, which all appeared to be in good health. It was therefore in a slightly better tempera-ment that he was striding back to his flyer with his guard behind him.

He knew that his ill temper that had plagued him through the latter part of the day leading up to the confrontation was due in part to the comm that he had received from Navesha. Being informed that his mate had already been targeted because he had brought her to this planet, and nearly lost her life due to it, did not sit well with him. The merchant had who had made an attempt on her life had been apprehended—and Veral would deal with him shortly—but he was forced to acknowledge that it was a matter of time before another attempted to succeed were that male had failed. If not for her connection to him, the presence of an alien would have been dismissed in the Great Dunes as something of little note since, unlike the greater cities, they had many species that freely came and went in their regular trade.

Mandibles clicking with poorly contained agitation, he boarded the flyer with his guards. The last thing he wanted to do was to put further distance between them, but Hitani's words couldn't be disputed. The only way to protect her while they were there would be to put distance between them so that none searched for an alien female tied to an Argurma male.

He sat down heavily in his chair and closed his eyes, but the subtle motion of someone settling in the seat beside him made him look sharply over at whomever had interrupted his solitude. Malraha inclined her head, her vibrissae shifting around her gently in an expression of sympathy, although it did little to temper the interest in her eyes as she looked upon him. He was not sure how to respond to either. A distant cousin of the house, it was not unusual that she had regarded him more than once with appreciation. Males and females frequently took mates from distant relatives on the Great Dunes, so her interest was not out of place if he were not mated. In respect of that, she had kept her distance until now.

She leaned in close and peered at him intently.

"Are you going to implement the suggestion of eastern house?" she asked in a quiet voice.

He appreciated that she kept her voice very low. The topic

was a sensitive one, and one that made him feel ashamed to even consider it.

"I will," he said in a quiet, rigid voice, hoping that it would be enough to deter her.

She shifted closer yet, making him tense, but he stiffened and drew back in natural recoil as she set a hand on his forearm covered with the dark material of his shafna that concealed his body.

"If you are willing to heed more advice, this goal might be best achieved if you took up with a female of Argurumal. Keep your human to a room within the household while she prepares to birth and take a proper female into your chambers. A female to be seen with among our people," she purred with a soft vibration of her mandibles.

His temper flaring, Veral ripped his arm away, his vibrissae hissing around him angrily. She was not incorrect, but it was beyond consideration. The female jerked back in the face of his fury, her own vibrissae rising around herself protectively. She knew that he would never harm her. Males did not harm females. But she would get the full taste of displeasure in this matter.

"You insult me and my mate," he hissed. "You are young, but not so young that you do not know that no Argurma would betray their mate with another."

She immediately dropped her head thirty degrees in a show of shame and submission. Her mouth tightened with obvious regret.

"My apologies, Veral'monushava'skahalur, I did not intend insult. I admit that I do not understand your bond with your alien. I did not believe that it could be as strong as it is between our species. I see now that I was mistaken in my assumption. I greatly admire you and would have been honored to have a strong male for my mate, even for a short time. I ask that you do not dismiss me for this error. It will not be repeated," she said earnestly.

Jaw working, Veral reined in his temper and forced himself to sit back in his chair once more.

"I will speak to Terri on whether or not you are still suitable to be within my guard. As per our ways, she has authority on such things. I will not have her insulted with your presence after your offer."

Malraha's vibrissae wilted around her shoulders, and she stood up abruptly from where she was seated. She gave him a sharp nod with a mumble of agreement before she fled from his presence. The vacated seat was claimed by his cousin Larth. Close in age to Veral, and close as younglings, from what vids he had seen before leaving the compound in his youth, Larth was the first among his cousins that came to Veral's mind when he assigned the head of his personal guard. The male's lips twisted with amusement as he dropped into the chair.

"Do not be disconcerted, cousin. It was evident to me that she was going to have to be spoken to, so this situation was the perfect opening to set her straight." The male lifted a shoulder. "It is not the first time she has set her interest on a male, but has never been so bold. No doubt she considered it logical without fully realizing the insult. She is young and eager to find a mate.

Veral huffed, his vibrissae lifting and snapping back down with impatience. "There was logic to it, I do not deny, but no Argurma would abandon his mate for logic." He cast a speculative glance at his cousin to see the male nodding in agreement. "Am I correct to assume that everyone heard?"

"Not everyone. I overheard, and a few of the guard positioned nearest to you. You are aware that there is little concealment with Argurma enhanced hearing."

"I find that I miss being among species that lack such abilities," he replied.

Larth chuffed, his eyes slitting with amusement. "It is inconsequential. She will be embarrassed for a time, but no one will think less of her. Her discomfort will pass."

"I have no concern for Malraha. Her offer was inappropriate. I do not look forward to telling Terri before word reaches her." He paused and met his cousin's eyes. "I ask that no one speak to her regarding the other matter. My mate is strong, but she needs that strength to carry our offspring. I do not wish for any further stress or worries to be placed upon her."

Larth inclined his head and settled back into his seat in preparation for departure. "Understood. I will see to it that none of the guards shares anything that they heard today with anyone in the household. There will be minimal opportunity for it to get back to her."

The silence that pervaded the flyer on their return trip guaranteed that Larth was instructing the entire guard on the tactical channel. Veral had access to it, but he had little interest in linking into it. He was beyond wearied, the separation from his mate weighing harder on him with every passing hour, compounded by the strain of his duties. He longed to take Terri and escape back into space. Without that option, he would have to settle for every moment he could steal away with his mate.

The hour was late, the sky black except for the glow of the moon and the millions of stars brightening it, when the flyer began to make its descent toward the large compound. The dark stone was a barely visible outline even in the strong lights of the flyer until they passed overhead as the craft headed toward the enormous, concealed docking area within the protective rocky hillside just behind the household. The face of the smooth, wind-worn black stone slid open, permitting entrance.

The moment they were docked, Veral hurried through the underground corridor that led to the courtyard. He could hear the guard behind him, but he did not bother to wait for them. He was eager to return to his mate. The pinch of anxiety that had burrowed within him all day did not ease until he slapped his hand on the access panel to their chambers and slipped inside. There, the sight of Terri curled up in their bed, her pale hair spilled out over their pillow beneath the moonlight coming in through the three narrow windows along the wall sent a warm rush through him.

He pulled off his shafna and draped it over one chair before stripping off his tunic and pants. His civix pushed against the pouch of his sheath, but he ignored it as he slipped into bed and drew his mate's warm body against his. She mumbled sleepily and curled her arm around his as her bottom scooted back to nestle against his pelvis. A quiet groan left him, but he would not be so selfish as to wake her. As had been pointed out to him, he had been selfish enough, although coming to Argurumal had been unavoidable. Sighing into her hair, his muscles slowly relaxed one by one, eased by the soft sound of her breathing.

He would do anything to protect her, even hide her in the deepest reaches of their territory, should the danger to her life continue.

He would deal with the latest threat and make certain that the male never entertained the idea of harming Terri again. With a protective growl rumbling in his throat, Veral dropped his nose against her head and breathed in her scent until it lulled him to sleep.

15

*B*linking against the sunlight pouring into the bedroom, Terri stilled as she felt a familiar bulk press behind her. Shifting her hips, she rolled over and took in his relaxed expression. In sleep his dark scales and harsh angular facial plating made him appear as some sort of beautiful graven image. In that moment, he was not unlike a few of the beautiful statues that had remained upright in the graveyard back home, though his mandibles that flexed lightly with every breath were a visible reminder of his strength and lethal nature. They drew her attention to his lips. Perfectly shaped, they were relaxed and slightly pouty in slumber.

Terri lifted her hand and traced the horned plating of his brow lovingly. Her lips quirked as one of his vibrissae slithered up and curled around her wrist. Even in slumber, he sought contact with her. An ache that had been building within her over the days eased. Dropping her hand, she snuggled into him, part of her ridiculously happy that his vibrissae still clung to her.

She had missed this.

His eyes behind his eyelids twitched as if on the verge of waking by her movement. His outer lids lifted, revealing the muted blue of his gaze, until the membranous protective eyelid also slid down as his glowing blue eyes met hers. A rattle escaped him with a pleased sigh as he leaned forward to brush his nose against hers, the tendril around her wrist slipping away at the same moment. Terri smiled at the demonstration of affection despite that loss of contact and stroked her hand through his vibrissae, relishing the way they twisted around her fingers in response.

"I've missed you," she murmured. "Since you're here, I take it you're done meeting everyone."

"I have met with all the households of the line."

She stretched against him, her fingers playfully flicking against the ends of his vibrissae.

"Thank goodness. I look forward to having more time to ourselves. I can think of some ways to pass the time," she teased with another flick of her finger over the sensitive tips.

He caught her hand, stilling her playful touch, but remained silent for a long moment as if were reluctant to answer. Just as her stomach began to twist in unease, he at last grunted in agreement.

"There will still be time that I must see to my duties, and you will remain here, but I will wish to be by your side while I am gone."

Terri frowned in confusion.

"There's no reason for me not to go with you for anything that comes up here. If I don't have to travel far…"

"No," his jaw tightened as his mandibles clicked pensively. "Recent events make it clear that it is best for you to remain here." He smoothed a hand against her cheek. "And perhaps increase your guards." His lips tightened. "Perhaps I shall assign Malraha to you."

She drew back, balking. This wasn't what she had in mind at all.

"But… Malraha is part of your guard."

Something flickered in his expression.

"Yes, and she is capable. She is a vigilant guard. I would trust her with your welfare, whereas I do not think she is suited to my guard."

She narrowed her eyes.

"Why?"

"She made a suggestion that I take the pretense of mating an Argurma female while I lead the house and offered herself at my disposal." Terri jerked upright, her mouth falling open, but his hand gripped her shoulder, keeping her focus on him. "She is young and ignorant, anastha. She did not realize that my mating with you was as strong as an Argurma mated pair. She was regretful of her error, but I estimate that you will not wish her to continue in my service."

"Fuck no I wouldn't," she snapped. She couldn't believe what she was hearing. She would have expected it of anyone else, and not have been bothered by the attempt, but not an Argurma female. A female who knew how the matings worked and actively sought to undermine them and attempt to replace Terri. There was no way in hell she would trust that female at all.

She blinked.

"And this is the female you want to watch over me? A female who I'm not going to trust and for all I know might not be aggrieved if I suffer from some sort of 'accident?' You think I'd be comfortable with that?"

Veral's lips tightened in acknowledgment.

"I did not factor the possibility that you would have these concerns. Malraha would not harm you, if you truly fear that. Her biometrics indicated that she was honest in her regret."

Terri snorted mirthlessly.

"Yeah, sorry she didn't succeed," she muttered. At Veral's frown, she sighed. "Okay well just so we are clear. Am I comfortable with her as your guard? Fuck no, and hell no about her being anywhere near me where I might be dependent on her. Regardless of her intentions and her abilities, I can't trust her."

He did not argue but inclined his head.

"It will dishonor her to return to guarding the compound. However, in consideration of events and your wishes, I will see to it that Larth reassigns her." His expression tightened. "Regardless, you will have a guard, anastha. I am sure my cousins will have suggestions of those best suited among the members of the house. And we will discuss what transpired."

Terri groaned. She should have anticipated that Veral would want to assign more babysitters.

"Just one," she offered. "I always have either Dreth or Navesha with me anyway, so just one more will be more than enough."

Veral narrowed his eyes in consideration.

"Two Argurma warriors should be able to subdue anything that might attempt to hurt you," he conceded, but expression hardened. "If there is any suggestion that it might not be adequate, I will make certain that you are sufficiently protected."

She grimaced but nodded.

"Okay, that's fair.

His hand stroked over her bare shoulder.

"Then we are in agreement. The market we will discuss later. For now, I wish only to reacquaint myself with the touch of my mate," he purred, his vibrating mandibles sliding along her skin as he dipped his head to kiss her neck.

Terri melted into his touch. This was much more like how she had expected their morning to begin.

She exhaled a soft sound of pleasure, a shiver blooming into a surge of heat as he rolled her onto her back. His heavy frame crouched over her; his eyes gleaming brighter with his desire as he pulled the bedding away to fully expose her naked body. She didn't like to sleep clothed, not only because she hated the feel of the fabric tightening around her uncomfortably, but for moments like these when there were needs demanding to be met. It didn't hurt that Veral also slept naked. He hovered over her in all his masculine beauty, his wide chest and muscled abs marked with the tiny networks of cybernetics. There were fewer on his forearms, biceps, thighs, and calves, but each glowed beautifully, begging to be touched and traced.

She pushed herself to a seated position, and Veral groaned as she dragged her tongue against a large patch on his shoulder, his body twitching with his desire. The upraised clusters of cybernetics, while resilient against attack from where they were implanted beneath his scales, were erotically sensitive spots wherever they were the thickest. It was a fun contrast that she loved to use to her advantage. His head thrown back in pleasure, she wasted no time in allowing her lips to travel down the muscle, her teeth lightly scraping and nipping in stinging bites against them.

Veral tolerated her explorations for several minutes as she tongued and bit at various spots on his neck and chest, his breath coming out in hard pants as he trembled with restrained desire. She knew that he had enough when his hand slid up to cup her neck. The curl of his fingers did not alarm her, nor when he yanked her back so she dropped once more on the pillows.

Her chest heaving, she grinned up at him as he kneeled above her. The hard muscles of his abs quivered, directing her gaze to his long, thick sex snaking through the air, the slightly hooked tip swollen with its rigid curve. Her mouth watered at the sight. She pushed herself just enough to grab it tight within her palm. Veral jerked, a muffled snarl leaving him as she stroked it, enjoying the way the tubes along the side excreted their slippery substance. With a moan, she licked and mouthed the head and shaft. When she finally took him into her mouth, she did so at a careful angle so that the curved flesh only lightly brushed upon her tongue.

It wasn't sharp. The tip would become more rigid only when

he neared climax. She had brought him to climax orally before and knew she was in no danger even then. Veral's civix stiffened, and as long as she kept him angled off of her tongue, he had no soft spot on which to latch.

But that wasn't her goal. She wanted him mindless with desire.

His civix twisted, and she sucked harder until he growled and yanked on her hair, pulling her mouth free of him.

"Enough," he rumbled.

With one quick movement, he turned her over onto her hands amd knees, her body swaying before she braced eagerly for him. His large hands slipped along her swollen belly for just a moment before anchoring against her hips. She drew in a breath and then he was there, his body arching over hers as his civix slipped between her folds and burrowed deep with a firm shove of his hips.

The movement of his civix twisting within her, burrowing relentlessly even when he yanked back to thrust forward again, lit up every sensitive spot within her channel. It churned, and tapped, thrumming within her as it sought the mouth of her womb to latch onto. Every hard thrust sent pulses of pleasure through her, until she was a panting, sweaty mess, rocking her rotating hips back against him, needing more of him.

Veral didn't hold back. As he rutted harder, his thrusts rocking her forward with firm slaps, one of his hands planted on the bed beside her, claws digging into the bedding while the other gripped her breast, tweaking and pulling at the nipple.

A tortured gasp left her as he tormented the hard, puckered tip as she felt him thickening with her as he stiffened. The pleasure-pain of his civix latching made her jerk against him as the first of her orgasms overtook her under her mate's approving growl. His pace then picked up. Now that he couldn't pull back more than very slightly, he ground into her with rotating hips, his civix's

117

tugging just enough to send spirals of heat coursing through her blood to coil deep in her belly.

His mandibles vibrated in a low, lusty purr just as his hand dove. The touch of his fingers sliding against her clit made her snap forward against them, creating more of the erotic tug within her. The snarl that followed filled the air as Veral continued his deep, grinding rut. Terri's muscles shook as her pleasure wound tighter. The build was exquisite, but she needed more.

"Veral," she whimpered.

The pinch of his fingers on her clit sent a sharp burst of ecstasy through her, and then she was falling over the edge of her orgasm. She bore down on his civix as she twitched and cried out in bliss. The hot burst within her and his own roar filling her ears was the pinnacle of everything in that moment. Another electric rush of pleasure followed the first as words of love and adoration were rasped to her.

erri scowled at the monitor. Veral had agreed to let her witness the merchant's questioning but only via cam from the safety of their room while he accompanied Navesha and Azan to the market. He hadn't been pleased to learn that the pirate was housed in the visitor's quarters of the compound, but he hadn't attempted to revoke his offer, nor did he hesitate to allow her to accompany him.

Of course the pirate he couldn't stand got to go. Terri got a damned vid feed. At least he left Krono for her this time. He sat beside her, head in her lap as she glowered at the image of her mate and his companions entering the jail and stopping at the reception. Terri scratched the dorashnal's jaw.

Dreth's vibrissae puffed and lowered in discomfort as he gave her and apologetic look from where he sat just across from her.

"I am surprised Veral didn't take you along as well," she remarked sourly.

Dreth chuffed, his eyes, considerably more expressive than Veral's, squinting with genuine humor.

"Someone was required to stay behind as your guard, and since he had not yet had the opportunity to select any others, it was logical that I be the one to remain since Navesha and the Blaithari wished to see the matter to its conclusion."

"As I would have liked to," she shot back. "I'm the one who nearly got killed."

"Which is why you are not involved," he replied, unruffled. "It is too personal. Your emotions will cloud your mind. Rather, focus on the objective of acquiring information."

"You are saying it's not personal for Veral?" she asked.

"It is personal, and he will likely kill the male when he is finished acquiring information," Dreth corrected. "But he is programmed foremost to keep to his objective and has the same personal training as all of us who must keep our malfunctions secret to keep his emotions second." He leaned back in his chair, eyes returning to the viewing screen.

Terri scowled at his profile.

"Should have known you would say something like that," she muttered, watching Veral as he followed the jail guard back through a locked door.

She blinked and sat forward as everyone jerked to a halt. What was going on? Even Dreth's lips fell in a puzzled frown. The tiny drone was just behind Veral's huge shoulders, so she had no way of seeing what was happening, but Azan's barked expletive and Veral's angry hiss was enough to tell her that whatever it was, it was not good.

Her mate rounded on the guard, snatching him by the throat with one hand as he shoved the male into the wall, his vibrissae whipping forward in fury.

"What happened here?" he growled.

He stepped forward, crowding into the male's space, and Terri drew in a sharp breath. The male lay crumpled on the ground, green foam spilling out from his mouth to mingle with the blood streaking down from his eyes and leaking from his pointed, frilled ears. Her fingers dug into the armrests of the chairs as she swallowed back her nausea.

"What the fuck?" she choked.

She could just barely hear the pirate mutter the same question as she toed the corpse with a shudder of revulsion. Since the drone was coded to Veral's bio-signature it stayed near him and the audio was filled with the guard's laborious breathing. He wheezed around the tight grip on his throat, his thick fingers digging into Veral's forearm. Although the Farhal was larger and impossible for Veral to pick up, the sheer strength of her mate kept him immobile despite his struggles. The guard's mouth gaped slightly as he drew in a ragged breath, however little Veral allowed.

Terri rolled her eyes as the excessive show of force despite the tiny thrill it gave her knowing that concern for her was largely what motivated the reaction.

Control of his emotions her ass.

"Yes, I can see he's keeping himself under control," she muttered.

Dreth shrugged. "The male is not dead."

"Answer," Veral commanded in a low hiss. "What happened?"

"Poison… It looks like poison," the male rasped fearfully.

From the angle of the droid Terri could see the deadly narrowing of her mate's eyes.

"And how," Veral snarled, "would poison have made it into the jail cell? Do you not remove your captive's personal belongings?"

The guard gave a jerking nod. "Yes, on my oath. We search all pockets, pat the clothing for anything in the lining, and search orifices. We also run a toxins and metals detector to catch anything we may miss. He was clean. There was no chance of him bringing it in with him."

"Who gave it to him then?" Veral demanded.

"I do not know! I just came on shift after the midday meal hour. I would need to check the security footage, but I do know that there haven't been any visitors. From what I understand, he did not move from the bench by the window all day."

"In front of the window."

"We know it is against regulations, but the window is very small. Not even the smallest species would be able to get through it."

"That is hardly the only potential concern," Veral snapped.

Her mate huffed then and released the male, the guard immediately rushing back up the corridor as Veral spun around, his eyes narrowing on the body. He barely glanced up to nod to another Farhal, one wearing a crisp black uniform jacket in contrast to the red ones worn by the other guard she had seen. This new male took position by Veral's side, his face hardening as his eyes skimmed over the corpse on the floor of the cell.

"Damned mess," the Farhal muttered as he pulled a datapad from a pouch inside his jacket. "I am head guard Shonk Vazan. You are Veral'monushava'skahalur, current head of the Monushava household investigating an attack on your household initiated by this vendor?"

Veral grunted in agreement.

Vazan did not react to the Argurma's non-reply, but Terri wasn't surprised. Over a year with Veral and she had become accustomed to it. No doubt the Farhal was accustomed to Argurma mannerisms because the male nodded his head and lowered his datapad to peer at the body.

"Guardsman Yarth gave me a summary of what happened, and I would like to assure the Monushava household personally that he is correct. No one visited, nor was any suspicious activity recorded in the cell." He squinted at the window. "He mentioned that you believe the attack came from the window. It is very narrow. It would be difficult to..."

122

"Not for an Argurma," Veral interrupted impatiently. "Navesha, check the male for any sign of damage on the back of his torso and arms—anywhere accessible from the window."

The female nodded and, before the head guard could object, headed toward the body. She stepped past Azan, who rubbed a bit of the mucus between her fingers and sniffed it. The pirate recoiled and wiped her fingers off on the body.

"If I were a betting female—and I am—I would wager that the culprit here is the dalif strobinis xerxi. It is a fast-acting poison contrived from the stinger of a deep-sea dwelling creature from Ogamulan. Any pirate would love to have a supply, but it is hard to come by and very expensive." She smirked up at him. "I nearly got a supply to take care of my dear former captain before we met up with you."

Navesha made a disgusted sound as she rolled the male over, no doubt from the foul odor coming from the body given the dark stain of bloody shit covering the seat of his pants. She didn't comment, however, as she ran her fingers around the male's head and checked his neck. Not finding what she sought, she stripped him of his vest and tunic and froze. Slowly, she pushed to her feet and glanced over at Veral who promptly strode, with a scowling Vazan, to her side.

"This is against protocols," the head guard rumbled, but other than that complaint he seemed in no hurry to touch the body.

Not that Terri could blame him with all the disgusting ooze all over the vendor.

The Farhal's remark was barely acknowledged by the Argurmas with more than a flick of their eyes upon him.

"Between his shoulder blades," Navesha growled.

Vazan shifted closer and whistled between his teeth as he lifted his pad up, no doubt capturing images, something that Terri knew the Argurmas were doing via their optical implants.

Cursing, Terri worked to aim the drone's visual recorder on

the corpse as her mate leaned forward. The view tilted as the drone swung at an abrupt angle, and she watched as Veral's fingers set on either side of a raised red bump the size of a nasty bug bite or sting. Slowly, he squeezed, and she felt her stomach churn as green puss wept from what had to be a pinprick opening.

"Fuck, that's disgusting. Like the zit from hell," she muttered, earning her an understandably confused look from Dreth.

"A what?"

She waved him off.

"Never mind. It's nothing your species has to deal with," she muttered distractedly. Clearing her throat, she activated her comm. "Now what?" she asked her mate, her voice echoing back to her on the viewing screen.

Veral's vibrissae twitched as his eyes panned the room before settling once more on the narrow window that let in only a thin beam of sunlight. Shonk Vazan's eyes slanted toward Veral's comm.

"Is this the female who was attacked? We may need to question her."

Her mate turned toward the guard, his posture stiff as he nodded. "She is. Ask your questions now. The female is an alien currently under the protection of my line and will not be leaving the safety of the compound while there is danger. The Blaithari was also present and may relate what she observed."

Terri frowned. A female under protection of his line? That was an odd way to address their mating. She had never heard him refer to their relationship in such cold, detached terms before. Perhaps it was normal, though. Navesha didn't seem to react at all to his statement and Azan only frowned slightly at him, the expression nothing more than a faint flicker across her face as she straightened from her crouch beside the body.

The guard scraped one thick hand against his wide jaw. "I did not realize that the Argurma were employing other species within their household."

Terri waited expectantly for her mate to correct him, but to her surprise, Veral said nothing. His lack of response appeared to be enough of a deterrent because the head guard shrugged, lifted his datapad once more, and proceeded to question Terri and Azan on everything they could remember. When he was satisfied that he had a full account of everything they witnessed, he slipped the pad back into his jacket and sighed.

"Not a lot to go on. Clearly it was staged in advance if the male was in place with his wares. Did anyone know that you were going to the market?"

Navesha shook her head. "No. I was asked only that morning to retrieve the items and brought the female with me that she might enjoy seeing our market." She turned a sharp look to Veral. "I was transporting the order for the household."

Veral clicked his mandibles in an annoyed tempo. "I will speak to Featha and ascertain whether she mentioned it to anyone."

Vazan slipped his datapad back inside his jacket and frowned. "I would like to question her as well."

One corner of Veral's mouth tipped. "You are welcome, head guardsman. Comm the household and make an appointment at your pleasure."

"I will. At this point, all we can do is question our local informants and see if anyone has heard or witnessed any strange meetings involving the vendor. I will be frank that it could simply be a matter of jealousy. Your kind does not have a history of taking other species into your employ or even your company. Someone might have seen the alien assisting this Argurma female and acted in hope of creating a possible opening of employment, or perhaps a member of your species retaliated against a breach of etiquette. It would not be the first time there has been a murder related to employment opportunities in the Shanah Guard, nor of Argurmas killing offworlders they find offensive."

Veral's eyes narrowed. "How regular are these incidents?"

Vazan shrugged. "More often than I would like. It seems like at least once a lunar we get a report of something of this nature occurring. Offworlders killing each other for scraps or getting killed by a local they have offended in their attempt to gain credits. There are limited employment opportunities, and competition is strong among those who come to Argurumal." He snorted mirthlessly. "You would think they would stop coming and go somewhere with wider opportunities. In any case, I would not worry too much about it as anything more than that. If I see any indication otherwise, I will notify you immediately. It still leaves the question of who killed the vendor, but if an Argurma can accomplish that feat, it is possible that a skilled assassin could too."

Veral's face remained expressionless, but Terri could tell he wasn't convinced. She, however, hoped Vazan was right. She stroked her belly with worry as she watched Veral leave with Navesha and Azan. She could feel Dreth watching her. She gave him a tight smile.

"He's probably right," she murmured. "Someone probably saw a good opportunity and took it."

Dreth inclined his head, his lips pinching. "That would be the logical conclusion," he agreed.

She wished that he was a bit more convincing because some small part of her trembled uneasily. She could feel metal tendrils sliding over her arm, her symbiont activated but in a resting phase with no immediate enemy to attack. Did she have an enemy? Someone had tried to kill her, and she could only hope that it was, as the guard said, a single event of opportunity.

*F*eatha stared blankly at Veral, her vibrissae puffed out, the tips moving erratically the only sign of her surprise.

"You cannot suspect me," she said after the passing of several minutes.

Veral had come directly to her the moment the flyer returned to the compound. There was logic to what the Farhal Vazan had said, but he needed to set his own mind at ease by speaking to his mother-kin. In truth, he did not believe that his aunt would do such a thing. Manipulating the order of the household was a different matter from assassination of one's mother-kin. And whether Featha liked it or not, Terri was included among them.

"No," he said at last. "Whatever disagreements we have, I am aware of your loyalty to the household and protectiveness of our line."

She stood from her couch, her vibrissae snapping through the air around her as she strode over to a table and poured water from a pitcher into a deep blue cup.

"Do the guards have a course of action planned?"

He inclined his head, aware that even though she was not

looking directly at him that she was aware of his every movement in her rooms.

"Aside from his request to interview you, the head guardsman Vazan will be sending his men out to make inquiries. There is little more that they can do. He believes the motivation may have been localized by her mere presence rather than an intentional strike against Terri or our line."

She paused, head cocking. "Do you agree with his hypothesis?"

Veral blew out a long breath, displeased to admit to his uncertainty.

"I do not know. It is a reasonable presumption based on the facts he presented, but I do not wish to dismiss a potential threat out of hand."

"If you would have my counsel…"

"I would accept it with gratitude."

The corners of her lips twitched.

"It has been many revolutions since anyone expressed gratitude to me." She sighed and sank down onto her couch again, her expression turning thoughtful. "When you are the Ahanvala, it consumes you, but you do not see the demands. Your vision is shorter and more immediate for the welfare of our people, so much so that you do not feel the weight of responsibility but bear it without prejudice. You are honored to bear it. It becomes a part of your identity within your processors. You become blind to what would never have escaped your notice. Until this moment, I did not recall how long since I had gratitude. My advice is do not become comfortable in your position. Protect your mate with strategy as you would beyond the borders of our star system."

"I am limited."

"So I have heard." She chuffed, the sound dry and lacking in any manner of amusement. "I agree with our mother-kin that this is a delicate balance that you must maintain on the edge of a knife. The charade must continue as you say, but do not neglect your mate. It has been… painful… to observe her grief at your absence." She paused and whipped her head around, giving him a sharp look. "You will not share my words."

"No. On my honor."

"Good. I would not desire the situation that you have, to be torn between your line and your mate. Now you will taste the unpleasant bitterness of being the Ahanvala and see it for what it is more acutely than any other before you. It has potential to bring you greater harm than any other. Do not make my errors and twist your reasoning to preserve what you consider necessary or right. I make no excuse for my actions. They were deliberate and planned out to what I thought was logical."

She paused, her mandibles clicking thoughtfully. "Our programming to seek logic blinds us all to a degree. It is easy to acknowledge why other species distrust us when we can be swayed to action by logic over loyalty when it comes to others."

"My mate has suggested something similar," he acknowledged, bearing the female's amused chuff in reply.

He did not credit it at the time, but being back on Argurumal, he was less certain in his conviction. He was still considering this later when he left Featha's rooms and the entire duration that he attended to his duties around the compound. How did one find balance with logic and reason when these were the highest ideals? The answer seemed to lurk beyond the ability of his processors to achieve. As the pain of separation from his mate grew throughout the day, he desired to confide in Terri and bask in the warmth of her comfort. It was a need that gnawed on him until he felt sick, but he continued to attend every task.

He could not let weakness win. He had to achieve the balance.

18

"Permission for quarter hour of your time," a feminine voice spoke, breaking Terri out of her reverie.

When Veral didn't come back to their chambers after returning to the compound, she had sought the solace of the gardens. Dreth stretched out in the chair at her side, his head angled up at the newcomer from where he had been going over something on the datapad he held loosely in his hands. He didn't speak, though his eyes narrowed subtly. Terri followed the direction of his gaze and squinted up at the female hovering over her.

Unlike Veral, whose body was littered with clusters of cybernetics, or even Navesha who had long streaks of them running along her face and forearms, this female had a few small patches, hinting at minimal upgrades compared to other whom Terri had met within the compound. Her build was lean and strong though, giving the impression of being capable of greater speed.

Terri set her own datapad down, reluctantly tearing her attention away from one of her favorite old Earth novels. Since downloading the human language programs that Veral's AI created from the information held in Earth's satellites, reading had become an enjoyable way to spend time and an escape when she needed it—like now, when she desperately needed a distraction from her dismay over Veral's recent strange behavior.

Maybe it's just pregnancy hormones and I'm reading too much into it.

Pushing the thought aside, she smiled curiously up at the female.

"Sure. How can I help you?"

The female shifted her weight subtly on her feet, her vibrissae flattening a bit with unmistakable unease.

"I am Malraha'monushava'fagri. I understand that Veral informed you of my behavior, but I wished to speak to you personally since I understand that I have been dismissed."

The smile fell from Terri's lips, and she straightened in her chair, immediately on-guard.

"About what, exactly? Veral asked my feelings on the matter. They're unlikely to change any."

Malraha's vibrissae twisted around her shoulders as her lips thinned.

"I do not fault you for your decision or expect you to reverse it. The boundaries involving mated males and females are clear in our society, and it was my own miscalculations that made me presume that it would be a different sort of bond formed with an offworlder. I did great insult to both you and Veral'skahalur and I wish to express my regret for that and to explain my actions so that you will have no further concerns."

Terri glanced over at Dreth and raised her eyebrows. Was this female for real? He gave a brief nod of his head though he looked over at Malraha with disapproval. Terri sighed. It was bold, but she couldn't say that the move wasn't effective.

"All right. Let's hear it," she said at length and gestured to the chair across from her. "Have a seat."

"Do not in any fashion distress Terri," Dreth rumbled from her side, the rebuke clear in his voice.

Malraha gave a short bob of her head and sat on the bench at the opposite side of the small table.

"First, I would like to formally request that I be permitted into your personal guard. Veral put a call out to interview those interested, and I came directly to you to make my case."

"Very bold of you," Terri said slowly. "But I'm sure you're aware that if I don't trust you in my mate's company, then I can hardly trust you at all. That wouldn't be very helpful for someone charged with keeping me safe."

"This has occurred to me," Malraha agreed. "And this is why I must explain my actions. I do not like that I have shamed myself, nor that I have reduced my standing so much among my mother-kin."

"Okay, I'm listening."

The female chuffed, staring off into the garden.

"I do not desire Veral. Not truly. But my proposal seemed like a logical move from my standpoint. He is a strong male of significant distance from me in blood and I admire the way that he has been handling his many responsibilities for our household. It was not an honorable request, and I would have been scorned by all our line if he had agreed."

She fell silent for a moment, her face expressionless except for a betraying tension around her eyes. "I am not a female of great standing or any importance. I was birthed in the northern territory household, and although I was reared in the facilities in the great cities of Argurumal's Black Stone Division, when I arrived to finish my final adjustments with my mother, it was to the realization that I have little to offer to attract a mate. I have little for any offspring to inherit outside of space in a minor wing of a minor household. I took a place in the greater household here and received two offers to attempt a mating bond. Both failed."

Her lips quirked in the barest hint of a smile. "That would have dismayed me too much. Navesha has failed four matching attempts to my understanding but still gets offers every revolution. I do not. I have offered to take the hormone, but the males will not agree to a hormonal bond with a female of low standing. They would rather wait to develop a true bond. Now that there are no more offers, it did not seem a great risk to offer myself to Veral. He would require no hormone, and I could find a place to belong and perhaps breed and bear offspring. It has happened before in the few instances where a male has survived the death of his mate to take another, though statistically rare. But now I understand that the mating is fully in place between you, I have no interest in pursuing him."

"And what would stop you from just murdering me and taking him then?" Terri asked bluntly. "You owe me no loyalty."

Malraha shook her head, her lips curving into a smile.

"Even if I desired that outcome, your mate would reject me. There is no profit in your demise, and I will not disgrace myself further in this matter. I do not owe you loyalty, but I am responsible for my position within the household and for my actions."

"Okay," Terri said slowly. "I can appreciate that. Still, it doesn't explain why you're interested in being *my* guard."

The other female's face hardened as she straightened further in the chair demonstrating every inch of the imposing warrior that Terri knew she had to be to have been assigned to Veral's guard.

"Because I am a warrior. I may not have as many modifications as many of my kin here since I am birthed from one of the minor households, but I compensated with training hard and applying myself to be the equal of any warrior here. Guarding you will restore my honor to a degree among my kin and to myself and give me a purpose that is greater than patrolling the compound."

"I see," Terri murmured with appreciation. "You do realize that guarding me won't exactly be exciting." She gestured to

Dreth. "This about sums up what you'll spend a lot of time doing. Are you sure you'd rather do this?"

"Yes," Malraha replied instantly, without wavering.

Terri's lips pinched together as she considered. She still wasn't happy with the female's attempt to poach her mate, but she had to admit that she liked Malraha's force of personality. Yes, she had made a grievous misjudgment, but she clearly had the integrity to admit when she was wrong, in addition to possessing physical strength and skill.

"Accept her already. You know you are going to do it, so you might as well embrace it now," Azan said cheerfully as the she emerged at a leisurely stroll, with a human woman on her arm, from behind a bush thick with fragrant flowers.

That the Blaithari managed to find her was both unexpected and unsurprising. There were numerous little paths and intimate clearings throughout the large courtyard, enough so that Terri rarely saw anyone in the small clearing nearest to the private rooms she shared with Veral. Even with that taken into consideration, she knew that Azan was particularly gifted with finding a way of being informed about everything. There was no reason that would be less true now than it was on the pirate ship. Because she knew that, she also knew she wouldn't escape without the female's opinion. Letting out a sigh, she leaned back in her chair, she regarded Malraha.

Might as well get it over with.

"All right. Why not? Consider yourself on my guard. I will let Veral know. I'm sure he'll be ecstatic that I have another person to hover over me," she sighed.

The female seemed to sag where she sat for a moment with obvious relief before she caught herself and straightened once more. Malraha turned herself at an angle so that she partially faced everyone. Her expression hardened in what Terri figured had to be her 'on duty' face.

"Relax. We are all friends here," Azan chortled, her laughter only increasing as Malraha's disapproving glower.

Terri bit back her own laugh, not wishing the female to feel alienated, but she caught the flicker of a smile that appeared at the corner of Dreth's mouth before disappearing.

"Is Veral capable of demonstrating ecstasy?" he inquired after a moment.

Azan snorted. "If you call cracking a faint smile a demonstration of ecstasy. The male otherwise seems to be limited to a range of expressions implying 'I will kill you.'"

Terri flicked her first two fingers at the pirate, the second slightly bent, in what she had come to realize was a crude gesture among the intergalactic communities. Azan barked out a laugh that Terri completely ignored, but she was privately delighted when Malraha's lips twitched. Returning her attention to the Blaithari, Terri raised an eyebrow.

"Was there something you wanted, or do you just randomly eavesdrop on everyone you meet?"

Azan shrugged with an unrepentant grin as she dropped down on a nearby bench, pulling her human onto her lap. "Not at all. Usually, it is more in the vein of information gathering. In this case, however, I was flat out straining to catch every bit of gossip shamelessly. I would have come and sat down to enjoy the show except my Wendy here objected. She has yet to learn that scruples are unbecoming of a pirate."

Tall and slender, and possessing thick dark hair falling to her waist, Azan's human hardly looked like a woman recently taken from Earth. Terri's own hair was only half that length and, like the rest of her once painfully thin frame, had only recently began to thicken. Wherever Wendy had come from, it must have been a kinder environment. It was only knowing that the other woman had been captured with the intent to sell her that kept Terri from feeling envious of what seemed like a much better lot in life.

"There's nothing wrong with wanting to be more than an ill-mannered space-thief," the woman shot back smoothly. "I keep telling you that the universe was not created to entertain and fund you. If I'm going to be unscrupulous, it will only be against those who are deserving of it. Friends aren't deserving of it."

Her eloquence wasn't what Terri would have expected of a recent survivor either.

"I differ entirely on that. Friends deserve it more than anyone else," Azan objected with a scoff, the lowest of her three arms on her right side banding around Wendy. "How else can those who care about them know the minute details that they can use to assist them? Prying into friends' lives is caring."

"That's disturbing," Wendy replied with feigned annoyance. She half-turned to Terri. "By chance, are you looking to hire a nanny?"

"You already have a youngling you care for as well as an entire crew of miscreants who would not know what to do with themselves without your firm hand," Azan quickly objected. She frowned for a moment. "Do not let me forget to check on said miscreants. I know I am going to regret allowing Garswal to stay on ship with them while we returned to the compound."

"There's really no need for you to stick around. I'm sure the guard is right and it's just a typical local thing. Probably nothing to worry about," Terri said, not liking the guilt that rose up from her gut.

"And leave it to Navesha to accidentally lose you or get you killed?" Azan scoffed as she flicked a leaf off her shoulder. "Not likely. I will not leave until I am assured that you and your youngling are safe."

"Navesha isn't trying to lose me or get me killed," Terri replied.

"I did not claim that she was but that she is negligent with the care of delicate little humans. That one is distracted by something," Azan said airily. "I will feel better with my own eyes on you, and those of your eager young guard," she added with a grin.

"No harm will come to her while I am present," Malraha hissed vehemently.

"See? *That* is the reaction of a good guard!" Azan praised. "If you could spit venom, I would be tempted to lure you away to join my crew. You cannot spit venom, can you?"

Malraha scowled back at the pirate. "Your foolish speech is making my head hurt."

Azan sighed dramatically and hugged Wendy to her. "This is why you are much better off with your fine Blaithari pirate and crew. Argurmas are not much fun." She slanted a wicked grin in Terri's direction. "If you change your mind about being mated to a fleshy droid, you are always welcome in our crew."

Terri didn't bother to hide her smirk when both Argurmas snarled in offense. Azan was just fortunate that Veral wasn't there to threaten her health, although her babysitters did a pretty good job at that by themselves.

19

*V*eral's eyes tracked his mate strolling up the corridor. For days, he had attempted to satisfy his need to be near his mate by covertly watching over her as she walked through the long halls of the compound. Their nights together were not sufficient to fulfil his need for contact, and inevitably at some point during the day he requested his mate's location and sought her out just to watch her for a moment or brush close to her in passing.

It was not enough. The whispers of contact barely took the edge off his need to be near her. His senses were deprived of her scent, touch and taste, and his processors were struggling, his concentration fragmenting into looping segments of data images of his mate. He required time alone with his mate without the chance of eyes on them. It was to that end he decided to stage a chance encounter to be near her without drawing attention.

He had been unprepared, however, for Terri to have two Argurma guards with her.

An annoyed hiss escaped him as he vented his frustration at the sight of Malraha and Navesha at either side of his female. Not only did her guards come close to blocking his view of his mate with their larger frames, but their presence was going to make his plans more difficult. With the addition of Malraha to Terri's guard —a decision that had pleased him solely for the reason of providing his female with extra protection—he had failed to calculate that it could potentially pose some manner of obstacle for him.

At least he could count on Navesha to be discreet. Even though she didn't know the details of his self-enforced separation from Terri, he knew that she had a reputation among the household for thinking quickly and doing what the moment required of her. It was the reason that Featha sent her on household business. It was an explicit trust that few others in the household enjoyed, though he knew that it also earned her some suspicion among some of his mother-kin, but that was not unexpected considering she had an intensely private nature, even for an Argurma. If she seemed secretive and prone to disappearing, it was never at a critical time, and her loyalty was unquestionable among the household regardless of personal feelings, conflicts and grudges.

Although he never knew what to expect from her, Veral saw no reason to discount her ability to fulfil her duties and he saw no reason to believe otherwise. Malraha, however, was an unknown factor. The female was young, and although she was an excellent warrior and guard—otherwise she never would have been selected by Larth for his guard originally—he did not have enough data to judge how she would help or hinder his plans.

He frowned at the narrow corridor. Strategically, this was going to be more difficult to accomplish than he had estimated. He had to fool anyone who might be observing that it was merely another random shuffle of bodies moving down the hall and to keep Terri ignorant of what he was doing. It was not the first time he had staged a passing contact with her when his need became too great, and yet he had to abandon his plans more than once when circumstances did not cooperate. If he was fortunate, this time he would be able to slip in, walk with them for a time, and steal her away from her guards to enjoy an embrace before anyone covertly watching his household—or even his mate—was the wiser.

His eyes narrowed as he judged the space, his tongues sliding over his teeth thoughtfully. With the Argurma females practically filling the corridor as they escorted Terri between them, he did not fail to note that there was little room for someone to comfortably pass them. He would not be able to go with his original plan, which required pretense of sliding past them as if going in the opposite direction to deceive anyone observing the exchange. He had miscalculated the space within this particular hallway. How unfortunate.

He debated withdrawing but dismissed it. Aborting was not an option—not this time. Need clawed too deeply in his gut for him to ignore. He needed to be with his mate. He would just have to revise his plans. He would join them from the rear and depend on those same large Argurma frames to shield his interaction with his mate.

Veral turned to face in the same direction in which the females were walking, muscles tensing in preparation for the exact moment he would stride out of the side corridor to drift seamlessly into their company. His lips curved in expectation as he counted their steps, judging their exact distance by the increase in volume as they neared.

A flutter of fabric appeared at the edge of his vision, and then the strong arm of Navesha came within view. Her eyes turned to him, widened as they registered surprise but then snapped forward again as if nothing happened. He was already moving forward, so when the female passed, he slipped out in an easy stride, his shoulder lightly brushing against his mate as he stepped behind her.

As expected, Terri glanced around at him, but he was gratified when Navesha shifted her body in front of the human to obscure their exchange. Her voice boomed out to Malraha, issuing a snide comment that had the other female bristling. It appeared he did not need to rely on the younger female. Navesha had everything in hand. Malraha did not so much as glance back at them as she snarled back, the back-and-forth exchange erupting into a loud, hostile argument.

Two things became apparent: it was easy to see why Navesha was unpopular with her abrasiveness, and that he owed the female his gratitude.

He nearly forgot himself and his own need for discretion when an expression of surprise and pleasure bloomed across Terri's face. His own lips could not be stopped from curving in an answering smile as she turned and wrapped her arms around him. His mate's open emotions never failed to charm him, even the way her brow furrowed in confusion as it did now. She tipped her head back to look at him curiously as she tucked herself beneath his arm.

"What are you doing roaming the halls? I thought you were in meetings all day as usual."

He dropped his head down, brushing his nose and mandibles against the top of her head as he drew her scent deep into his lungs.

"I am," he rumbled. "But since I have you in my arms at this moment, I am happy to take advantage of this meeting."

"Are you?" she asked, her voice breathy with desire, but beneath that, a continuous warmth that welcomed him home.

"It is fortuitous," he rasped.

Just ahead he noted that Navesha had drawn to a halt a short distance away, her argument escalating rapidly as their bodies completely blocked the entrance of the corridor. The female no longer appeared amused and briefly he wondered what they were so hotly discussing that was making her eyes narrow dangerously.

He considered interceding, but she slanted an impatient look his way from the corner of her eye, her expression darkening.

The message was clear. He may be Ahanvala, but if he wasted the opportunity that she was providing, however unpleasantly, he would not be granted another one. He drew Terri closer to the wall and caged her there, his dark cloak blending in with the stones. He drank in her startled gasp as he dropped his head and brushed his nose against her throat, drawing out a soft chuckle as his lips and mandibles caressed the skin.

"Even more fortuitous considering I have a gift for you," he said against her soft, silken flesh.

Reaching into the pouch at his belt, he felt around for the fragile bloom contained within it. He had seen it by chance in the courtyard and had admired its golden petals that reminded him of the strands of his mate's hair caught in the sunlight. Pulling it free, he brushed the petals against her cheek, its rich perfume scenting the air around them.

Terri gasped, the sound soft and exquisite as she brought her hand up to cup the flower.

"Veral, it's beautiful," she whispered.

"As is my mate," he rasped, enjoying the way her lips quirked with amusement.

"Your mate has swollen feet and is waddling everywhere. I'm hardly a beautiful, delicate flower," she laughed, "but thank you."

Lifting the flower out of her grasp, he tucked it into her hair and admired it there for a moment before pulling her back into his arms. He sighed, relishing the feel of her body pressed against his. His civix woke hungrily, but he was able to ignore that need for now. His most demanding need was not about sex but connecting to his mate and offspring. As if on cue, he felt his daughter kick between them. He wondered if she sensed his presence pressing against her home within his mate's belly. Well, she would have to enjoy her mother for a bit. He chuffed as he drew Terri in closer, allowing himself the peace of connecting with his family.

If Terri had been Argurma, he would have connected with her on their private communication line, but just having her there in his arms was enough. This was what he needed. He was aware, however, of their limited time trickling away. He could feel Navesha's attention impatiently returning to him, and he reluctantly drew back after drawing in one last scent-laden breath deep within himself.

"I must go," he whispered reluctantly.

Terri groaned but did not otherwise protest as she nodded in understanding.

He bit back his own snarl of frustration. Soon this charade will be over. He was eager to be done with it all.

Brushing his lips and mandibles against her neck and jaw once more, he withdrew and stepped away in one fluid movement. He did not look back as he slipped down the corridor, leaving his mate with her guards. In the distance he could hear Navesha finally growl in warning and it must have been enough to get her point across because the argument stopped. He was still curious as to the subject and turned it about in his mind as he swept through the corridors to his office. Glancing down at his comms he frowned as he noted a transmission request from Vazan. It seemed that the Monushava House would have company from the Shanah Guard.

*V*azan's arrival was greeted with a cool reserve and formality that Terri found fascinating. The presence of the Farhal made everyone in the compound cease their activities when he neared and adopt a focused regard as their eyes trailed his progress. Many followed after him, stalking him through the corridors to the central meeting room. Terri wasn't sure how she had been swept up in all of it, but there she was, pressed in among the crowd, fighting to see what has happening between the larger bodies of the Argurmas surrounding her.

Grunting, she pushed her way past the two males standing just in front of her. It was like wedging herself between two solid walls, but she huffed triumphantly when she stood near the front, her place mostly concealed by the Argurma pressed in closely around her. Still, it gave her enough of an unimpeded view that she saw her mate stand from where he was seated.

She knew the moment he detected her presence among the crowd. Veral stiffened visibly, his nostrils flaring as he drew in her scent, and even his vibrissae immediately lifted in a gentle coil at their ends with awareness, but he did not otherwise acknowledge her presence. She shifted in place, uncertain of how to feel about it. He was clearly busy with the Farhal, but it was so unlike him to not so much as turn his head even slightly in her direction in a subconscious action to seek her out. Instead, his expression remained flat and unaffected, his entire attention focused as he watched the guard approach.

She snorted softly to herself. Now she was being ridiculous if she was getting upset that he failed to look in her direction just because she entered the room with his people. All the time away from her side to attend to his various duties—and her hormones—was messing with her head.

He had a lot of new responsibilities; he couldn't continue to hover over her day in and out. She didn't expect him to, and besides, having a bit of freedom to wander through the complex —even with the guards in tow—had been nice until the novelty of it wore away. Just because they had been joined at the hip for months didn't mean it could always be like that.

She just needed to take a step back and stop being so paranoid.

Unfortunately, that was easier said than done. His standoffish behavior and her recent brush with death had done a good job in making her anxious. If that wasn't bad enough, it didn't help much with her control over her symbiont, either. The bio-tech reacted to every little provocation lately. Even now, she could feel the cool metal siding over her arm and hand in a state of preparation—for what, she had no idea.

Sweat slickened Terri's hands, and she swallowed back bile as she wiped her palms on the thighs of her leggings.

Everything is fucking fine.

An annoyed growl sounded just behind her, bringing a welcome distraction. Terri glanced over her shoulder as Azan made a path for herself with her six arms spread wide. The disgruntled sounds from the males died, however. It wasn't because the pirate patted her blaster with a certain amount of affection, but because of the hard, focused glare of Malraha at the Blaithari's side as they took point at Terri's rear. The presence of the two females glaring protectively from where they stood behind her eased a bit of the anxiety clawing at her.

Rolling her shoulders, Terri forced herself to let go of the tension gathering between her shoulder blades and focus on what was important. The investigation. She hoped that the guard's inquiries would provide some certainty as to what happened in the market. It was the not knowing that put her on edge and visited her during her dreams at night. She only hoped that his presence at the compound meant he would have something to report soon. She had the impression that he would visit after he exhausted local inquiries.

Veral gave a very abbreviated nod to the male.

"Greetings, Shonk Vazan. Welcome to the Monushava House. My mother-kin, Featha, is expecting you in her chambers," Veral said, his voice cool and hard.

The male grunted, his datapad already out and held firmly between his fingers.

"I take it that you will be escorting me to meet with Featha?"

"You assume correctly. Although she is no longer the head of our line, she still has many duties she oversees. She asked me to escort you to her private office once you arrived."

"Understood. And what of the alien who was attacked? Will I be meeting with her as well?"

Her mate did not react for a moment, but eventually his dispassionate gaze swept over the crowd without pause before resting once more on Vazan. Veral's mouth tipped up in a glacial smile.

"I can acquire her location if necessary, but at this point her coordinates are inconsequential. You have already questioned her and recorded what little useful information she was able to provide."

The guard frowned. "Do you mean that you do not know where she is?"

"Should I?" Veral asked so chillingly that Terri drew back a little in surprise.

What?

Anger rose sharp and hot within her, and she bristled with indignation. As if in a perfectly timed response to the tide of emotion rising within her, she looked down in horror, watching as her symbiotic gauntlet came to life, projecting numerous hard-edged spikes. The Argurma nearest to her blinked down at her arm blankly before giving her a calculated look and shifting away.

Perfect. Now she was more or less literally wearing her emotions on her sleeve. There was little hope of preventing her display from becoming gossip among the entire household that Veral's mate had a violent temper.

Pressing her lips into a thin, strained smile, she attempted to rein in her fury to regain control of her symbiont and appear calm and unruffled, but it was no use. Anger and confusion beat at her persistently. She was his mate; if anyone would know or care it would be him! What the fuck was going on?

"I am the head of the line," he continued matter-of-factly. "I can locate anyone in the complex if necessary, but I do not make it my business to concern myself with the coming and goings of my mother-kin, much less of an alien. If you had need to question her, it would have been expedient to have relayed your need ahead of your arrival."

She blinked in disbelief, her mouth falling open.

An alien?

Was that all she was now?

Terri stumbled back, nausea boiling in her belly as a mortified heat crawled through her, warming her cheeks. She pushed her way past her guards and could feel the weight of their concern as

147

they turned. Malraha seemed to say something, but her words were lost in the roar of confusion in Terri's mind. The scowl of disapproval on the Blaithari's face turned to a look of sympathy, but even that didn't help or stop her from trying to flee. She shrugged away their hands, her head shaking from side to side, no longer giving a fuck if she was overreacting.

She couldn't believe that he just said that. And in front of everyone—his entire family—as if she were nothing at all.

Her breath stuttered as she wheezed, trying to draw a breath past the knot of emotions constricting her throat. She couldn't breathe! She could feel the pressure of tears behind her eyes and at the back of her throat threatening to choke her with the crushing weight of her embarrassment.

She needed to get out of there.

Blindly, Terri spun around, colliding with the males still observing from behind her. One of them grunted, but they mercifully didn't otherwise react as she pushed her way through. Not that it surprised her. They had barely even glanced her way when she slipped between them despite all the wiggling and elbowing involved on her part. Whereas it hadn't made her efforts to get past them any easier, this time it at least did her the favor of being able to make an exit without drawing too much attention.

Pushing her way back through the crowd, relief filled her in a cool rush as she broke free into the main corridor. Bracing herself against the one wall with one arm, Terri drew in gulping breaths of air, the unshed tears that she refused to let fall stinging her eyes. A tremor ran through her, and she shuddered with pent-up emotion.

Something had changed, and she felt helpless to understand it or circumvent it. Veral had changed since they arrived on Argurumal.

Now that he had gained the leadership of his family, was he regretting mating with her? Did he suddenly so dislike the idea of having a human mate and half-human offspring? Was it just a matter of time before they were stuck in a room somewhere in the compound to be cared for but forgotten?

A few days ago, Terri would have laughed at such speculations. Never before had she been plagued with worries like these. From the first when Veral made his intentions known, she had been secure in their bond. But now... everything was different, and she was faced with uncertainty for the first time.

She hadn't been able to ignore the fact that Veral was delegating her protection to guards, a perception confirmed by how pleased he had been when she accepted Malraha into her guard... Was it because he couldn't be bothered with her?

He hadn't even accompanied her to the last few visits with the medic.

She squeezed her eyes shut, attempting to push away the doubts and slow her panicked breathing. She didn't allow herself to think of anything else but the rhythmic flow of air in and out of her lungs.

And the burning anger that wouldn't be ignored even as her anxiety dissipated. If anything, it felt like it was climbing through her blood. Blinking back her tears, she glared at the red threads of mineral in the black stone beneath her hand. She didn't look up from it as she listened to the approaching footsteps.

"You are well?" Malraha asked, hesitant.

"Of course she is not well," Azan snapped with heat. "He just humiliated her out there in front of everyone! I am half-tempted to go neuter him in your honor," she offered, slanting Terri a hopeful look.

"I'm sure that offer comes from a good place somewhere within your heart, but no, that's not going to help anything," Terri said with a weak smile at her friend.

The pirate grunted, unconvinced. "I find it changes a male's behavior quickly. I would enjoy fighting my way through his guards to make a point… but if you insist, I will not."

Malraha curled her lip at the Blaithari, her mandibles widening and closing in clear discomfort despite her sneer.

"You do not understand Argurma society. Veral cannot appear weak…"

"Oh, so it is habit among your kind to pretend as if your mate doesn't exist?" Azan said, a brow cocking in challenge.

"No," the Argurma admitted. "But we should trust him to act in the best interests of the line. That includes his mate as well as all of us."

Azan shook her head, her three pairs of arms folding over her chest as her eyes narrowed with suspicion.

"I do not like it. This is not the same male I remember. That male would not have spoken in that manner. Nor would he willingly be parted from his mate as he has allowed. Something is wrong with this scenario," she snarled.

Slowly, Terri straightened, adjusting the thin white material of her robe that flowed over her belly. She couldn't see the hem any more than she could see her ankles around which it fluttered. She smoothed one hand over her symbiont gauntlet, watching the way tiny metal tendrils lifted from its surface at her touch, like grains of metal to a magnet. Unlike everything else around her, her symbiont was the one thing she still had some measure of control over, even if it was responding.

"I agree," she said slowly, drawing the attention of both her guards. "But there's not much I can do about it. Not until I'm able to speak privately with him. I'm tired of just waiting around for him to have time for me, rarely venturing beyond our chambers or our private part of the courtyard gardens. Time to do something constructive."

The Blaithari gave her a curious look, the Argurma stood

stiffer at her side. Terri grinned at them as she lifted her right hand.

"I do believe it's time to resume training. I don't know if someone is trying to kill me, or what the hell is going on with Veral, but I am not just going to sit around waiting to be saved."

A wide smile split the pirate's lips.

"*There* is the female I know so well!" She glanced over impatiently at the female at her side. "So where can we take her to train with her symbiont properly?"

The Argurma's vibrissae puffed and flattened uncertainly as she considered.

"There is a training yard…"

Azan clapped the female on the shoulder. "Excellent! We shall go there!"

Terri's lips curved as she allowed her arm to be taken by her friend.

"This day is suddenly becoming a lot more interesting. I will have much to regale Wendy with this evening."

Terri arched an eyebrow at the female's sudden exuberance.

"Speaking of Wendy… does she mind you being gone guarding me like this?"

The Blaithari chuckled. "I will have to tell her that you asked that. According to my dearest human, I need to find a hobby so that I am not forever plaguing her while she tries to work on our accounts and logs. It is a bit of a mess she inherited, and she is still trying to put it right. She is likely thanking you for every hour of peace she gets on the occasional shifts I take to relieve Navesha," she grumbled.

Terri had to agree that it was odd how frequently Navesha needed to tend to some matter or another. While Dreth took a secondary guard position, following at a greater distance, he was always present. Navesha was the only one among them who regularly disappeared. It was difficult to wholly trust the female to be reliable. She had suspected her briefly after her attack until she learned that Navesha had been visibly recorded on all monitoring systems attending to her tasks. But the female's absences—who had sworn to protect her—were almost as strange as Veral's. Argurmas took oaths very seriously as far as she understood...yet lately she was starting to feel like she never understood anything about the species at all with the strange behavior being displayed.

Blowing out a deep breath, Terri followed Malraha's lead along unfamiliar corridors as Azan fell into step behind her. Many Argurma paused in surprise as they passed by, but none so much as those who halted in their sparring as she entered the large, padded training room.

Terri slowed, aware of their eyes upon her as they watched her cross the floor. They stopped when they finally came to a series of target droids that Malraha decided to select from. As the female leaned forward to peer over at them, Azan craned her neck to watch.

"Do not go easy," she advised as she wrinkled her nose at a sleek droid.

Malraha gave the Blaithari a doubtful look, but at Terri's nod, she returned the droid and went down to another section, earning a grunt of approval from the pirate. Even as the female's eyes scanned them, fingers deftly selecting one droid after another of various shapes and thickness, most of them larger than a human, Terri couldn't help but to fidget under the weight of attention.

A male nearby chuffed to the female at his side as they watched the droids trail behind them.

"It is Veral's shame that he mates with a weak offworlder—we have all seen how he distances himself from her, as she must also—but now she thinks she will impress us with this display? For what purpose?"

"Perhaps to win her mate's affection back?" the female murmured. "It is admirable to attempt to return honor to her mate, but those droids will injure her, and it will just make her situation worse, especially for a gravid female. A foolish endeavor. Should we stop her?"

The male's lip curled ever so slightly at the corner in a smug smile.

"Allow her to humiliate herself. Perhaps then she will creep back to her quarters where she belongs rather than force her presence among us."

Terri's back stiffened with indignation, but she was gratified all the same to hear the female hiss angrily at her companion.

"There is nothing objectionable about her presence here. She is his mate. I would prefer any offworlder to being alone if I failed to bond."

The male grunted, unmoved by her anger. "Be pleased that you bonded with me rather than a lesser being. Veral had found in his mate a being of nothing but soft, weak flesh. A female who is easily broken. I share no concern for her. The droids will not harm a gravid female. If she suffers a bruised or broken limb, it is something easily repaired by the medic. What is not so easy to repair will be her humiliation. She will learn that she is not fit mate to an Argurma."

A low growl escaped from between Terri's teeth. *Weak, my ass!* Sure, she was pregnant, but she had been training throughout, not sitting on her ass eating candies. She was accustomed to activity and sparring. Gritting her teeth, she strode over to her guard and pointed to a boxy droid with enormous metal hands. She had practiced with target droids before on *The Wanderer*. All it took was enough critical successful strikes for it to register her victory. This model was one she had recently graduated to.

"Malraha, this one first."

The female nodded and activated the droid's programming. A bright strip of light that ran down the side of its head flashed, and it turned and approached Terri with aggressive strides. As expected, it moved easily on its feet, making it an effective target, its huge hands grasping for her. Terri ducked out of the range of its hands, her arm lifting as she summoned her blunted whips. It moved quick, lunging at her in progressively faster strikes, but Terri managed to stay just barely ahead of her as she snapped her whips out, catching it time and again with loud, cracking blows. Though sweat noticeably slickened the back of her robe from exertion, she didn't hold back her triumphant grin when the droid flashed red and dropped away.

A laugh escaped her amid the approving murmur of her gathered audience. A second and a third droid followed, each of them dispatched after a grueling battle, and each bolstering her confidence a little more as her symbiont responded with deadly accuracy. She was actually having fun!

It seemed to be catching, because even Malraha appeared to be affected by it. Her vibrissae were twitching with obvious excitement as she readied the fourth target droid.

Loud growls and hisses, however, had her turning her head to meet Azan's grin from where she was propped against the nearest wall. Terri bit back another laugh at the female's satisfied smile among the glowering males surrounding her. She had known what she was doing when she told Malraha to not go easy and now was reaping the profit. She had clearly been engaged in taking bets with the Argurmas near her.

Shaking her head with amusement, Terri turned to face her newest target. The droid was considerably larger than the others had been, but it was a natural progression as far as Terri could tell. Unlike the others, however, it was studded with spikes, including two club-like appendages extending from its arms. She whistled low as she looked it over. Definitely going to be more of a challenge. She didn't relish the thought of being whacked with those mallets, no matter how it was programmed. It was sure to leave bruises on her arms and legs despite the fact that it wouldn't be more than a sharp sting to an Argurma. It was nothing that would kill her, however, and the droids didn't target the torso so she had little to worry about with her baby outside of being a bit more winded and weighed down. At worst, she would be sore and humiliated.

She braced as the droid immediately spun in her direction, far quicker than she expected. She jerked in surprise when it rushed her, the club-like extensions of its arms lifting as it swung at her in deadly earnest. It moved so fast that Terri barely managed to hop out of the way, her eyes widening with worry as she felt the sharp breeze fan her face from its swing. That would have done more than bruise if it had connected... It would have taken her head off!

Was that supposed to happen?

An alarmed growl sounded behind her, indicating that it sure as hell wasn't.

"Comm Veral. The droid is malfunctioning," Malraha barked in panic to Azan. "It is somehow set on combat settings. That should not be possible! All the droids for target training are supposed to have locked programming. Its programming must be corroded. Clear the room!"

Terri's whips snapped out, the blunt ends expanding into blades that barely seemed to score the metal as she dived out of the way of another swing of one of its lethal arms. She cried out as something crunched hard against her calf, dropping her to the ground in agony. Its massive arm rose again, swinging down. Her whips snapped out, coiling around the metal leg of another droid, the momentum and the whips' quick retraction sending her skidding across the floor to the opposite end of the room.

Through eyes glazed with pain, she wheezed as she watched the droid turn once more toward her. Malraha attacked it from the side, but it flung her away effortlessly. Not even the plasma bolts from Azan's blaster seemed to slow it as it advanced.

a waste of time. It was simply what it was.

Veral despised wasting time as much as he disliked wasting resources, and within a relatively short amount of time, he concluded that the visit from Vazan amounted to exactly that. Little that Vazan had thought to ask Featha had differed from Veral's own questioning, and those points which did were of such inconsequential detail that it was maddening.

What did it matter what exact needs Featha had for her supplies? Plants for the ever-expanding courtyard and household common goods did not require such detailed explanations. He had seen the records for himself and had noted that it bore little difference from her usual monthly expenditures. The minute details of how everything was to be used and their purpose had no bearing on his mate's attack. It had taken all his self-restraint to keep from throwing the male out. He could have sent that information, along with his own data file preserved in his processors, to the head guard and saved everyone the time and effort. He could have been spared hurting his mate.

He knew within a .0043 percent probability that he had fractured the trust in their bond with his attempt to direct attention away from her. Although it had seemed necessary at the time, it now filled him with self-disgust. His sensitive hearing had registered her gasp, and he had covertly watched as she retreated into the safety of the compound's labyrinth of corridors. She was safe from the guard's prying and from the world outside the household.

But the cost was far greater than what was tolerable.

As attuned as he was to her vitals when she was near, he had been all too aware of the unsteady rhythm of her breath and the sudden quickening of her heartbeat. Her blood pressure elevated as well. But it was the sound of grief and the patter of her stumbling steps as she fled from him that cut the deepest.

Because of this, he was angry at Vazan's presence, but not nearly as angry as he was with himself.

Featha sighed impatiently, adjusting her robe over her lap as the Farhal finally stood with a respectful nod.

"I appreciate your time and forthrightness on this matter," Vazan said politely as he tucked his datapad into his uniform jacket.

"My pleasure to assist," she replied, her mouth thinning with displeasure as the male made no hurry to leave.

Veral was of the same mind. He twitched, his fingers digging into the back of the long couch on which his mother-kin sat in effort to not hurry the male out. He needed to seek out and soothe his mate, and that was not going to happen until the guard left the compound. Only then would he be free to amend things. The leisurely way the guard moved—stretching slowly as he glanced around thoughtfully—put Veral's teeth on edge.

"This is concluded?" Featha finally asked, her voice sharp from her strained patience breaking the silence.

Vazan inclined his head, one corner of his mouth quirking.

"My apologies. I have not been able to help myself from admiring your household. It is truly one of the finest I have seen.

It is just curious for a household suddenly taking in aliens that I have yet to see even one in service here."

Featha shot Veral a dark look from the corner of her eye but straightened, her back stiffening at the male's assumptions. True, they were ones that Veral had intentionally seeded within the male, but not ones that his mother-kin would tolerate.

"Who we have in our household and what role they have is our business alone. You doubtlessly have been on Argurumal long enough to know that our compounds are self-sufficient. We have no need for aliens everywhere. Our human guest's position here is a private matter, like things among Argurma."

"Of course," Vazan said graciously, his smile widening. "I should have expected nothing else. Forgive me for my assumptions."

"Is there anything else I may assist you with?" she inquired icily.

"No. You have answered all of my questions. Thank you," he murmured as he stepped away from the seating area.

Featha inclined her head for an instant before dismissing the male altogether as she stood up and left to return to whatever duties currently occupied her time. Veral fell into step beside the Farhal, his vibrissae churning with impatience as he dutifully escorted the male from his mother-kin's quarters.

The head guard gave him a sidelong look and sighed. "I appreciate your time and patience with this matter. Featha's testimony regarding her errands just confirms what I have suspected, that the attack on the alien is a localized, reactionary incident. I will keep the file open in case we receive any more information on who is responsible so they can be punished appropriately, but it is safe to assume that the attempt on her life was an isolated event."

Veral grunted. The guard's conclusion was satisfactory, so why did he not feel appeased by the report?

He resisted the urge to run his hand down his face to relieve the tension pounding behind his eyes as he accompanied Vazan to the compound entrance. Without betraying a hint of emotion—neither relief nor concern—he inclined his head respectfully as the male muttered his thanks and drew up the high collar on his jacket to ward against the lightly blowing sand.

The Farhal stepped out, and an unsettling itch ran through Veral, forcing him to step out behind the guard.

"Shonk Vazan?"

The male glanced back at him curiously.

"Is there something else, Ahanvala Monushava?"

Veral chuffed quietly at the formal address, his eyes turned toward the towering compound behind him. Something still unsettled him, and it seemed to lurk even closer at the Farhal's pronouncement. The compound itself seemed too much like a crouched predator threatening his mate. He was uncertain how much of that was a fantasy derived from the organic part of his mind, and how much of it was a reasonable conclusion reached by his processors. It was disturbingly difficult to tell.

"I do not require such ceremony. I am interested in what probability you have witnessed in which crimes were perpetrated from within a unit rather than from an outside source?"

Vazan worked his jaw thoughtfully.

"On Argurumal, I can honestly say less than ten percent of the murder cases involve close relations and trusted individuals. It is rare among Argurma, especially with your allegiance to your maternal lines and kin, but it does occasionally manifest in terms of disagreements—typically in regard to station and inheritance on rare occasion."

He slanted Veral a cautious look.

"I had suspected a possible attack orchestrated by Featha, but there is nothing I can see to implicate her. All of her actions since you have taken position of Ahanvala have been typical of her normal activity. There have been no documented outbound messages from the Monushava compound at all over the last half lunar. But you know your kin better than I. Should you be concerned?"

Veral's vibrissae swelled and flattened for a moment, the soft hiss of their writhing lengths betraying his current unease as well as his uncertainty. He did not care to share information about himself, but he required the male's insights from the outside advantage.

"I have been occupied elsewhere far from Argurumal until recently. I have few close connections with many of my mother-kin. My only certainty comes from my programming. The line and my mother-kin are held above myself. This is what we are all programmed with, to consider our line and household first. To break this programming would require extraordinary circumstances to necessitate it."

The guard nodded thoughtfully.

"So you would say it is unlikely that a murder would be planned casually by any one of your kin."

"The probability of such occurring is low, below 2.68 percent without a considerable incentive worth the personal cost of breaking one's programming."

The Farhal cocked his head as he gave Veral a curious look.

"And what would happen if you broke your programming?"

Veral lifted a hand in helpless surrender, uncertain of how to describe what he innately knew through his programming.

"There would be considerable pain and a fragmenting of the mind as the processor attempts to rearrange the codes of our programming. They would have to consider it a significant necessity to their own survival and welfare to risk it."

"Does anyone within your household strike you as such?"

Veral considered his kin, and while there were those who were secretive, he could not logically ascertain anyone who would fit the model. He met the guard's eyes and hissed with quiet frustration between his teeth.

"No. Not one fulfills the criteria."

Vazan nodded as he wound a sheer scarf over his lower face. "Then we are in agreement. Accidents and the reckless behavior of those outside your environment cannot be helped. I would not be concerned. If you learn of anything more, please comm the guard barracks and ask for me."

Veral did not reply as the male faced away and stepped out into the building winds. There was a sandstorm pushing in, as earlier reports had already informed him, but still he remained there at the door, his protective lids covering his eyes as he thoughtfully watched the guard board his flyer and depart.

He expelled a hard breath and started to turn back into the compound when his comm went off, flashing red in an emergency communication. Veral accepted the transmission as he strode indoors, cutting through the courtyard in his haste as he once did covertly with Terri when they first arrived. Now it was worry rather than caution that propelled him.

"Speak," he growled into the connection.

"Ahanvala!" a male shouted into his comm to be heard over the loud sounds of chaos erupting in the background. "Report at once to the training yard, the battlements room."

Veral frowned and redirected his trajectory. "I am coming. I will arrive in 5.7 minutes. State the emergency."

"A battle-class target droid is malfunctioning and is locked in combat mode. It has already dealt injury to your mate and despite our advances against it I estimate…"

Rage roared through Veral, and his mandibles widened as he released it in a vicious bellow, his mind blanking for several heartbeats before his processors kicked in against the overwhelming emotion. As awareness returned, it was to the observation that he was running at full speed through the corridors en

S.J. SANDERS

route to the training yard. The battlements room was a padded room that should have been the safest place in the entire facility for his mate to spar with droids as she had done onboard their ship—and yet he now faced the real possibility of his female in danger of dying there.

Without slowing his ground-devouring pace, Veral sprinted, the heavy thump of his feet preceding him, alerting everyone in his path to his approach. A bitterness filled his mouth as his worry spiked until his entire existence became centered on that one thing alone.

His mate.

His Terri.

He would not fail his anastha. He would not fail his offspring.

Muscles tightening, Veral breached the room at full speed, his processors analyzing everything he saw at the very moment, calculating his next action. Terri lay back against the floor, her arm raised in defense as several spikes burst forth between the razor-sharp whips that did little to slow the droid's advance. It was only together with the Argurma rallying to his mate's aid that they prevented an all-out assault from the droid. All the while, it flung its attackers and beat back the symbiont's protections with the steady ruthlessness of a machine, giving Terri only limited time and space to drag herself at a painfully slow rate across the floor, her damaged leg limp behind her.

She was vulnerable and without her protectors. Malraha lay unconscious, crumpled against a wall while Azan tumbled and fell as she attempted to rise.

Two males and a single female vaulted onto its back, lances stabbing deep as they aimed for the delicate circuitry in its neck. Each blow failed to meet its mark as plating shifted protectively, and it swerved violently, upsetting their balanced perch. Within the next breath, it ejected them from its back with a single snap of its arms as it drew close to Terri, overshadowing its target.

Veral did not hesitate to follow his hasty calculations. With every bit of speed that he could summon into his limbs, he sped forward and jumped, his foot only briefly coming into contact with a shelving unit, propelling him higher so that he achieved enough elevation to drop at an angle that gave him the perfect opening. Drawing out a blade from its sheath against his thigh, he stabbed down with all his strength. An arm snapped up, hitting him with enough force to send him sailing through the air. He only just barely managed to catch his descent on the balls of his feet, his eyes narrowing with rage at the droid drawing back its arm over Terri, as a roar tore from his throat.

He rushed forward again, allowing his claws to slide out. Although the reinforced metal claws would be slow working on the droid, he refused to give up. His claws dug with loud, metallic shrieks into the droid's back as he hit it. Raising one hand, he slashed at the protective barrier at the back of its neck, dread forming in his gut as he met his mate's frightened eyes. Pain filled him, replacing his anger with torment as the droid's flexible hand half-hidden behind a spiked club reached back and seized him.

It wrapped around his torso, pinning one arm to his side. His right arm was free, giving him the ability to dig his claws into the metal around its central spine, but it did little good. With a single sharp tug, he was pulled free. He bellowed as the thing held him dangling in the air in front of its metal head. The vise-like hand was crushing him, his vibrissae churning and snapping as he struggled to free himself. Azan was firing at the thing as she attempted to drag Terri away, but his female fought against her hold.

"No!" she shouted, her arm extending again.

Her whips came up, striking simultaneously with a strong enough blow that the droid faltered and turned toward her, opening itself up for a metal spike that extended like a lance from her arm to burrow deep into the droid's neck.

S.J. SANDERS

A loud crack echoed through the air, accompanied by the vicious sparks that leaped into the air seconds before the machine dropped to the floor, releasing Veral as it fell.

Hitting the ground hard, Veral grunted in pain, breath fleeing his lungs at impact. With a loud, painful intake of breath, he rolled into a crouching position before forcing himself to rise and stumble to his mate's side. A low, painful growl escaped as he took in his mate's countenance, the red welts on her delicate skin already purpling with vivid bruises. Allowing himself to drop to his knees at her side, he drew her up into his arms, his face burrowing into her sweat-slickened hair.

"Anastha," he rasped, his body shuddering as he felt her hands slide up his back to tangle among his vibrissae.

"Veral," she whispered brokenly. "I'm okay... I think. My leg hurts and I have this really painful aching in my... Oh my... Fuck!" she cried, her body tightening as she curled in on herself, her arms circling her belly.

Ignoring his own pain, he encompassed Terri in his arms, pulling her up fully into his embrace as he pushed up onto his feet with a pained hiss. Her cheek leaned into his chest, a cry escaping her at being jostled.

"Veral," Dreth murmured at his side. "Is she well?"

"I do not know," he growled. "I am transporting her to the medic immediately."

The male nodded his head, casting an uncertain glance toward Malraha's prone body as Veral adjusted his grip on his mate. He lay a hand on his bicep, drawing Veral up short for the briefest of moments. "Know that it was an accident. We all witnessed the malfunction. Malraha did all she could to alert us to the problem and to stop it. If you had been even a moment later..."

"It is fortunate I was not," Veral interrupted, brushing his cousin off with annoyance. "See to our mother-kin, but I ask that

164

you do not detain me any further," he growled. "My sole concern is my mate and offspring, and nothing more at this moment."

The male drew back and lowered his head deferentially, but Veral swept past him without acknowledgment. His entire being focused on the small female clinging to him as her body trembled with silent cries. He lowered his head to rest his cheek against her brow, mandibles vibrating in a soft purr.

"The baby… Oh, shit, it hurts so much," she cried out into his chest. "There's something wrong."

"I have you, anastha," he murmured, his voice hoarse with the emotion tightening his throat as he rushed through the halls. "I will not allow anything to happen to you or our offspring. I swear it."

A dull, sick feeling rose from Terri's stomach as Veral ran at a breakneck speed through the dark halls. She wanted to beg him to stop before she either passed out from the pain or puked all over him. She wasn't sure if it was due to the speed at which she was being carried, the horrible pain in her leg, or the cramps stabbing deep into her abdomen, but any possibility was far too close for comfort.

Truth be told, she half-hoped for the former. Each step sent currents of pain ripping through her but also waves of some light-headed feeling. Being unconscious would have been a mercy, but as much as she hurt, she was also afraid that she wouldn't wake again.

It scared her in ways that she hadn't experienced since the days she was forced to sleep in the old crumbling buildings of Phoenix.

She was thankful that they seemed to make it to the medical quarters in record time. Tarik looked up as they burst through the entrance, barely clearing the doors that hadn't yet opened all the way for them. Veral twisted at an angle to get her safely through, although he grunted at the solid thunk of his shoulder, or perhaps its large spine, colliding with the door in passing. Teri winced, knowing that he was banged up too, but it didn't slow him.

The medic snapped to his feet, hands immediately going for his scanner as Veral swept in, heading directly for the med bed. Tears sprung to her eyes at the way he almost reverently set her on it, his expression soft as he met her eyes. He lightly dragged his fingers over her cheek, his claws only then receding. That alone told her of his panic, that he hadn't even thought to retract them while hauling ass to the medic. He leaned down and nuzzled her before pulling back, his expression hardening once more as he looked over at Tarik.

"My mate has been injured. Fix her."

The medic nodded but did not otherwise react to her mate's hard growl as he swept by him with the scanner. Veral stepped back, his eyes never leaving the male, but Terri wanted to cry with relief as the medic's face dropped close to her to look at her eyes before glancing away to skim the rest of her face with concern. She knew that she had to look terrible with the beating she took if the way she felt was anything to go by.

Fuck, please let him have good meds.

A wash of blue light flickered over her and he looked down at the scans taken by the med-bed. His mouth tightened.

That wasn't a good sign. Obvious concern from an Argurma was rarely nothing.

He met her eyes again and leaned in closer, his hand lightly touching her arm in a gesture of comfort.

"Your leg is broken. That is easy to repair. The trauma to your body, despite taking no observable blows to your abdomen, has hastened delivery."

She choked back a watery sob. "My baby... is she going to be okay?"

His expression smoothed, lips tilting up in an expression that looked kindly for an Argurma, his mandibles held tight against his jaws, projecting calm.

"She is fine. She is fully developed and has sustained no injury. Unfortunately, due to your own injuries and the progression of your labor, there is little I can give you to ease the pain. This will not be pleasant," he said honestly.

A new pain rippled over the surface of her belly, and she recognized it for what it was… Contractions. Her little Argurma-human baby was coming whether they were ready or not.

Tarik pressed something, his eyes flashing as he linked to the bed, and instantly several metallic extensions came out to raise and support her legs. Her broken leg was encased, and an excruciating pain seared through it, drowning out the pain of the contraction as Tarik worked at repairing it. At least the encasing was solid and concealed whatever it did from her eyes. As painful as it was, she certainly didn't want to see what exactly it was doing.

Whatever it did, it was thankfully over fast enough, and her leg was lowered beside the other propped-up limb, the casing slipping back to form an identical support for that foot. A soft band wrapped around her chest, and she squeaked in surprise when the bed tilted, setting her body at sixty-degree angle. Her fingers wrapped around the sides as she gave a wild look at Tarik.

"What the fuck…?"

Veral growled and moved closer, his vibrissae writhing aggressively in response to her alarm. Tarik's gaze darted over to the male without concern before focusing on Terri, holding her gaze as he brushed back her hair with one gentle hand. She could hear Veral's coils rattling and hissing as he moved threateningly to Terri's other side, his gaze locked on the medic and his hand.

"The medical supports are now in delivery function," Tarik informed her, his voice mellow and soothing. "This angle will ease your infant's progress, allowing gravity to work in our favor. It appears that your symbiont's communication with your infant is increasing to ease it during birthing. This is good." His eyes raised to Veral. "Calm yourself, Ahanvala. You need to project calm to your mate and assist her, not threaten me."

Veral's growl cut off so suddenly that Terri's eyes shot up to her mate. His lips twisted with self-disgust, but when he met her eyes, his expression relaxed and warmed as his right hand skimmed over her cheek lovingly. This was the male she had mated and spent the last many months with. Her lips quivered with emotion as she leaned her cheek into his touch.

She had missed him so much.

The tiny cybernetic sparks within his glowing eyes multiplied, his eyes brightening with emotion and the adoration that she glimpsed in their most private, most tender moments.

"Please tell me you aren't recording this," she joked with a ragged whisper, gritting her teeth as another wave of pain washed over her.

His smile widened slightly. "I am merely making record, anastha."

"Great, and with me looking like a high-speed collision," she muttered.

His leaned forward, lips brushing her brow.

"You are beautiful, anastha. Always."

"Veral…" she whispered, her eyes meeting his.

It was on the tip of her tongue to ask him why he had been so distant with her. Where he had been. She opened her mouth, but a scream tore from her as her belly and back tightened with a deep, clenching, unending spasm. A four-pulse chime went off on her bed that had the medic taking his position.

Tarik moved in between her parted thighs, his hands covered in some sort of membranous material as he crouched down low. He glanced up at her reassuringly.

"She is coming."

Of all the pain Terri had ever felt, those experiences had

nothing on childbirth. She literally felt like her pelvis was going to explode from the pressure. Her loud curses at the medic and at her mate's civix filled the room in between her screams when she had enough breath to spare despite the mild pain inhibitor that Tarik gave her. She was even briefly reduced to begging tearfully to be knocked out. Veral even tried to threaten the medic if he didn't ease her suffering, but there was little Tarik could do but give her a booster of the inhibitor during the worst of it.

It was worth it, however, when her body gave one final push and she felt the relief of her daughter's head push through, her warm little goopy body slipping free into the medic's hands. For one amazing moment, she saw a true smile light the Argurma's face as he cleared her mouth and nose and gently placed the baby on her chest. Immediately, her arms wrapped around her daughter, love filling her.

Something warm slipped over her pelvis and belly that sent flashes of heat into her. It was soothing, taking away any lingering pain. She felt a mild pressure as something else slipped from her body, but she was too caught up in her baby to pay much attention as Tarik worked around her legs.

Veral leaned over her shoulder, his mandibles humming with a soft purr as he leaned in close, his expression a mixture of love and wonder. His full lips parted, showing the barest glimpse of his sharp teeth and his eyes widened briefly before relaxing, the corners shifting slightly to tilt with absolute infatuation.

Her mate was clearly in love with their daughter... and who could blame him?

Terri smiled at the squirming infant in her arms. The baby's body was pearly gray with scales scattered in strategic clusters rather than the dark silvery scales that covered her father. She was beautiful, and very Argurma in appearance, just as the scans had predicted.

Running her fingers lightly over the baby's face, Terri's smile widened as she took in her perfect tiny features. The little spine buds were visible, as were the double black tongues that peeked out from her mouth. Her brow sloped a bit more like Terri's, giving her features a more delicate, compact look, but she had the perfect horned plating of the Argurma, with little mandibles resting against her cheeks and curling vibrissae that plucked curiously at Terri's clothes and hands. The lack of plating on her chin and her little human nose made her look all the more precious. Terri laughed in wonder at the glowing blue gaze that stared back at her with equal fascination. A tiny right arm curled up against her chest, the small green jewel-like symbiont winking in the lighting of the medical unit.

Veral nuzzled Terri's hair with his broad nose and mandibles, his breath stirring the blond strands even as it warmed her skin.

"She is as beautiful as her mother," he murmured.

Terri laughed and leaned into her mate's strength. "I don't know about all that. She looks a lot like her father, I think."

He fell silent, a soft rumble rising in his throat.

"She… looks like my mother. I do not remember her… not truly, just glimpses that rise through my processors as times. She has fewer scales, and her coloring is unusual for our species, but she does look like her."

Terri sucked in her bottom lip thoughtfully as she watched his hand cup their daughter's tiny head and she shifted her face up to her father to give him the same curious, unblinking stare.

"What if we name her after your mother?"

He paused, his eyes turning toward her.

"You would do that? It is the mother's right to name their offspring," he stated, his voice hesitant and yet carrying an undeniable longing.

Terri turned her head up and smiled at her mate. "I would be happy to name her after her. You obviously loved her very much."

He swallowed, his eyes flickering with intense emotion, and leaned in close, brushing his nose against that of their daughter.

"Welcome, my daughter, Harahna'monushava'terri."

She cocked her head at him. "Was that my name in there?"

He inclined his head. "I loved my mother—I am certain of this—but I love my mate with all of my being. I would be pleased if all our young were honored with your name to distinguish your line. If you were Argurma, they would carry the name of your line. I wish for them to carry you with them in any way they can."

Terri swallowed back a lump of emotion, her smile turning watery as she cuddled Harahna close.

"It's a perfect name," Terri sighed.

23

*T*erri stretched, enjoying the pull of her tired muscles. Harahna was asleep in the small, padded sleeping structure, just the right size for her, that was tucked beside their bed. The sight tugged at Terri's heart, a fond smile on her lips. Harahna's tiny fist was wedged against her mouth as she absently suckled at her knuckles in slumber. Veral stood just to one side of the tiny bed, eyes fastened on their daughter as if he couldn't get enough of looking at her. Terri understood the feeling. Part of her just couldn't believe that they had created such a perfect, tiny being.

Veral glanced up at her, eyes warming to a summer-sky blue.

"I thank you for this gift, anastha." He paused, seeming to consider his words carefully. "Among my people, we give many symbolic gifts. In our histories, they represent the first life that came from the Great Mother Kalithan, she who births and devours all life, to represent each gift offered by her mate Monshar, the lord who shapes life and innovations, from their coupling. All of the gods that were born into the great being of the cosmos are born from their mating to give our world their numerous gifts which sustain us."

"That's beautiful," she said quietly as she drew closer to him. "You've never mentioned your gods before. I didn't know that you believed in anything."

The corner of his mouth twitched.

"Relics of our past. Most Argurma have forgotten the gods. I am not even certain as to my own views. It is difficult to see the gods acting in the world, and I refused to think much on it, but it is hard to dismiss them when we see the gifts they give. You and Harahna are evidence of them, as much as the presence of the sand dragnar that came to be tamed by the hands of my ancestors were to them."

Tilting his head, he regarded her as he expelled a soft sigh.

"Our species forgets such things. We see ourselves as advanced, with all our superior technology, and separate from their gifts, though we still hold onto this ritual. The minor households who live deeper in the Great Dunes at the edges of the territories still keep to the old ways. The land there is dangerous, and so it is rare that they leave their households, and rarer still that the council is able to determine anything that pertains to them. It is to their benefit to keep the council from stealing their offspring for processing—something we cannot prevent on our own, not without risking war with the council."

Terri drew back at his words, heart hammering anxiously.

"I am *not* allowing your council to process our daughter!"

He shook his head, amusement flickering in his gaze but behind it a hard, deadly resolve.

"They will not. Just as I will not allow them to experiment on and eventually process you. As soon as it is safe to leave Argurumal's gravity with Harahna, we will depart. Her inheritance will be secured for her, but we will not remain any longer than necessary."

It was as if something snapped into place, and she felt the cold brush a dread skitter over her skin as her heart raced with real fear. Her symbiont pulsed, but Terri locked down her control on it. It didn't stop it from pulsing hotly on her arm, nor the tiny metal tendrils shifting below her skin, but she managed to keep it under control this time.

"You're worried. That's why you've been acting strange. You don't want them to suspect that I'm here and come for me."

Reluctantly, he inclined his head in a nod, sending another spike of fear through her.

"Yes." He sighed again. "My mother-kin will protect us as much as they can, and this household is a safe zone where not many can penetrate, so few will even dare without good reason. Our presence here is not known to the council, but if they learn you are here, then it would give them legal reason to tear this household apart looking for you."

He paused, his eyes narrowing as she sucked in a ragged breath.

"Calm yourself, anastha. I will not allow it to happen. This was why I did not wish you to know. I do not want you to fear. It was especially concerning when you were carrying our offspring, but even now, I do not like the way your vitals are jumping."

"Well, obviously keeping it from me didn't help at all," she snapped, her anger causing her words to hiss out, though she kept the volume down so not to wake Harahna. "Not only did I not know just how much danger I was in while under your family's so-called protection, I also had to go through all the bullshit with your secrecy. Do you have any idea how the fuck that made me feel? Pretty shitty. Like I was being shunned for some reason that I couldn't even guess at—and all in front of your family." Her eyes narrowed dangerously at him. "Did they know? Did everyone know but me?"

He shook his head, a flash of remorse crossing his face. "No.

Although the entire household knew to keep our presence a secret, only those who went with me to meet with the minor houses knew and were sworn to silence. It was brought to my attention that if I distanced myself, the knowledge of an alien female present who is mated with an Argurma male—something that has never happened in our history—would stand a better chance of containment."

Terri drew in a sharp breath, her eyes widening.

"Malraha knew then, and that's what provoked her offer."

"Yes, she thought it would make it more convincing if I hid you deeper within the compound and publicly took her as my mate," he agreed, his eyes flashing as he looked up at her. "It was beyond considering. I would do anything to protect you, but I would never consider that. I did not wish to cause you pain or fear with this secret. I did not wish you feel any harm from it," he admitted, his composed mask slipping for the first time as his lips pulled back from his teeth in a sorrowful grimace, his eyes squeezing shut.

Something about the broken rawness touched her wounded heart.

"I don't like secrets—ever. I've spent too much of my life knowing that survival is dependent on being aware of the dangers around me."

"I did not wish that life for you now that you are my mate," he said quietly. "I would do anything to protect you."

"Well, that's great, but what you have done is prove that I can't trust you, that I have to watch your actions like everything else around me," she said bitterly. "You hurt me. I hope you understand just how much."

His head dipped low, eyes squeezing tighter, making hard lines in the fine scales around them.

"I will take any punishment you offer for the offense," he

rasped. "I knew that I wounded myself with my deceit, but I feel it even greater now. Never have I regretted anything so much as causing this pain and breaking something important within our mating bond."

"I can't even begin to wrap my mind around all of this. I need time," she huffed, her fingers rubbing at her temples. "I do want to know one thing... Did you ever, even for a second, regret our mating and wish that you could have taken an Argurma female as Malraha suggested?"

"Never!" he snarled passionately.

She swallowed back a surge of emotion and stepped closer to him, her hands brushing the side of his face. His nuzzled her hand even as it stroked back to brush against his vibrissae. They promptly wrapped around her hand and fingers devotedly.

"And if the council finds out about us?"

"Then we will seek our far mother-kin in the Blowing Sands," he growled, his eyes snapping open to meet hers. "They will give us refuge. We leave them in peace, knowing that they cultivate in their mines the wealth of our people even as we extend our protections and resources from other parts of our territory to them. We keep their locations secret and our trade routes among the sands known by only a few. They do not trust anyone else but their mother-kin, and so we will be safe among them until we can leave."

A shudder rippled through her as she tried to imagine being out in the wilds among strangers even more brutal and terrifying than those within the household.

"Very well," she whispered as she allowed herself to be cocooned in her mate's arms.

There, she took solace and grabbed whatever peace she could as her heart attempted to stitch itself back together and heal. She would find a way to trust him again so their bond could be repaired once more, just as he had to find a way to make amends for it.

They owed that to themselves—and to their daughter.

Her eyes dropped to Harahna, her innocence clutching tight to Terri's heart. Their family would survive this.

$\mathcal{N}$ ormally, the arrival of a daughter of the line, especially one destined to someday be Ahanvala, would be a huge affair. All the minor households of their line would have been invited to the compound as well as the Ahanvala of neighboring territories. This could not be the case for Harahna, and Veral was irrationally angry about it even though it had been his decision. Only those of the household were in attendance in the central gathering room, their expressions lit with curiosity as they drew in close to meet Harahna.

His daughter should have been traditionally greeted, and he could not ignore the fact that excluding the minor households was a grave insult, but one he hoped to remedy with the visual record he was taking of the event. Their entire line would know and bear witness to Harahna's arrival, even if they could not attend in-person.

He wanted them to know her. Harahna would not have the same opportunity. She would mature far from his mother-kin.

It was a disservice to his daughter, but it could not be helped at this time. As tempting as it was to remain and allow Harahna to be reared among her people, he was too aware of the dangers to allow it. He would teach her and prepare her all he could—and perhaps engage in occasional covert visits—so that she would someday be ready to take her place when she came of age.

That would mean submitting her name to the registrar, but Tarik was handling the data so that her name was legally within Argurumal's databases. It would be unpleasant to deal with the registrar official. Whomever the offices sent would be there for Veral's seal as the Ahanvala on all completed official documents, and there was no way to circumvent that. At least with Tarik's data, he did not have to worry about unauthorized data-leaks regarding his offspring. It was all sealed in the medic files that would require council override to access or his own seal of approval to open.

All the registrar office would have access to would be the most necessary data regarding her vitals and her name. Terri's name would be withheld from all documents in the record, her presence reduced to an unlisted mother. Only his people would know who she was. He liked that even less than concealing his daughter. He was proud of his mate, but the secrecy was necessary. The officials would not think anything of it since it was not uncommon for females to carry young with the donated genetic material of mateless males. The council, of course, would know differently, all too aware of the fact that he mated outside of his species. He hoped that they would be away from the planet before they discovered his parentage on Harahna's file.

His daughter... his offspring. He would protect her and her mother with everything he had. With his life. If that meant never returning to Argurumal, the sacrifice was worth it. He had never planned to come back anyway, although this would be the first time that there would be no option unless he were willing to risk them in a war against the council.

He was not.

Veral glanced down at his daughter, her delicate, round face relaxed in slumber. She was unlike any other Argurma infant on Argurumal and yet, despite her apparent vulnerabilities inherited from her human parentage, she was all the more precious to him. With both a mate and a daughter to care for and adore, he was having trouble restraining his emotional output. He even had the disorienting experience of his vision, and other vital sensory systems, shutting down late at night during one such emotional surge. Although it had taken 8.4 seconds to reboot, he had been caught off guard by it while he held his mate close to him and listened to the soft, even breathing of Harahna.

Terri's arms shifted to support their daughter's sleeping head at a more comfortable angle as she gave him a wry glance.

"So how long do the baby meet and greet showings usually last?" she whispered low enough for just his ears.

He bit back a chuckle. She was understandably overwhelmed by being surrounded by so many of his mother-kin. With the exception of the day they arrived, and the visit from the head of the guard, she was unaccustomed to being around so many of them. All around her were the honorary gifts sent for her. A shaft of tharwal grain that grew in the protective canyons of Argurma's far northern reaches, a soft fur of the amakhal to keep their offspring warm during the cool desert nights, a delicately carved cup to represent the cool springs hidden deep within the caves, and a golden distaff.

Each of these gifts of the firstborn children of Kalithan: Ashanhara, the lord of the crops who developed the first seeds within all males and planted the first crops; Tarihi, who fashioned all beasts from mud and water and taught Argurmas the art of hunting and husbandry; Ehanel, the goddess whose body fed the springs and who was the spirit of Argurumal; and Kathan, the youngest among them, who taught their people all manner of technology. Of all these gods, only Kathan was half-remembered as the educational centers, the kathanvals, were named for him. Terri, as a female, the living embodiment of the great mother, sat with their daughter upon her knee among the divine gifts.

At least his mate had received some reprieve. Many of his mother-kin had been eager to hold Harahna, the first among which had been Malraha. She had inspected his daughter with a careful curiosity as if searching for something. Perhaps some sort of answers that she thought his offspring might have. Navesha, in contrast, did not touch Harahna at all, and instead eyed her shrewdly with an almost fearful reluctance that Veral could not decipher. What did a large warrioress have to fear of a baby?

"Not much longer, anastha. Ninety-seven percent of the household has paid their respects. Food will then be brought out, and equan liquor, but we are not required to stay," he murmured. "We can have food and drink delivered to our quarters. It is expected for a new mother to rest with her offspring, regardless of the effectiveness of our healing technology."

He paused as Larth approached. The male's eyes fastened on Harahna curiously. Since Veral and Terri had been sequestered with their offspring for the initial days following their daughter's birth, he too, like everyone, was seeing the newest member of their line for the first time. Veral's vibrissae puffed out proudly. Larth was of his close mother-kin. He was among the last who would greet Harahna since the closest of their household would be welcome to linger nearby and even escort them to their chambers when they were ready to leave.

"How strange," Larth observed, eyes narrowed with fascination as he brushed a fingertip against the back of Harahna's hand. "The first of our kind to be born mixed with another species. I would have dismissed such claims before you returned to Argurumal with your mate. Now here the evidence is for us all to witness."

"Well, everyone present," Terri corrected with a soft laugh.

"This event is being recorded for the minor households to be distributed to them later. They will share in this momentous occasion, if from afar," Veral amended.

His mate glanced up at him, her brows rising with surprise, but she did not object. She understood. They had spoken earlier of the matter and his inability to properly include those among his extended line. This was the only viable solution.

Larth's lips thinned as his focus shifted to Veral, his head tilting at the slightest of angles in consideration.

"What of the other households? This is too great of importance to keep among ourselves," he stated, his voice harsh with incredulity.

"My mate and I owe nothing to all of Argurumal," Veral replied stiffly. "We are programmed to adhere to the welfare of our line."

"And to serve Argurumal!" Larth leaned in and growled. "You may have broken that programming when you left our planet, but it is still there. Our people require this knowledge. The Council uses our inability to develop mating bonds and breed outside of our species as a method to control us and our reproduction. They already do so by encouraging early mating, but this is another facet. They wield this data to discourage us from mating with other species with claims that it is unnatural and to do so would be a reckless endangerment to our own survival. Yet at the same time, they tell us that our mate-bonding is an unhealthy, primitive process that impedes our ability to form strong, productive households. It is all misdirection to achieve their own purposes. It is our responsibility to correct it."

Veral glared, his body becoming rigid as his vibrissae rattled in clear warning. He stepped forward just enough to partially block his mate and offspring as he stood in visible confrontation with the male. Although he could feel eyes turning toward them, he did not back down but met his cousin's indignation with his own suppressed anger.

That Larth dared to suggest that Terri and Harahna belonged to his people in any sense infuriated him.

"You are suggesting that I expose my mate and offspring to our entire population when it is my imperative to keep them away from the council as long as possible?" Veral snapped.

Larth threw out in a hand in the first sign of frustration he had ever seen from the male.

"If the council were successful, they would terminate you and take your female and offspring without anyone knowing of their existence, and without the wider implication being understood— that we can develop intense mating bonds outside of our species, and that such bonds are natural. Whether we are able to breed or not, that possibility will change the lives of many Argurma. If the council were forced to accept interspecies mating with the human species, it would open the door to interspecies mating planetwide."

"What about Earth?" Terri asked, her voice breaking through their argument effortlessly. She looked at them both curiously, her jaw tightening. "Although it is clear that it is impossible to keep Earth a secret, as Azan and Kaylar both have shown us, if the Argurma species knows that humans are compatible... what's to stop them from going there to harvest what remains of our population?"

She glanced up at him, her lips twisting wryly.

"Not that Earth has anything to recommend it at the way it's falling apart, but to take women and men from our homeworld without rules or some kind of protection doesn't sound like it would be very beneficial for my people."

Larth inclined his head in acknowledgment, though reluctantly.

"You are correct. However, no one will consider taking the matter before the Intergalactic Nations if no one knows about it. Argurmas can protect humanity if we are allowed to do so without interference from the council. They seek to eradicate the necessity of mate-bonding from our species entirely. Too many of us are relying on artificial means of starting the bonding process due to the efforts to diminish it. Only the council has knowledge of this outside of our line. There is no circulation among regular communication lines—or even private underground lines that I have access to—that one of our own successfully bonded and bred with another species. We require knowledge, not silence," he said wearily. "I just ask that you consider it, Ahanvala."

Veral felt the tension uncoil from within his frame as he met his cousin's imploring gaze, the formal words cooling his blood. His cousin addressed him now not as mother-kin but as the head of their household, reminding Veral of his greater duties. A frustrated growl tore from his throat, but it was the soft touch of his mate's hand on his arm that diminished the hostility raging within him.

"He makes a good point, Veral. It may be worth the risk to break the silence. It could keep us safer in the long run if they don't have the option of making us disappear in order to keep their secrets," she observed, her agreement surprising him. A resigned amusement filled her eyes. "It's better if there are no secrets, wouldn't you agree?"

"I agree," a stern voice broke in.

Featha frowned at all of them as she pushed her way forward, her expression softening only the slightest as she inclined her head to Terri in a gesture of support that surprised him.

"I came to see what was delaying my greeting of the new female only to overhear your argument. While your concerns are valid, Veral, I support Larth and Terri's arguments. I care little of the people of the Black Stone lands in their towering cities, but we of the Great Dunes struggle the most with finding mates. Despite my ambitions, I do wish Dreth to have the opportunity to find a mate if he cannot find one among the Argurma. I know I am not the only mother in the Great Dunes who feels this way. I have spoken to many females throughout the territories in our correspondences and this is a subject of much grief for our people. Your mate would represent hope for everyone."

Her lips twisted in the faintest of smiles, and she leaned down and gently touched his daughter's head. "It has given me hope."

Veral met the proud female's eyes, struck by her admission.

"What would you have me do, Featha?"

To his further surprise, her smile grew.

"You have two weeks until little Harahna will be ready to depart. It is enough time to make the Council regret their lies and secrecy. We gather our records, and when you depart Argurumal, we will send out an anonymous signal relaying it over our planet and through Argurma-held space so it is received on all of our people's open lines of communication."

Veral closed his eyes against the weight of the decision he was being presented. It was crushing. He knew that they spoke with reason but the fear that clawed through him over the slightest chance of losing his mate and his daughter bit deep into his heart.

Terri's hand tightened on his arm.

"Veral, you can share the weight of this decision with me," she whispered. "You're not alone and don't have to shoulder the responsibility for everything all on your own."

Opening his eyes, he met her warm brown gaze, a small tremor running through him with an agonizing crack of pain as some final resistance broke with in his programming. If he were capable of manufacturing tears, he would have; instead, he held her gaze, seeking comfort within it as he drew his family into his embrace.

"I do this all for you, anastha. What course do you think we should take?" he asked.

Her eyes moved, sliding over him, her expression filling with love.

"I don't think I want anyone to miss out on this kind of love. Let's do it. Let's share it with everyone," she said firmly.

25

*T*erri smoothed her loose robe with a free hand, her eyes straying to her mate as they walked through the training area. His brow was lowered as he inspected the droids carefully, reviewing their programming. He had been at it for days now.

She didn't know what he expected to find, but he had been uneasy since the target droid malfunctioned. So much so that he hadn't allowed her anywhere near the training yard unless he was with her. For extra security, Dreth and Larth trailed behind them, their bodies aggressively tense as they stood, their legs braced wide, just behind them.

Terri sighed and shifted Harahna's weight in her arms.

"Do you really think someone messed with the droid?" she asked around a yawn.

As much as she loved the fact that Veral was including her in his regular duties around the compound, she was looking forward to sitting down. She didn't understand how she was so tired. She had little to do during the day that was demanding—not compared to what she survived on Earth or the often brutal pace of salvaging. She only had to be on hand to care for Harahna's needs that amounted to little more than feeding and changing her baby every few hours day and night. Taking care of a small baby should have been easy.

Instead, she felt like she was walking half-asleep, with less and less patience for Veral's fixation on the droid malfunction. For the last week, he had stopped nearly every day to test another idea on the target droids' programming to see if he could replicate what had happened. In fact, he applied himself to it with more enthusiasm than she had seen him take to anything else in his meetings and duties for the household.

Veral grunted, eyes narrowing as he opened the compartment on the droid in front of him. "That is the question," he rumbled as he slid his fingers over the inner panel, connecting with the droid's system. "Malfunctions among droids are common, but I do not like that it occurred with the target droid you were sparring with. You were attacked once before," he reminded her.

"Yes, she replied. "But even you agreed that evidence pointed to it being an isolated event. I don't see any connection between the two. Do you?"

His eyes flashed, and he stilled until reluctantly he shook his head and pulled away to promptly turn to the next one.

"No," he growled, frustration seeping into his voice.

"See?" she said with a small smile. "Anyway, I'm sure if the council knew I was here that we wouldn't be having this conversation. They would just send in the troops to kill me or disable me in some way so they can get their grimy hands on me. They wouldn't have any need to make it look like an accident."

Veral gave her a confused look.

"No, they would not 'send in the troops,' as you say. They would wish to keep the matter secret. They would likely employ skilled bounty hunters and assassins to capture us if possible or kill us. It would not be an attack that we would see coming," he grumbled as he pulled open another access panel and hooked himself in that droid's system.

"Sometimes an accident is just an accident. My daddy always said that bad luck came in threes. I guess I'm due one more fucked up thing happening if he's right," she teased.

Her effort to lighten the mood, and hopefully engage Veral in something a bit more interesting than his current preoccupation, fell completely flat.

She sighed and exchanged a look with Dreth. Veral was over-the-top protective, but this repetitive examination of the droids was unlike him. There were certainly other things that required his attention than malfunctioning droids that had already been inspected by no fewer than six different individuals. Instead, he should be patrolling the grounds, taking comms with his mother-kin in various parts of their lands, and arranging meetings—all of it boring, boring stuff that she was obligated to try and be enthusiastic about now that he was including her in his duties, if that was what she could call trailing after him as if she were a dorashnal.

She glanced down at Krono where he lay at her feet, his huge head resting on his forepaws. His sides heaved with a sigh, but he did not otherwise even twitch as his eyes tracked Veral. The poor creature rarely got out of the rooms since he couldn't accompany Veral in many of his tasks. He kept Terri company while she rested, but when she was accompanying Veral, he was left in the room alone for most the day. Although she was assured that most Argurmas kept their dorashnals in their private quarters, Krono was accustomed to free rein throughout *the Wanderer* and regular intervals sprinting over open ground whenever they were salvaging planetside.

The corridors of the household were hardly comparable to the freedoms they enjoyed. Terri couldn't help but note that, despite being out of the room, Krono didn't look any more enthusiastic than she felt.

Krono was bored, she was bored, and she would have bet money that Veral was bored, too.

There had to be more to his insistence on investigating everything himself so intently. He committed himself to it despite numerous reports from the household's technical specialists, and even a report from the manufacturer regarding common droid malfunctions. Everything said clear as day that it wasn't uncommon for programming to become corroded and the machine to switch to its auxiliary programming. With a droid also programmed for battle, corrosion could be lethal.

She knew that he was on edge—the droid's malfunction still gave her the occasional nightmare, after all—but she wondered if there was a chance he was also using it as an excuse to avoid his duties. He would deny it, of course, since he was obsessed with her safety, but… was he tired of being the Ahanvala and looking for any reason to escape it as soon as possible?

Not that she could blame him. For as long as she had known him, he was a male who was in a constant state of activity. There were a few leisure opportunities that they enjoyed, but for the most part they were either traveling to a job or working one. It was the life they were both accustomed to.

Terri wouldn't admit it out loud, but she was getting increasingly restless. There was a lot to be said for living in the relative safety of the compound with anything she wanted practically at her fingertips, but she had to face it—she wasn't made for this life. Staying within the four walls and courtyard of the Monushava compound—which had originally sounded like a good idea when she was pregnant and wanted to be near someone with medical knowledge—was slowly making her crazy.

It was too dark and too claustrophobic, and lately she was feeling the constricting weight of it even more. There wasn't a day she didn't feel it as she walked the same routes through the hallways, trying to ignore the way the monotony of it all crawled under her skin.

Changing her route did little to help it. To make matters worse, she was hopeless when it came to contributing to an Argurumal household. Unlike everyone who was programmed and trained to fulfill a duty, she was useless. There was not one productive thing that she could find to do in a place than ran like an efficient machine. Even when she accompanied Veral, she had nothing worthwhile to do except enjoy his company until she decided to return to their rooms with Harahna.

In truth, the only thing she *had* to do was take care of their daughter. When not occupied with feeding, she could attempt to amuse herself with either a book or walking through the courtyard and various parts of the compound—and wait for time to pass. Unfortunately, dark, endless walls and the same flat conversation among those who regarded her more as a curiosity than anything else wasn't nearly stimulating enough, and the courtyard gardens could only serve as a distraction for so long in her day before she became restless there too. Not even accompanying Veral, as had become normal as of late, had done more than taken the edge off for a little while.

"Veral, perhaps your mate is right that this is futile," Dreth offered, his voice breaking the thick silence surrounding them.

Larth made a choking sound in the back of his throat, his eyes widening at the younger male.

Veral snapped his head around, his hand paused on the systems panel of the droid he was currently leaning over. He straightened and glared openly at the other male, his vibrissae writhing in irritation. Dreth inclined his head toward her wordlessly. Veral's head turned her way, and immediately his vibrissae flattened. His expression morphed into one of chagrin as he took in her tired—and probably somewhat impatient—expression.

He removed his hand, turned away from the droid, and

approached her as a tiny light flickered on the panel's inside casing.

"Uh, Veral…" she murmured.

What was with the light? Was that supposed to happen? She didn't recall seeing any of the other droids light up, but she also admitted that she hadn't been paying particularly close attention.

Mandibles purring with their vibration, he leaned in, his knuckles brushing her cheek lovingly. Immediately, she melted into the touch. The light thing was probably nothing. Aliens put alarms on everything, and it was only blinking.

"I know, anastha." He sighed. "I am—as you like to say—obsessing. You have been standing there patiently yet again as I inspect the droid futilely. Not even surveillance has picked up anything suspicious, but when I look at all the data, I am processing that there is something that I am missing here. Perhaps it is due to my own suspicious nature and my fear of harm coming to you. I will cease now. Thank you, Dreth," he added in acknowledgment to the male standing just beyond them.

The light behind him flickered faster, and Terri's heart began to race. Okay, that wasn't good. Still no alarms going off, though. Her eyes darted to Dreth and Larth to gauge their reaction since neither of them had remarked at all on it. Larth frowned in confusion as he met her eyes.

Shit, they were standing right between the guards and the droid. They were probably blocking any view of it. She had better say something fast. Better safe than sorry, as her dad was fond of saying about… well, everything when it came to the ruins of Phoenix.

"No, Veral. I mean, yes, you're right… but that's not what…"

Nearby, Krono stiffened and whined anxiously, his vibrissae standing around him like a halo.

Her mate frowned down at her, his body straightening warily as he glanced over at Krono and back at her again.

"Krono? Anastha, why is your heartbeat increased?"

The guards frowned and started walking toward them. Placing her hands on either side of his face, she yanked Veral's head toward the droid.

"What's that?" she asked as her mate snarled, his muscles tensing, and the droid began to emit a sharp beeping sound. "Oh shit. That would be an alarm. Fuck!"

Terri barely got the curse out when Veral's arms banded around her, lifting her up against him, with Harahna protected between their bodies. He snarled, a sharp curse—her human cussing was clearly rubbing off on him—as he pivoted away and took off at a full-out run away from the beeping droid. Larth's eyes widened in realization as he grabbed ahold of Dreth, jerking him back as they too spun around, falling in at Veral's side. Despite their size, they were quick as they raced to the opposite side of the compound at a speed beyond what Terri would have managed.

Even so, no matter how fast they ran, the beeping followed them, becoming louder and sharper until a cacophony filled the air.

White noise filled Terri's ears, muffling all sound as metal fragments flung toward them. At the wall Veral and Dreth dropped down low, pulling Krono tight against her and wedging her and the dorashnal against the wall, the Argurma's enormous bodies surrounding them completely as the males turned their back to the explosion hurling toward them.

A shout of denial left her lips. She wasn't about to allow harm to come to any of them. She mentally shouted to her symbiont, projecting her need of a barrier as she moved her right hand from Veral's shoulder where it was firmly clasped around the spine jutting up through an opening of his robe to grab ahold of Dreth's shoulder spine instead. Somehow realizing her intent, Veral grabbed ahold of Larth and yanked him in close at her other side, his eyes staring at the mass rising from her symbiont.

Metallic tendrils flew free from her wrist, more than she had ever seen before as they burst out like a tangle of thousands of whipping vines. She could feel her strength waning as they wove an ever-expanding tight net of metal until a woven shell surrounded them. Within a matter of seconds, they were completely covered by living metal as the first of the projectiles hit.

Terri whimpered as she felt the dampened impact vibrating through her along those subtle lines like a spider feeling the vibrations of its prey caught in its web. It didn't hurt, but was an overload of sensation buffeting her all at once. The shocks seemed to hit everywhere, and she couldn't help the small cry that escaped her. Veral growled in her ear as his arm tightened anxiously at her back. Harahna squalled, her little body wriggling against Terri's chest, the sound muffled by the ringing in her ears.

Then there was blessedly nothing. No more vibrations or shrieking metal. Only Veral's continuous, rolling growl and Harahna's cries.

A tremor of exhaustion filled her as she allowed the barrier to collapse and draw back into her. The shock of the metals re-entering her bloodstream made her shake uncontrollably. Veral didn't let go her for many minutes, his growl shifting to a soothing purr as he stroked a hand down her back. She was distantly aware of Dreth shifting as he stood and stepped away to provide them with some privacy, but at that moment she couldn't have cared less whether anyone was witnessing her recovery.

When at last it was under control, she lifted her head from her mate's wide chest and looked down at Harahna still caught between them. Her daughter looked back up at her, her face still scrunched unhappily as she sucked on her hand, her tiny mandibles still quivering with distress. It was only then that she noticed the metal tendrils that were wrapped around Harahna as well as her, securing the baby to her.

Terri stared down at them, unable to tear her eyes away as the metal slowly retreated to the small, glowing symbiont on Harahna's arm. Their daughter had instinctively protected herself and secured herself to her mother when frightened. Terri's lips parted in awe as she exchanged a surprised look with Veral.

Despite his surprise, her mate seemed to be especially proud of his offspring's ability to protect herself. His vibrissae puffed and he crooned down at her encouragingly. She wondered how long it would be before the entire compound knew of their daughter's achievement.

Harahna wasn't as impressed. She looked at both of them with her big glowing eyes before she pulled away her fist and her bottom lip began to quiver once more. Veral's eyes widened, his vibrissae puffing and flattening at their daughter's distress as he tilted his head down toward her and began his rattling purr once more. Terri drew her up closer, kissing her plated brow and murmuring nonsense until their combined efforts quieted their daughter.

Assured that his offspring was unharmed, Veral gently set Terri back a bit so he could stand, pulling her to her feet in the process. His brow lowered as he inspected her.

"You are well, anastha?" he rasped.

She nodded, eyes straying over the wreckage of the droid.

"Yeah, I think so. What happened?"

Her mate twitched uncomfortably, but Dreth chuffed from where he stood a few feet away, his vibrissae snapping with his lingering tension.

"Veral discovered a way *not* to corrode code," Larth remarked with mild amusement as he brushed the wrinkles from one sleeve.

Her mate shot him a dark look, but as he glanced down at Terri, Veral's lips twitched wryly.

196

"I attempted to corrode the system's control code. A forced corrode was the only probability of an intentional malfunction I had not yet tried. It seems that the reports were correct about forcing certain codes to corrode," he admitted. "It was in the manufacturer's warning that there was potential for an unpredictable system reaction. I had estimated that the droid locking into battle mode could have been result of that, since the manufacturer was not clear about what systems reactions to expect. Seems that explosion is one of them," he commented dryly.

Despite his cavalier words, he still had an arm banded around her as his vibrissae slipped through her hair, betraying just how rattled he was. She patted his arm reassuringly as she looked at the metal fragments littering the floor.

"You would think 'warning: deadly explosion' would have at least gotten a mention," she observed.

Veral inclined his head in agreement as Dreth let out a soft chuff and kicked a bit of the rubble with one boot.

"What now?" he asked, his head tipping at angle to glance at Veral.

"I have exhausted every idea. There is no evidence of sabotage—as it seems a stronger probability that you would have been blown up—or tampering with the codes. It is just too perfect to be coincidence," he growled.

"Okay, so let's go to the next plan. We will go hide with your far-kin. We only have a couple of weeks left before Harahna will be clear to travel offplanet. We can take the medic and a small guard and get away from here," she suggested.

Veral gave her a questioning look.

"Are you certain? Even most Argurma avoid the Blowing Sands," he said solemnly. "I admit that I desire to take you there and have since you birthed Harahna, to keep you both safe. I did not because I was concerned that our daughter's inner throat filters were not developed enough. However, these few days have provided her with extra time for the filters to strengthen. If we go, we will have to keep her completely covered, but it would be possible if you are in agreement."

Terri shifted nervously. "She won't be harmed any out there, right?"

A soft smile curved her mate's mouth.

"No. We will take all necessary precautions and have the medic examine her just to remove any doubt. She will be fine," he assured her, his hand smoothing Harahna's vibrissae lovingly.

Taking a deep breath, Terri smiled, warmed by a sudden surge of excitement.

"Okay! Let's do it. We'll lie low out there for a while, and as soon as Tarik gives the 'all clear,' we're getting the hell off this planet," she grumbled. "Who knew that space would be the nice, safe, civilized place to be? I think I'm ready to go back to being a simple salvager."

Veral chuffed and brushed his nose against her temple.

"Give me two days, anastha, and we will do just that. Soon enough, it will be just us," he promised with a raspy rumble and a heated promise that made her toes curl.

"Two days," she sighed in agreement. "I'm going to hold you to that."

Larth groaned. "Two weeks in the hidden caves and crawling through high-wind sandstorms... I should have stayed enlisted as a warrior," he muttered.

Dreth looked over at him curiously.

"Is it that bad? Our far-kin live there without problem."

"Worse. Our far-kin is accustomed to having their expelling vents clogged with sand, but clearing them out is unpleasant. You will see," he muttered. "I will prepare everything we will we need and alert Hitani that we are heading east once more."

"You can always stay here," Veral said, unperturbed by his cousin's disgust.

The male immediately bristled.

"And leave the guarding of you to who? Navesha is preoccupied, Dreth has never been there and does not know what to expect, neither has Malraha or most of the household guard. I will go. I will just require a few things," he muttered.

26

*B*ehind his polite mask of indifference, Veral seethed at the presence of the local registrar. He knew it could not be delayed since they were leaving for the Blowing Sands early the next day, but he disliked everything about the registrar on sight. To make matters worse, the male just would not leave. He insisted that there was data that required further verification.

"What further verification do you require, Registrar Akal'-sivkoran'tanil?" Veral demanded as he held in a growl.

It would be easy to break the male in front of him if he lost his temper. The registrar was smaller, his implants clearly designated more for interfacing with the databanks of the High City Ki'karthilan than the modifications given to one of the warrior class. Despite Akal's limitations, he regarded Veral with dispassionate disdain. If it were not for Larth standing at his side, Veral might have been tempted to act on his murderous impulse.

Veral was well aware of what the Argurma of Ki'karthilan, and all of Amhim'voreth thought of the people of the Quarnet'safet. The Dunes bred wild males and females, difficult to break to the council's will, corrupted, and lacking in intelligence. Perfect to train as warriors and sacrifice indiscriminately. The only people lower were those hidden in the Galithilan and offworlders.

At least Akal's tongue was kept in line by Larth's presence, saving Veral from being forced to pull it out. Few had the imposing glower of his guard, and Larth took sadistic pleasure in making his prey squirm. And despite his obvious distaste, the registrar shifted uncomfortably under the male's glare.

Arak made a rough sound in the back of his throat.

"I do not know the reason, only that I was informed to collect the necessary verifications," he said stiffly.

"You have received all documentation from our medic," Veral reminded him, his voice dropping to an icy temperature. "Further verification is outside what is lawfully required."

The registrar lifted one shoulder and huffed.

"It was deemed insufficient. The birthrate in the Amhim'voreth has dropped drastically over the last fifty revolutions, and the Reproduction Department has asked us to help in this matter to determine why. I have asked to run further verifications and do additional testing on the female Harahna. As the mother is unlisted as per private agreement, we will not be requiring her to be produced, but I will need to take some samples of your genetic material and nanos in addition to that of your offspring."

"No," Veral growled, keeping just enough bite from his tone that it did not veer into inappropriate for an Argurma. "The situation of the Amhim'voreth has nothing to do with my offspring. I will not permit collecting of genetic material or any form of testing on her. That is the end of the matter. I have placed my mark on your documents and that is all I will give you. Take it and leave."

The male frowned, surprise registering on his face with the slight uptick of his vibrissae. "You would deny the Reproduction Department? They have the authority of the council behind them.

If you refuse this minor process, it can bring undesirable attention to you and the Monushava House."

Veral leaned forward, his eyes narrowing.

"Do you threaten me?" he growled.

Akal blinked, his expression blank aside from a tightening around his mouth. He straightened his sleeves and rested his hands once more in his lap. A betrayal of nerves. Argurma who claimed to be uncompromised emotionally still had their little tells. Even the famous rages of the Argurma warriors were an emotional outlet where few others allowed more than a trickle of something through—deny it however they like. If one knew what to look for, it was easy to process.

"No," the male replied. "It would not serve the purpose of the registrar's office to threaten our citizens. If you are certain that is your official standpoint, then I ask only to visually verify the health of Harahna, as is my legal duty. As to your objection to further testing, I will forward it to the reproduction department." His eyes glinted with the barest hint of satisfaction. "You can expect contact with them within a lunar."

Let them. Veral would be gone with his mate and offspring long before then.

Careful to not betray his thoughts, he inclined his head and turned to Larth, issuing him instruction on their private channel. His cousin stepped away and walked out of the office to retrieve the medic and Harahna.

Veral had hoped to avoid a physical examination because his daughter had traits unlike those of an Argurma, but Tarik had assured him that there was a strong probability of such features being merely dismissed as a mutation and noted as such rather than raising suspicion. He would rather not have had any such speculation of his offspring, but the medic had warned them during Harahna's pre-departure checkup the day before, that physical verification of health was not unusual. It was considered normal in cases where a mother was kept classified.

It was for that reason alone he had prepared by having Harahna brought to the medic in case it was required.

As he waited for Larth to return, Veral stared wordlessly at the registrar, the claw of his forefinger tapping sedately on the armrest of his chair. Akal glanced over and adjusted his seat. Veral held back a grin at the sign of discomfort. He had no intention of conversing any further than necessary with the male, and if the silence made the registrar uncomfortable, then that at least was satisfactory.

"Harahna is not a name that we see often," Akal observed. "After her mother?"

"No," Veral replied.

"Is her mother-donator of a nearby household? We do not normally inquire of such things, but with the Reproduction Department seeking answers, cases of successful births are worth noting for households having difficulties conceiving or carrying to term."

Veral did not reply, allowing silence to fill the space left by the question.

Akal's eyes narrowed, his mandibles twitching, only to practically leap to his feet when the door slid open again, admitting Larth. The medic trailed in behind the warrior with Harahna wrapped in a sheer blanket in his arms. Akal made a move in their direction but was stayed by Larth's ominous growl, forcing the registrar to sink back into his seat.

Tarik's expression remained cool as he carried Harahna over to Akal. Although he gave the impression of being an unassuming, obedient male programmed to his service, there was no mistaking the warrior who dwelled below the surface. It could be seen in the way his eyes pinned the male as he drew near with Veral's daughter.

"Do not touch. She is still very young," the medic warned as he pulled back the light blanket concealing her.

The warning should have been unnecessary. Argurma culture did not approve of anyone outside of their line touching their offspring. That very fact had caused issues with offworlders before in the marketplace, even when Veral was in his training. He was glad that the medic thought to remind the male because Akal's hands dropped to his side at the reprimand as he leaned forward.

The male's eyes scanned her, verifying her biometrics. Upon completion, his lip curled as he pulled out his datapad before reluctantly leaning in close once more.

"Overall biometric stats are perfect. Size is small for an Argurma, but the offspring is in good health despite being malformed and mutated. Female's head is narrow and misshapen, and she is lacking both the nasal ridge plate and chin plating. Female offspring is also nearly scaleless and possesses a sickly coloration," he observed aloud as his datapad processed his notations.

Veral's claws dug into his chair, fury making his vibrissae rise around him. He just barely kept them from whipping menacingly and held back the snarl that rose into his throat even though he choked on it.

If the registrar did not conclude soon, it would be his death sentence.

As if answering some unspoken wish, Akal hissed as his head whipped back, narrowly avoiding the tiny, clawed hand that raked unhappily at his face. Veral's lips twisted in a proud smile. That was another reason that strangers were not permitted to touch their young. Argurma young developed faster than most species, especially with their long incubation in the womb, which made them potentially dangerous to those who got too near and frightened them.

Although Harahna did not seem frightened, her eyes tracked him, her tiny nostrils flared, and her small mouth pinched, her distaste for the strange male hovering so near her clear. Her hastened gestation had not affected her development as far Tarik had been able to tell, and was evident in her reaction.

The registrar's vibrissae twitched in displeasure. Wisely, he reined in any other sign of irritation as he leaned down at a modified distance. "Eyes are clear, and nanos are numerous and healthy," the registrar continued, oblivious to Veral's rising temper. "That is unexpected, given her severe mutations. How are her internal organs, medic?"

"Fully formed and healthy as any Argurma offspring," Tarik replied with a subtle sneer.

It was gratifying for Veral that the medic took a protective attitude when it came to his daughter. While everyone of the line would protect her out of loyalty to the household and line, that sort of protectiveness was usually reserved only for the closest of kin. He had never even seen Gargath act any less than professional with any of their line. Veral's estimation of the medic rose. At the medic's side, Larth was hovering nearer, his vibrissae puffed out with unspoken menace. One wrong move from Akal, and it would be the last one he made by the time they got through with him.

"Noted," the registrar said as he straightened and put his datapad away. Lifting his comm, he spoke into it. "I am finished here. Be prepared to leave this place." The voice at the other end confirmed, and Akal dropped his arm to his side and inclined his head politely. "That is all that I require."

Veral's lips lifted slightly in an appropriate smile of acknowledgment, one he did not feel but that was expected for sake of propriety. Smiles were seldom about emotion, but the sort of smile dictated by appropriate social interactions and cues, and occasional humor—one thing that the council had never been able to irradicate despite its annoyance to those in command.

That was something Terri still struggled with. She gifted her smiles freely and with genuine emotion. With the exception of her sardonic expressions, her smiles related joy and pleasure, and he greedily wanted to keep every one of them to himself. He even found himself responding with smiles to things that he truly found pleasing. In this case, however, he offered nothing but the slightest diplomatic quirk of his lips that said nothing of the seething turmoil within him.

He would have liked to show just how close to death he stood and awakened the latent fear lurking within the male that he could see the faintest shadow of—but it was better if he did not. He did not wish to give the registrar reason to alert the council of possible dissent coming from the Monushava House.

"Larth, escort Registrar Akal'sivkoran'tanil to his waiting flyer and send *her* in."

His cousin smirked as he immediately herded the registrar toward the door.

There was no need to specify who Veral meant. His cousin knew very well that the pirate was lurking in the shadows just outside the room where Veral had asked her to wait. He would signal her to go in, and Veral would engage in the next step necessary for departure.

With the registrar gone, Veral slanted an approving look to the medic as he stood from his chair. Tarik watched him cautiously as he approached and stiffened further when Veral set a hand on his shoulder spine. The gesture was one that could preclude an attack or a mark of trust and closeness between Argurma… It was a paradox that guaranteed no one knew for sure where they stood and demanded trust of the recipient. Caution was smart, but in this case unnecessary.

"You honor me. I thank you," he grunted before releasing the male and walking away to the opposite side of the room, peering out the window that overlooked the entrance of the compound. A genuine smile curled his lips as he watched Larth give the male a non-too-gentle nudge that came too close to sending the registrar sprawling into the sands. "Is everything ready?"

"Yes, Ahanvala. I have loaded all private data regarding Harahna's medic records into your personal AI system aboard your starship and have deleted everything within our own systems in case the council forcibly accesses our systems."

"Good. Return Harahna to Terri and tell her that I will be there soon."

"Yes, Ahanvala," Tarik murmured.

Veral did not watch him go, his attention on the vast sand dunes that flowed out from the compound as far as his enhanced vision could see. The red sands of the Quarnet'safet rose and fell in their graceful peaks and valleys. He had trained in the dunes, suffering the strains of deprivation from food and drink, facing the harsh climate there. He had even trained at the edges of the Galithilan to earn his marks in the worst of what their world had to offer—an accomplishment few of Argurumal's warriors could claim. A flicker of something that he processed must be excitement flickered in him.

He would be out there again... away from the petty control of the council, back in the wilds.

It wasn't space, but he looked forward to introducing Terri to the rare and deadly beauty of the Galithilan. He would comm Hitani and ask that she see to it that he and Terri enjoy a night alone at one of the hidden oases.

The soft sound of feet against the floor met his ears. The pirate was good, but no matter how lightly she stepped, she could not get by an Argurma's enhanced hearing if he were not distracted.

"Azan," he greeted, without turning around.

She sighed, and her footsteps altered to their normal rhythm as she strode the rest of the way across the room, stopping just a short distance behind him.

"You rang?"

He looked over his shoulder at her in confusion. "What?"

The female grinned unapologetically.

"Something my human says. From what I understand, it is from an old Earth vid. I do not understand the reference... something about a household of peculiar humans who delight in the unusual. I have been curious for lunars, so do not be surprised if we raid your vids while we have your starship in orbit," she informed him gleefully.

"You remember that this is not a pleasure excursion," Veral growled as he turned to face her.

"As if you won't be tasting a bit of pleasure yourself," Azan snorted mirthfully, and he felt heat rise into his scales. How did she have such insight into his thoughts? "We will keep to the plan, but it is many days of waiting, so we will entertain ourselves as well. But do not worry, we will not sully your bed overmuch."

"You will use the furbished crew quarters. Do not enter our rooms," he hissed in abhorrence.

The idea of anyone lying where he intimately held his mate made him itch.

Laughter burst from the pirate.

An annoyed growl vibrated through him. He was not in the mood to be toyed with.

"Relay your instructions to me so that I know you will stay on task," he grumbled.

Azan stretched her upper arms lazily. It was deceiving; there was nothing lazy or fickle about the pirate, despite her eagerness to cultivate such impressions. He was not surprised, though satisfied, when she produced a flawless recital of her instructions.

"We are to take *the Wanderer* and set down in an obscured

landing zone on the dark side of the smaller moon Gali'sowren. There, we await further orders. We are to employ no outer lights or leave the ship for any reason other than an emergency. Once we receive signal from you, we will drop down into orbit heading to the coordinates you will provide. We will pick you and your nice little family up and meet with my crew at our agreed-upon location."

Veral grunted.

"We will be leaving tomorrow night after dusk, but I want you out of Argurumal orbit before sunrise, during the shift changes. You will have exactly twenty minutes to be clear of our planetary tracking. The coordinates you are going to is an emergency facility kept by my line and a few of our closest relations. Once you are there, it will keep you off the long-sweep radars," he grumbled. "And one other thing," he said as Azan turned to leave. He shot her a dark glower. "Try not to get too overeager with the replicator. I do not wish my mate to lack in her favorite sweet things and drinks."

"No luxuries... Heard and obeyed," the female said with a precise salute.

"You have your orders then... Now leave, Blaithari. I wish to return to my mate" he ordered. "I will see you in two spans."

Azan's grin widened knowingly, but tucking her hands into her numerous pockets, she sauntered out without another word.

Perhaps there were gods after all... If so, then they just might have blessed him at that moment.

Letting out a sigh, he returned to his desk to finish what little work remained before he could return to his chambers for the evening. Now that it was upon him, he was eager to get away from all the detailed data entry work. He longed for the simple data logs and hours of privacy and leisure during travel that came with salvaging.

Soon.

*T*arik offered her one of his tight but warm smiles as he handed Harahna to Terri.

"Do not be concerned. The registrar did not question what his eyes saw. While his comments were unflattering, he did not suspect anything regarding your offspring's mixed heritage."

A relieved sigh escaped Terri as she hugged her baby close. She dodged the little hand playfully batting at her face before distracting her daughter by wiggling her fingers until one was captured and stuffed into an eager little mouth. Despite being only a couple of weeks old, Harahna was developing at a rate that didn't cease to shock her.

"Did the registrar see the symbiont?" she asked.

The medic's smile widened slightly.

"No. Argurma protocols kept him back far enough that I was able to keep her right hand between her body and mine."

"Good," she sighed in relief.

"And I brought something for you," he added, directing her attention to a small bag he lifted.

A familiar honey-sweet smell filled the room, making her mouth water with anticipation.

"You brought me vansik?"

"On Veral's instruction," he clarified. "He wanted you to have an appropriate treat from the oases of the Galithilan. It is one of the few exports that come from our far-kin, and he said that you never had the opportunity to have it fresh. Only replicated."

His lip curled slightly, betraying his opinion on replicated food. Terri offered him a commiserating grin. She had some imported foods on space stations, but until she reached Argurumal, she really hadn't had the opportunity to taste the difference between replicated and fresh foods. A sniff affirmed that this was the fresh stuff. The difference in the aroma of the vansik was incredible.

Terri took the bag and brought it close to her face, inhaling as a chuckle escaped her.

"It really does smell better too. I can't believe how much I love to eat these little things considering I'm not usually one who enjoys eating bugs," she confided.

A surprisingly raspy chuff escaped the medic that was echoed by Malraha from where she was seated in a chair next to the baby's bed. Navesha smirked from her position by the doorway.

"You would be surprised to know that many Argurma hold the same aversion, and yet vansik is among the few exceptions that appeal to us all," the female commented as she looked at the bag with what might have been longing.

Her smile widened at the thought but dropped when the door chimed. Navesha straightened and touched the door panel.

"Registered identity is Featha'katala," Navesha reported.

Malraha immediately stiffened, and Tarik stepped back quickly from the doorway.

Featha. Wonderful.

Biting back a sound of dismay, she nodded to Navesha, who promptly put in the acceptance code.

S.J. SANDERS

The door opened to the tall crimson robed Argurma. She stood there, her eyes trailing around the room before she stepped inside.

Tarik's mandibles drew close to his cheekbones deferentially when she gave a sharp glance in his direction before raising her hand and flicking her fingers in a dismissive gesture.

"Leave us, Medic."

"At your orders," he replied stiffly.

He wasn't happy about it—his body language screamed it—but he complied. It seemed that no one argued against Featha. The female had such a strong presence that Terri could suddenly understand how she had kept order in the Monushava House.

"And you as well, Malraha and Navesha," Featha directed. "Stand guard outside the doors. I will not be long. I wish to speak privately to Veral's human."

Terri opened her mouth to object—after all, they were her guards—but thought better of stirring the pot when they were so close to leaving. She would let Featha have her moment and pray she wouldn't have to see her again before they left Argurumal. The female was a lot to take.

Malraha gave a wide-eyed nod before slipping out behind Tarik. Navesha, not as easy to impress as the other guard, hesitated for a moment, her expression thoughtful as if she considered arguing the matter. At a hard, uncompromising look from Featha, she finally inclined her head before she stepped outside.

Terri privately pitied any mate who Dreth ended up bringing home.

Forcing herself to calm despite her natural desire to run and hide from—or take out from a safe distance—the imposing female, Terri smiled politely in the way that was considered appropriate among Argurmas and gestured to the small table and chairs at one corner of the room.

"Would you care to sit?"

The female returned the smile—if the arctic expression on her face could pass for a smile—and dropped her head at an angle to decline the invitation.

Damn all the social cues. Terri wasn't sure what she should do next. Thankfully, Featha saved her from having to guess.

"Your hospitality is noted, but I will not be long," the female stated imperiously.

Once again, Terri was reminded of some of the nobility she had to deal with and couldn't help but feel a renewed sympathy for Dreth. Terri had little doubt that she was formal and exacting in everything. That didn't dredge up images of a warm childhood. Terri might not have had much, but her parents loved her with everything they had for the time that they had together. Between her and Dreth, she was pretty sure the other male got the short end of the stick when it came to happy childhoods, regardless of how much he was materially provided for.

Since it was obvious that Featha wasn't there for a social visit, it was time to cut to the chase.

"How can I help you, Featha?" she asked woodenly.

The female's brow arched, but instead of immediately replying, she glanced down at Harahna.

"There is nothing you can do for me, human," she said as she stepped closer. "I merely wish to see my sister's namesake before you leave."

She paused for a moment, a look of uncertainty crossing her face as she glanced up at Terri from the corner of her eye, gauging her response. Finding something there that apparently set her at ease, the female relaxed and held out her arms.

"May I hold her?" she asked.

"Hell no," was the first thing that came to Terri's mind, but she kept it locked tight behind her lips. But as cold and impersonal as the female was, Terri had a hard time finding reason to deny such a simple request. Featha was Harahna's family, after all, and she had sworn to protect her. Hell, Harahna might even

return someday. If so, it would be good to encourage some kind of bonding.

Sucking in her bottom lip nervously, she pulled her finger free of Harahna's mouth with a pop and handed her to the tall Argurma.

Featha's expression softened as she took the baby, her fingers smoothing the blanket away from her face before brushing through the unruly mass vibrissae. The coils tended to knot around each other so hopelessly that Harahna would squeal with frustration but at that moment they plucked curiously at her mother-kin.

"She looks nothing like my sister," Featha said, and Terri nearly snatched the baby back, prepared to defend her daughter's appearance. "She is lovely, though," the Argurma amended with a smile—something a bit closer to genuine. "She will grow to be a great Ahanvala."

Terri blinked at her in surprise. That... was unexpected.

"You really think so?" she murmured, glancing down at her baby, who seized her mother-kin's hand and happily began to slobber all over it.

Featha chuffed.

"I have little doubt. She is smart and reacts quickly. These are traits I recognize from my sister. And the fearlessness. Many Argurma do not know it until after they are taken away to be conditioned, but your Harahna has it, just as mine did."

A shadow of pain passed over her face.

"I love my sons, but I always wanted a daughter. I would have named a daughter of my immediate line after her if I had managed to bear one. I speak of the disgrace of my sister's emotional breakdown, but she was not. I say such things to keep my people strong and prepared because of how our world will treat them if they are not cautious. My sister was brave and fearless, even in her agony. She did not care what the council thought of her heart.

They broke it when they took Veral. And they broke mine when they took her," she whispered as she brushed her cheek against the baby's.

Harahna's two chubby hands grabbed the female's vibrissae as if hugging her back. A soft chuff escaped Featha as she gently untangled herself and glanced at Terri.

"My sister had been so close to outsmarting them. I see where Veral gets it. She wanted to hide him with our far-kin in the Galithilan. I begged her not to and told her that our household could protect him. I was foolish. They came a day early—I have never been able to discover why—and took him. Then she left me, leaving me her youngest offspring."

Terri startled in surprise. "Veral has a sibling?"

Featha inclined her head.

"I do not wish for him to be told. He did not know, and it is up to Navesha when she wishes for such connections to be made. She has been angry for many revolutions, believing he was the cause of her mother's absence just by existing. That her mother had grieved for him and left her because of it. I had thought that processing would help her forget her pain, but it seems that the trauma she experienced in her youth preserved her memories— the precious and the ugly. Although she has mellowed since he returned, I do not know her heart on the matter. As you know, our species is programmed not to be intentionally expressive or emotional. I tried to be a mother for her, but I have failed her as much as I have failed Dreth."

Terri winced slightly at that. Even though she had similar thoughts just moments earlier about Dreth, as a mother it was hard hearing that come from his mother's mouth. Instead, she focused on the most incredible thing: Navesha—control freak of the biting remarks—was actual family. Veral's sister!

"Wow…I really can't imagine how lonely and painful it has been for her," she murmured. "I really hope she decides to tell him. I think Veral might like knowing that he has her. And having him might help her heal too."

Featha cocked her head inquisitively.

"Do you?" she asked before brushing her lips against the bony plating of Harahna's forehead and handing her over.

Terri stared back at the female, appalled as she cuddled her daughter against her. Tiny claws pricked as Harahna attempted to get through her tunic. She was hungry again. It appeared that she would be enjoying her snack momentarily as her daughter nursed her own.

"Of course. She's his family. That makes her my family and Harahna's family. I want her to be in our lives."

"Would you say that includes all of his line, or just his imme-diate birth-kin? You did not seem so interested until now."

Terri grimaced. As much as she had endured just flitting around the compound aimlessly, she really didn't know any of his mother-kin. She had been too caught up in her own boredom and her own morose thoughts about her mate's absence to have made much effort in that direction. At times, she might have even resented the way that they eyed her in passing. She didn't even know Featha and immediately judged her on outward perceptions—half of which the female destroyed within five minutes.

She definitely hadn't liked Kaylar at all.

Terri held in a groan. She had been alone so long that she had forgotten something about what it was like to have family. She was going to have to do better.

"Yes," she said at last. "I know I haven't done a great job of it, but I want him to have his connections with his family and for our daughter to enjoy them as well."

A small smile tugged at the corners of Featha's mouth.

"Perhaps there might be something to the human species that I did not see," she said casually as she glanced around the room, her eyes falling on the packs of Terri and Veral's belongings. "You are prepared to leave, then?"

"We are. First thing in the morning. Hopefully Harahna sleeps well," she laughed weakly.

It wasn't much of a joke. She was going to need as much sleep as she could get before they faced trekking over the Galithilan. The transport to the eastern minor household would be a short one. That would be the easy part, but she hoped that Harahna cooperated and allowed Terri to get all the sleep she needed.

Featha chuffed in understanding and walked over to the baby's bed. Her hands reaching into the bedding.

"My sons did not sleep well unless the bedding was drawn perfectly tight," she commented as she worked, drawing the bottom blanket snug against the sleeping mat. "Argurma offspring may develop quicker than other species, but they can be difficult…Wait, there is something moving just over…"

Featha jerked back as something that resembled a spider but with far too many legs and a long abdomen like a scorpion, with three whipping tails four times the length of its body, jumped up from the bedding. Its tails flailed as long, thin legs reached for her. The Argurma let out a startled roar, her arm coming up protectively.

Terri ran forward, distantly aware of the long cords of her daughter's symbiont wrapping around her as she initiated her own. A long double-edged blade extended beyond her hand, and she nearly stopped in surprise at the new weapon, but she pushed back the shock as she swung the blade forward.

The sound of the blade cutting through the alien arachnid hit with a wet crunch not unlike the sound that the vansik made when eaten. The wet sound, however, was mostly from the head falling away and followed by a soft thud as it landed on the floor, the body crumpling right beside it.

A wheeze escaped Terri as she looked down at the remains and Featha drew in a shaky breath. From the corner of her eye, she watched as the blaster was lifted. Her body froze, and it exploded with heat.

The plasma bolt slid right by Terri's head, blowing apart another of the creatures that had, unknown to Terri, materialized from the bedding. Featha then pointed the weapon down and proceeded to blow the ever-loving hell out of the bed until it was nothing but wreckage. The whine of displeasure that came from Harahna in objection to all the noise was the only other sound in the room outside of blaster fire.

That and her guards suddenly piling into her room with weapons drawn.

Terri remained rooted to the spot, not even looking their way, as she stood there beside the bed, numb with shock.

Those things could have killed both her and the baby the moment she put the baby to bed.

From the corner of her eye, she watched as Featha leaned down to pick the things up by their tails—or what little remained of the second, anyway—and threw them at the feet of the guards. Both females stared at the remains, their expressions stony. Never before had Terri hated the outward impassiveness of Argurmas more.

"Hathals—in the offspring's bed! Where did these come from?" Featha demanded, her mandibles and voice vibrating with anger. "These creatures come from the Amhim'voreth and the Ahmhim'shal'va. Someone brought them here and put them in this room. I want to know who!"

Navesha frowned down at the arachnids, her boot toeing one.

"The eggs would be easy to hide, no bigger than a claw or capsule, and they hatch fast. It could have been anyone. We can review the security footage and see who has been near the room. I will…"

"No," Terri snapped, panic tightening her throat. Featha's errands, the egg capsules, Navesha's secretiveness and harbored grudges. Was it one of them or someone else? She didn't know. All she knew was that she wanted everyone away from her and her daughter. "I need everyone to leave the room."

Featha looked at her steadily and inclined her head. "We will give you some privacy. I will comm Veral at once. He needs to leave with you tonight. There is no more waiting. This was not an accident."

With a flick of her fingers, she dismissed the guards. They balked at Featha's command but at Terri's pleading look they drew back.

"We will be outside the doors," Malraha said quietly. "If you need anything…"

"I know," Terri murmured as she dropped her cheek against Harahna, breathing in the warm smell of her daughter. "Thank you."

She heard the footsteps as they left, her body tense as she opened her tunic for Harahna's questing mouth. As her daughter latched on, she relaxed, but it was only when she was certain that there was nothing around except silence that she allowed herself to weep.

*I*ce swept through Veral's blood as he held his mate close under his arm, escorting her to the flyer prepared to transport them east. Krono clung close to their side, his vibrissae moving through the environment, sampling every energy signature near it. Veral's vibrissae were doing the same, flooding his processors with information, much of it useless. It did confirm the absence of threats, however, and that was all that mattered at that moment while his body was still flooded with terror.

He had come dangerously close to losing both his mate and offspring. There was nothing casual about this attack. Nothing that was devised to look like an accident. This was a blatant attempt at murder. Whoever the perpetrator was, they were no longer making any effort to hide what they were doing. They were also going to die—painfully.

Larth inclined his head from his position beside the entrance to the vessel, remnants of red sand still clinging to his armor. The male had not made it far into the compound before Veral commed him with new instructions. That his cousin arrived before him and readied the vessel eased some of his tension.

There would be no delays.

Returning the greeting to his mother-kin, he stepped aboard.

The flyer was small and compact, made specifically to carry passengers for short distances. Although rarely favored by many Argurma since it didn't have space to transport cargo, it was sleek and fast, and less likely to attract notice. That served the households of the Quarnet'safet perfectly.

Since the main cabin connected directly to the piloting station, Veral spotted Dreth immediately in the pilot's seat. A large dusky dorashnal lay wedged in beside his station, staring back at Veral. The male glanced up from the controls and gave a terse greeting as he set his hand on the control panels, hooking into the systems once more.

Good. Veral was not interested in any sort of pomp and ceremony. He just wanted to get his mate and offspring far away from the compound.

That Dreth ignored the manual controls and tapped directly into the system told Veral something of the male that he did not know. Despite his mother's grooming, Dreth had received at least intermedial training as a warrior to have specialized enough to earn piloting updates to his system.

"Engines are readied. We are ready to depart, Ahanvala," Dreth reported.

"Acknowledged," Veral replied as he made sure his mate was seated and fastened securely, just barely avoiding Krono's large body in the process.

The dorashnal took a protective position by the females' side, and Veral brushed his hand over the coiling vibrissae on the beast in a gesture of approval. Krono let out a grunt and stretched out on the ground, ignoring the other dorashnals on the flyer as he was trained. Veral could trust him to protect his mate and offspring.

"Good boy, Krono," Terri whispered, and the animal tipped

one long ear back at her, although his eyes never left Veral's daughter.

Unaware of her anxious dorashnal guard or the protective stance of her father hovering over her, Harahna looked up at Veral sleepily, one fist propped against her mouth where she had been sucking on it. The metal coils of her symbiont still cocooned her securely to her mother's chest. It was a wonder that they remained initiated for so long. It had to take an incredible amount of energy that would need to be replaced.

As if responding to his observation, his daughter turned her face into her mother's chest, nuzzling aside the fabric to latch on to one pink nipple. Veral stroke a hand down Harahna's vibrissae before brushing a kiss against his mate's cheek, his mandibles tucked in so not to scrape her with their sharp edges.

A small smile crept onto his mate's lips despite her obvious physical and emotional exhaustion. He was coming to understand just how much such intense emotions could be detrimental to one's welfare, and he was not sure if he missed the absence of them or was grateful to be spared that misery. All he knew was the fear that settled inside his core and the anger that pulsed through his processors.

"Rest, anastha," he ordered quietly.

Her smile widened, and a soft sound of amusement escaped her.

"Only because I'm exhausted and because you asked so sweetly," she replied as she lay back against the head rest.

Veral slid his hand along the controls of the arm, and the seat tipped at an angle to help her rest more comfortably. His eyes lingered on her, watching as her features softened and her eyelids fluttered tiredly. Within seconds she had dropped off to sleep, and it was only then he realized that he had been crooning to her even as his mandibles purred to ease her into rapid slumber. It was something that he had never thought to use against his mate, since it seemed too much like a violation of another's will, but in that moment, he wanted nothing more than for her to get the rest she needed and forget for a short time her narrow escape from death.

Harahna also slept, her mouth still working even in her sleep.

Tarik slipped into the seat across from her. It was a bit close, but Krono ignored it and the medic did not so much glance at the animal. That was odd enough, but more so was the absence of his own dorashnal to accompany him into dangerous territory. With rules in the compound to ensure safety, it was not odd for dorashnals to be absent from the main corridors, with certain exceptions where their presence was required. The quarters and private courtyard were spacious enough to give the animals plenty of privacy and freedom to move. But they always accompanied their bonded Argurma outside of the safety of the compound. While there were females who did not bond to a dorashnal, it was rare for a male to be seen absent of one. It always spoke of tragedy.

"Where is your dorashnal, medic?" he inquired.

The male met his gaze briefly.

"Died," the male replied. "When I was young, I was attacked by a razithihis. Vagirith killed it, but he could not be saved. My father terminated him before he was in too much pain. We endure the weight of our actions doing what we must for those we are bonded to." His eyes looked meaningfully at Terri and Harahna. There was no judgment in the male's expression. Instead, his mandibles twitched with approval.

"You made a wise choice," the medic commented, closing all further discussion of his dorashnal.

Veral grunted to indicate his understanding and allowed his gaze to rest on his mate and daughter.

"I do not want her to be anxious. Her emotions tire her. And Harahna as well, even though she seems adept at keeping herself secure to her mother. Will it present any damage being engaged so long?"

Leaning forward, Tarik swept a scanner over the offspring to gather more data than the simple bio-scans that warrior and medic-class Argurma possessed.

A soft grunt escaped the male, and he settled back into his seat.

"It takes less energy for a symbiont to protract and remain that way rather than constantly fluxing as Terri tends to wield it. The nanos are compensating for the energy draining, pulling from her fat reservoirs. She will merely eat more while they are engaged. I see no reason to be concerned, but I will monitor her. It is possible that her symbiont, being a second-generation production, has modifications that were made by the parent symbiont to counter possible deficiencies. It is fascinating to see such bioengineering. Other than our nanos—a technology we acquired and implemented from an elder race—our technology is far more limited. Even our nanos, while capable of multiplying and being passed organically to our mate through insemination, are incapable of improving on themselves to such degrees."

Whereas not too long ago Veral would have found the depth of the medic's scientific fascination annoying and suspicious, it now amused him. The male was devoted to his females' welfare, and so Veral no longer possessed any issue with Tarik's endless curiosity. If that kept his mate and daughter well provided-for, then he was pleased.

A small flurry of activity surrounded the flyer at that moment, drawing Veral's attention as several guards peeled away to safe zones away from the flyer. The vessel vibrated slightly as Larth stepped in, a brute of a dorashnal close at his side. Larth ducked his head to clear the entrance and dropped into the seat closest to him. He was immediately followed by Malraha, who did likewise across from him, her own dorashnal, a thin, rangy thing that was still clearly growing into her paws, sitting awkwardly at her side.

Navesha slipped in alone just after them, her expression tense as her mandibles flared.

"I regret to report that I will not be traveling with you. Featha is remaining behind to investigate what occurred here, and I have decided to do likewise," she growled. "We will also be watching for any sign of movement from the council. The registrar's presence coinciding with the attack is too convenient. Someone knew that male was coming and likely is in communication with Ki'karthilan."

It seemed that he and his cousin were of a similar opinion on the data presented. That was something that Veral was also worried about and why he agreed with Featha's judgment to leave immediately. Not only because it was an obvious direct attack with deadly intent, but the timing was too close to his departure and the arrival of the representative of the registrar's office too convenient.

"Noted. Comm if you have any updates to our situation."

The female nodded stiffly and departed, the hatch door sliding shut behind her. The drone of the engine increased as the flyer began its final preparations for liftoff. He caught a glimpse of Navesha before she disappeared behind the safety barrier. They were all clear for departure. From his peripheral vision, he could see the tension radiating through Malraha as her hand tightened on her spear and her other gripped her dorashnal's vibrissae tight enough that the animal whined and turned her head in warning. Malraha immediately loosened her grip, though her body vibrated with tension.

"Speak your mind now while you have the opportunity, Malraha. There is no returning after we leave if you have concerns."

The female expelled a hard breath and met his eyes.

"I think this is foolish. If the council is involved, there is no escaping them for long," Malraha's replied. "Fleeing may only mean delaying the inevitable. It would be wiser to take a stand here at the compound where we have defenses we can utilize."

Veral met her gaze, his jaw hardening.

"My task is not to defeat them. Whatever victory we gain in direct confrontation would only be short-lived before they destroy us completely. It will take more than our household to effectively fight against the strength of the council and all the united forces of Argurumal under their yoke. My only intention is to delay discovery until it is safe to depart. With my absence, the council will lose interest in the house of Monushava. As of now they have no direct proof of your complicity against them and I will keep it that way for as long as possible. Featha has orders to deny all accountability and knowledge of our status and to renounce me formally to preserve the standing of our house. Tarik and Dreth are fully aware of their risks by joining with us. You are welcome to remain with the rest of the household if you are concerned," he replied in a firm voice that invited no argument.

The female flinched, but she did not speak further, nor did she leave her post. Despite his annoyance, he did not fault her for being concerned and so did not reprimand her further. The offer was a reasonable one, not one born of resentment. Those who did not wish to be entangled in their fight with the council should remain behind. He did not begrudge anyone who wished to look out for their own safety and those of their immediate line.

Veral glanced over at Larth. Even the large male appeared on edge, his vibrissae flaring aggressively as his eyes snapped everywhere, never staying in one place long. It was the look of a male readying for formidable battle.

"What of you, cousin?"

Larth grinned from his seat, the points of his fangs and a hint of the edge of his sharp teeth showing between his lips.

"It has been revolutions since I have practiced stealth maneuvers against war droids on the edges of the Galithilan. They do not operate well in those conditions for the same reason it is too risky to take flyers beyond that point, but they still will be set regardless of how many are brought down. I would not wish to miss participating."

Veral smirked. An expected response from a war-blooded male. With all advanced programming set as a warrior, it would never depart him, regardless of his post. Nodding in approval, Veral turned and slipped into the seat beside the pilot behind the emergency flight controls. Dreth glanced over at him, and at Veral's signal the engines roared as the flyer lifted and snapped forward to dart out of the entrance.

"Inputting coordinates for the eastern holdings and increasing speed," Dreth relayed, the flyer maneuvering through the air at a sharp angle as it adjusted its course. "Projected arrival three hours, twenty-three minutes, and five seconds."

Veral grunted in acknowledgment as he settled into his chair.

Silence filled the ship. There was no need for useless chatter, and he suspected everyone was resting however they could manage to do so. Dreth leaned back, dozing with the AI hooked directly to his temple to rouse him at any change in their path.

Veral could not sleep. Instead, he watched the dark sky stretched out ahead of them, his eyes falling on the dunes as the faint operational light of the flyer reflected off the sand. The view gradually brightened and became more vivid as the sun crested the horizon framing the tall, dark structure of the compound that rose up before them.

As their flyer drew in on its approach, Dreth immediately straightened and wordlessly fell into procedures to initiate landing. Just behind him, he could hear the subtle shifting of Argurma and dorashnal through the flyer as everyone slowly awakened. Terri sighed, the sound making his civix tighten, but he ignored the sensation as he spun around in his chair to face his mate.

Her face was flushed with sleep, but she gave him a drowsy

smile until she woke enough to recall where she was and straightened, her seat sliding back into its primary position. She glanced down wryly at Harahna, who didn't seem to be inclined to release her breast anytime soon, but had merely at some point switched to the other one. A gentle pat at their daughter's back, however, had the tendrils of their offspring's symbiont retracting promptly. Harahna shivered slightly as they withdrew back into her skin, but she did not otherwise wake.

The minor household did not have a secured, hidden docking bay such as the primary household possessed, but it was still in a well-sheltered position between the household and a long artificial wall that shielded one side of the compound to keep the dunes from encroaching. There the flyer and any other vessels were not readily visible, and the area around it was constantly monitored.

It took them only a few minutes to gain the necessary clearance and land. The alert had been raised upon their departure and the entire eastern holding was on alert and readied for them. Veral was not surprised when he and his mate were greeted by Hitani and Vand the moment they exited the flyer. Although the pair wore steely expressions, they inclined their head in formal acknowledgment before their gaze strayed to Terri and finally landed on Harahna.

"So it is true," Hitani murmured, a fleeting look of wonder on her face. "A daughter of the line was born to the Ahanvala and his alien mate, and successfully survived her first tiani days."

Her eyes turned to Veral, her expression easing into one of respect and something like warmth—something he never would have recognized if not for his mate-bonding with Terri.

"What are tiani days?" Terri whispered at his side.

Hitani regarded Terri with an inscrutable look, and Veral bit back a growl. Terri would not know such things and should not be judged for it. The female did not comment on the lack of knowledge but answered the question in Veral's stead.

"Tiani days are those in which our offspring, while more advanced than weaker and less developed species, are most vulnerable. The tiani, whom we call the spirits of fate, may take them during that time and so we call the days after them and ask their mercy that they do not steal our young to replace their own that they lost to eons of time."

The female's attention snapped back to Veral. "We have prepared a convoy as directed, including the special instructions you requested," she said. Her head tilted at a very slight angle. "It seemed unnecessary at the time, but it is evident that your female can use the rest and time to re-establish necessary bonding with her mate after such trauma that we were only recently made aware of. This I understand and approve of."

Veral did not really care if she understood or approved of his plans or not, but he inclined his head all the same in acknowledgment of her words.

"And our transport?"

The first hint of a smile appeared on the stern female's face.

"The sand dragnar are being readied as we speak."

"**F**lyers and other vessels do not operate well in the Galithilan," Hitani said as they approached several animals gathered in front of the entrance gates of the compound. "To travel deep into the Galithilan, we do as our ancestors before us have done. The sand dragnar carry us safely to and from the abode of our far-kin, and so they will carry you."

Terri swallowed nervously as she stared at the creatures that were supposedly going to carry them across the sand.

That was a sand dragnar?

It didn't look like a tame mount, but almost like images of mythical dragons she had seen, except that it was smaller. It had a single thick pad set just above its first pair of legs that was just barely big enough for two people to ride it. Unlike any dragon she had ever seen illustrated, its body was longer, like a snake, with eight short legs and a head pointed like a wolf or a fox, though with mouths filled with rows of small teeth that made its entire jaw look like a serrated weapon.

Despite is ferocious appearance, the dragnar closest to her made a bassy crooning sound as it dropped its head to eye-level. The blue slitted pupil expanded in its flame-red iris as a billow of its warm breath swept over her. Terri gasped when the dragnar nudged his huge nose toward her, ignoring the anxious growls from Krono. With a soft chuckle, Terri pushed its nose back so she could admire it.

Like many lifeforms on Argurumal, it seemed, the dragnar was covered in scales and shockingly fine vibrissae that crowned its head and ran down its body. They were very thin and seemed to be constantly moving about it. At the tail, the vibrissae were thicker and longer, forming what looked like a fanned fin. That tail rose, the vibrissae expanding outward for a moment before it slapped back down to the sand with a soft thud.

"Sankal likes you," Hitani observed, a faint smile of approval pulling at her lips. "She will serve as a good mount for you and your male." The female gave the sleek neck a pat before addressing the rest of them as she made her way around to the largest of the beasts. "You will ride in pairs. Mount and hold on. The dragnar are trained to follow their alpha female, Girshwin. They move fast, so be prepared."

At a dual octave chirp from the Argurma, the dragnar lowered flat against the sand, providing an easy mount for Hitani and her mate as they slid onto the padded seat. The moment they were secure, the dragnar rose to her feet at another one of the chirps, her proud neck curving.

"Mount up," Hitani ordered. "We have far to go to make it to shelter before sundown. You do not want to be caught on the Galithilan after nightfall."

The sound was apparently an Argurma thing because everyone around her effortlessly made it. Larth called out to one, chirping at it so that it lowered for him to mount. He offered a hand to Malraha, and the female looked like she would rather chew nails than ride with him, but she ignored his hand and vaulted up onto the dragnar's back behind him. From the stiff way she sat behind the male, Terri was certain that there was no love

231

lost between the two and wondered if there was a story there, but she was promptly distracted from her musings when Sankal dropped in front of them in response to Veral's command.

The big eye watched her, a resonant croon echoing from the female dragnar's throat as they walked down the line of her neck to the padded seat. Veral lifted Terri easily, setting her in the front before launching himself into the spot just behind her. The contact sent a delicious thrill through her, which only grew in intensity as his arms wrapped around her to grip the vibrissae fluttering just in front of them. Moments later, the padding shifted again as Krono scrambled up, his retractable claws digging into the padding just behind Veral, his whip-like tail coiling around her mate's waist. Terri could feel it between them, and as strange as it felt, it put her at ease knowing that her entire family was securely together.

Sankal surged to her feet then as he gave another chirp, and the startling shift beneath her might have been concerning to Terri if she hadn't felt so secure in her mate's arms. Even Harahna rested quietly in the sling across Terri's chest that served to hold her daughter close even when the baby's symbiont was inactive. No doubt the slight ease of weight from one foot to another as the dragnar tested her passengers was a soothing motion to their offspring.

With one of his free hands, Veral drew the light blanket completely over their daughter, fastening it to the strap of the sling. His hand then lifted inside Terri's hood and drew out a stretch of fabric from the layered material there within the shafna. This he wrapped around her lower face, tucking and pinning it in place before doing the same for himself.

Despite Argurma's vents and high tolerance for sand, apparently the Galithilan was troublesome even for them without some extra protection. His eyes fastened on her, dulled by his secondary membranous eyelid with a look of affection as he tugged a visor over her eyes. It was not unlike her goggles back on Earth but made of metal and had a technical enhancement that brought their surroundings into sharp relief. Enjoying the novelty of not having to squint against the grit, Terri sat up straighter, winding her hands in the dragnar's vibrissae with Veral's.

Her neck curving, Sankal's scaled head turned back to watch them carefully with an intelligent gleam in her eyes. Two enormous vents at either side of her jaw blew, spraying a light dusting of sand as she continued the process. Vibrissae fluttering like mad, she made tiny adjustments to her balance until finally she stopped moving for the span of a breath before the dragnar leaped forward, her body sliding lightning fast across the sand.

Hitani hadn't been exaggerating when she said that the dragnar were fast. It was easily beyond what many people back home had called "hold onto your ass" speed, except that rather than barreling down empty streets in barely running pickups and beat-up cars, Terri was practically flying across the desert on the back of a creature that seemed straight out of a fantasy novel. If she had anyone to wager with, she would have bet that Sankal could beat most basic flyers out there. She couldn't imagine why his people would have stopped riding them, and she might have asked if she was certain that she could breathe and talk at the same time.

Flying across the sand at an astonishing pace, Sankal broke over the dunes like a boat cresting waves. While the other dragnar lagged behind their alpha, Sankal was to neck-and-neck with the large female, playfully singing to the other in bassy trills. The other female barely turned her lupine head in her direction but increased her speed, her upper body diving gracefully as she dropped down the side of the dunes.

Sankal moved to go the same direction, but Veral called her attention with an unfamiliar chirp and redirected the dragnar away from the grouping. Behind the cloth mask, Terri frowned in confusion. The wall of sand rose around them, and though it barely bothered her through her protective gear, she worried about being separated from the others. Turning in his embrace, she attempted to shout over the air whistling by them created both by the dragnar's speed and by the wind blowing all around them.

"Veral, what's going on? We are going to lose them!" she shouted.

Her muffled voice sounded hollow to her ears, as if it had been thrown back at her. Veral didn't speak, though his arm tightened briefly around her as if attempting to allay whatever tension he felt coiling within her. Unfortunately, as attentive as he was as a mate, he didn't seem the least bit interested in where the rest of their group disappeared to.

Unable to communicate, Terri blew out a frustrated breath against her mask and leaned into him to wait out the ride. As fun as it was to come close to flying on a near mythical creature, her joy was dulled by the worry that pinched at her nerves, especially as the sand blew harder until all she could see through her vizor was a curtain of red haze all around them.

Now she saw for herself why the area was called the Galithilan—the Blowing Sands. That was all there was as far as she could see. Time and space seemed to disappear there, and she had no idea of how far or how long they had traveled until a rocky ridge protruded out of nowhere.

Sankal let out a bassy trill of pleasure as she whipped straight for it. Within minutes, the blinding red sand dropped away as they passed into the cavernous alcove of stone, the opening at the top allowing sunshine to pour in to give life to the most beautiful thing Terri had ever seen. The dragnar dropped gracefully into a thick bed of sand at the entrance, her enormous body coiling there, blocking out all wind and flattening her neck so they could dismount with ease.

The moment her feet hit the ground, Terri hurried toward the sight, her breath hitching. She had seen tropical planets and those with prismatic sands that cast rainbows across golden oceans, but nothing compared to the sight of life flourishing in the heart of the worst part of the deserts of Argurumal. Her eyes skipped over one feature and then the next, eager to take it all in.

A pool of water filled much of the space and all around there were plants of various hues from the deepest lavenders to magenta and maroon. There were even a few yellow fronds with the slightest hint of green that swayed with an errant breeze. The sand went only halfway into the cavern before terminating and leaving nothing but an exposed rocky floor that, as they drew closer to the spring, became almost spongey with some kind of mineral deposits.

Krono darted forward, his paws kicking up the substrate as he dashed straight for the water, plunging in. He splashed a bit but then dropped his head to drink, his vibrissae lashing around him contentedly.

Terri lifted a hand to pull away her mask and visor, the opposite hand going up to push back her hood, dropping the visor into the pocket of her shafna. She didn't want anything to block her view.

"What is this place?" she asked, her dry throat making her voice unnaturally raspy.

Veral chuffed and wrapped an arm around her as he drew back his own coverings.

"A gift to make amends to my mate," he purred. "Only in the harshest sands of Argurumal can an oasis be found for those who know where to look." His hand tucked on her chin tipping her head back to meet his eyes. "I neglected my mate, and now I will correct it. We are completely safe and alone in a place where no one will find us... alone for an entire diurnal," he added.

Her heart leapt but she swallowed back her excitement. It seemed awfully frivolous when they were trying to hide from the council.

"But the council…"

"Will not know where to look."

"And your mother-kin, they must be…"

"They are aware of my plans," he interrupted, his low voice rumbling enticingly in her ear.

Terri squirmed against him, her breath sharpening with a lick of burning desire.

"That certainly explains a few things then. Hitani disapproved of the plan?"

"Initially," he admitted. "She could not have stopped me. I know this part of the Galithilan from my youth and recalled the way here. But she would have been displeased. Now she is not. She sees the necessity in it."

"Because I've been traumatized," Terri reminded him dryly.

"Because you require your mate," he corrected. "And there will not be much privacy where we are going. Our far-kin live in a close communal household. You will see. For now, we will enjoy our time."

Terri groaned in delight. They had spoken before of taking a small retreat—and this was as perfect as it came and exactly at the right moment. They had been working to save credits with the plan of taking a standard galactic revolution off and enjoy their first year with their offspring. The timing was…

Almost perfect.

Terri chuckled and reluctantly drew away from her mate as Harahna fussed, her little body fighting to get down from her sling. It was frightful how strong she was getting every day. The medic told her that it was normal for an Argurma baby, but it still caught her off guard.

"It seems Harahna wants to enjoy this place too," Terri remarked as she pulled her glowering baby out from the confines of the sling.

Harahna squirmed harder, wanting to be put down, but Terri

held onto her tightly as Veral hurried back to the dragnar to retrieve a large, flat bundle fastened to the rear of the seating blanket, beneath the folds of fabric. Dragging it over one shoulder, he returned with it, striding past her into the soft growth.

Terri followed him to the edge of the greenery and was delighted when he set it down near the pool. He strode about the area as if inspecting it, but then returned and began to pull out supplies. Within minutes, he had constructed a lean-to shelter beneath which he set their woven sleeping pallet and bedding. There was even a blanket for Harahna to play on that he spread out over the grass just outside the shelter.

He looked up from their assembled camp, his vibrissae tense around him with uncertainty. He gestured to her, and she began to walk toward him but stopped suddenly.

"Uh, Veral... what about predators? This is a water source. I'm sure we won't be the only things out here."

Veral chuffed, his vibrissae dancing lightly with amusement.

"No predators. The passage is too small for the larger creatures, and the smaller ones will not bother us. There are no vansik colonies on this side of the pool, and many of the dangerous insects and crawlers live farther into the trees," he said, gesturing toward the far side of the oasis, where several trees grew up against the side of the cavern.

Muttering under her breath, she went to him. As she neared, however, a smile replaced her worried frown while she looked at everything he thought to provide for their little retreat. There were sealed packages of food and drink—and even her packaged vansik that she had left unopened in their rooms. Her heart melted at the gesture. Even in their desperate flight from the compound, he had been thinking of her.

Despite the fact that it was a bit disconcerting that everyone knew they were frolicking at an oasis, Terri decided to enjoy herself. Setting Harahna on her blanket, Terri stripped off her shafna, tunic and leggings until she was just in her underthings, luxuriating in the feel of the breeze cooled by the pool of water. Reclining next to their daughter, she watched greedily as Veral removed his own shafna, armor, tunic and leggings until he was stripped down to the red sadt that covered his bulging mating pouch. She had no doubt that its slit would be parted and damp as Veral strained to contain his civix.

Terri licked her lips, eager to play with her mate even though they couldn't enjoy each other while Harahna was awake, and a grin curled her lips at his husky groan. She admired his control as he shuddered and dropped down beside her as if he hadn't struggled with himself just moments before.

The fronds of plants beside her brushed her skin. Some were thick and leathery, but there were a few fuzzy ones. The most numerous were plants with long, thin blades that sprung out in clusters. She didn't see any flowers beside their camp, but she could smell them. Perfume blanketed the entire area. They had to be hidden somewhere among the plants.

The day passed lazily. They ate from the wild fruits that grew in the oasis and played with Harahna on the soft banks of the pool. When they weren't out in the shallow water with their daughter, they reclined together on the shore, enjoy the drowsy warmth of the day. Veral had even brought Knucklebones, a game of chance, surprisingly one that appealed to Argurma.

It was the closest that Terri had ever come to experiencing a true paradise. There were no threatening predators in the oasis due to its narrow passages—and further encouraged by the dragnar's presence—and no demands on their time. The sun warmed them, but the cavern cut off the worse of the rays so they were comfortable without Terri and Harahna—who lacked enough scales to be fully protected from the brutal sun—being sunburned. For once, Terri had no fears hounding her as she drank in the simple joy of just being there with her mate.

When Harahna was finally laid down in her little nest, her tiny body half-curled against Krono's belly, Terri straightened to feel Veral's hard body aligned with hers. His breath stirred her hair, and his mandibles slipped through the strands, followed by his vibrissae. A sweet perfume filled her nose and she breathed it in as something petal-soft was drawn across her cheek. She turned her head to see a dewy, deep red flower with a thick conical center.

"Eat it, anastha," he growled lustfully. "The heart of the kari flower is the sweetest, but not as sweet as my mate's cunt. I wish you to enjoy this pleasure while I enjoy mine."

He slipped the bulbous end into her mouth as he drew her down until they were on their knees, his thighs supporting the backs of her legs. She sucked in the treat, a burst of sweet flavor coating her tongue as a moan escaped her. That moan was followed by another as her mate tilted her forward, bracing her over a thick roll of their bedding. His teeth slid across one ass cheek, a tingle of awareness following their path.

Then he was there, his mouth sucking and licking at her folds, his dual tongues teasing and plunging until she was panting, her cries muffled by the flower that leaked more of its sweetness into her mouth. He sucked on her like she sucked on her flower until her body convulsed with pleasure and a deep growl of satisfaction vibrated through her from her mate's mouth.

He rose, his lips abandoning that sensitive spot to trail back up her ass and down the slope of her back. He braced over her, his mouth planting tiny kisses on her shoulders as his hips brushed her bottom. The hot touch of his civix felt like a brand, enflaming her desire once more as it writhed, already slickened from its own secretions. It flicked once against her folds and nudged her clit, making her tremble and sigh. The feel of it whipping against her stirred her blood so she nearly cried out, if not for that damn flower, when the civix plunged deep within her.

Veral snapped his hips home, his hips against hers as his arms tightened around her. Her cries muffled, her mate recoiled and snapped forward, his twisting sex plowing and dragging through her so deliciously that she was a quivering mess beneath him as he rocked and ground them together. Unlike their usual frenzied couplings, he seemed to take his time, drawing out each touch, heightening every sensation as his civix flicked and thrashed within her, seeking for that special center where it could latch on. The swollen, hooked end bumped deep within her as it failed to gain purchase, pushing her into a renewed wave of pleasure.

In this position, she felt everything—every bump, every snaking whip within her that put sudden exquisite pleasure in her most sensitive internal places. The moment he connected, his tip lodging against the mouth of her womb, an explosion rocked through her, mounting rapidly into renewed waves of heat that climbed through her as the pressure built once more. The sensual tension made her tremble against him as he ground deep, his own grunts and growls muffled against her shoulder. But everything bloomed in white fire when Veral caught her clit between his two knuckles and squeezed with enough pressure to bring the slightest pinch of pain as he ground deep and released with a throaty roar against her flesh.

Her cry, muffled by the flower, ripped out of her, enhanced the smell of exotic blooms and the soft brush of plants around them.

As her ecstasy claimed her, she decided that she was correct… It was a true paradise indeed.

*T*heir arrival at the coordinates of his far-kin's house was just how Veral remembered it. The dragnar entered through a narrow underground canyon by following the vibrations of the groundwater that rose there. It was the same way that the beast was able to home in so perfectly on the oasis. His ancestors had discovered that ability generations ago, and it had been all but forgotten by most of the Argurma civilization.

He had the coordinates, but they would have done him little good amid the storms and red walls of sand that rolled over the surface of the Galithilan. He would have been helpless to find the entrance, even with the best flyer at his disposal. He would never have found it without Sankal's precise echolocation. Her deep croons pierced down through rock and sand until she discovered the most immediate path into the hollows of the water reservoirs.

Sliding from the beast's neck, he gave her an absent pat as he faced the weathered female staring at him, her vibrissae coiled tight against her body in careful watchfulness and her mandibles flared to further draw in his scent and that of his mate.

Keeping to tradition, he did not turn his back on her as he helped his mate down, but the moment she was at his side, he lowered his body to a crouch, touching his hands against the stone floor and the canyon. Terri moved to follow his gesture, but he shot a hand up, catching her and pushing her back upright.

This was not for females. Males had to prostrate themselves to prove they would heed the commands of the mother of the house. Even kin who had been gone far longer than what was considered acceptable.

"Veral'skahalur," the female spoke, her voice raspy with incredible age. "You are welcome, son of our house."

Veral glanced up and slowly stood to approach the elderly female who held her arms out to him. He embraced his father's mother's mother in the way of the people of the Galithilan, his hands cupping her head and his brow touching hers.

Although Veral's father, Goralth, had been among those gathered by the council in his youth, he had returned home and went through the agony of breaking his programing under his family's care. It was only by chance that he had met Harahna, Veral's mother, and left the Galithilan. Veral had been brought to his father's mother-kin during his training period after his first round of implants. He had been told that he had once played there when young with Larth, but he had no true memory of it other than a sense of coming home whenever he returned.

"It has been so long," he said aloud, echoing the feeling that rose from within him.

His far-grandmother chuffed and patted his shoulder spine, her glowing eyes brightening as they turned in delight to Terri. A wide smile stretched across her face, baring all her teeth in a smile that would shame any civilized Argurma. Veral was even uncomfortable to see it, due to all his programming and training but, on his grandmother, it was natural and right.

"I am pleased that you have brought your mate and offspring. We will have a naming ceremony for your daughter that she knows this part of her line as well, and we will feast for many days to celebrate return of our favored young."

She glanced fondly at Larth as she spoke, reminding Veral that his cousin was from the eastern holdings, though their fathers were brothers who left the Galithilan. The male smiled at the elderly female, not even bothering to restrain himself. Dreth and Malraha seemed to be the only ones uncomfortable amidst their far-kin, but that would ease as they become accustomed to the ways there. Even the dorashnal could be seen wandering with their bonded Argurmas rather than confined. Although the people held to very strict traditions, they were freer of themselves with their kin.

Veral had forgotten much of this himself. He had been away long before he even left Argurumal, and his programming had been resistant to the culture of his father's mother-kin. Although it had become a second home at times, he had never really understood it and had eventually immersed himself in his official training, which took him further and further from the Galithilan. Eventually, he left the Quarnet'safet of his mother-kin altogether and resided for a time in Ki'karthilan for the final phase of his warrior training. Returning to Galithilan, he felt like he was experiencing it viewing recorded data of a fragmented memory.

He turned away and gathered his mate under his arm to follow as Mahame directed them deeper into the canyon where the house rose, carved from the rock itself. The long stretch of the cavern in front of it was an enormous courtyard filled with dragnars, dorashnals, Argurma offspring chasing each other. Malraha and Dreth may have been close behind him with obvious desire to avoid the male and female warriors scrutinizing them, but Veral was not concerned.

They would become accustomed to it.

"This place is incredible," Terri murmured at his side as the entered the cool, dark interior.

Despite the dark stone of the corridors, the walls were rough, and rather than polished to high shine to show of the minerals in the most elegant way possible, they were brightened by woven tapestries and lights. Some of the path lights were from the market, but there were also simple candles made from the raw material extracted from the vansik colonies. With a slightly sweet fragrance, their warmth was not only from the light they sustained but also from the rich perfume that released as they heated.

"Okay, no offense, but I'm not going to lie. I kinda wish we came here first," Terri admitted in a hushed whisper.

Mahame chuffed happily ahead of them.

"You found a good mate, Veral," the elder observed. "Not many would appreciate the beauty of our halls, preferring the sterility of endless dark stone. The flatter and darker the walls, the more they like it. I have been to the Monushava House once, revolutions ago, with my daughter's son, and it was like living underground."

Veral had never seen the house from that perspective, and he wondered if that was how Terri thought of it, too. She had never showed any comfort or true admiration there as she was now. In fact, as he thought back on it, she had almost shrunk back from everything there except the courtyard gardens. Here, she was looking at everything, her expression lit up even though the corridor was still dim. He had to admit that it did not have the endless dark, sleek beauty of the Monushava House. Instead, it was comfortable. Perhaps that was the appeal.

Someone grunted skeptically behind him at Mahame's observations, clearly not of a similar mind, but he did not acknowledge the response by so much as turning around to discover its source. His kin were content to ignore it, and so Veral chose to as well, rather than give anyone an opportunity to make a complaint. The time for changing their mind had long come and gone. They were all going to be guests for the next couple of weeks while Harahna weathered her final tiani period. After that, she would no longer be too vulnerable to remove from the planet surface and his mother-kin would be able to return to their regular lives.

They arrived at a set of doors and his great grandmother squeezed a lever on the door handle and pulled it open. Electricity was limited there so it was natural that they wouldn't waste it on something like sliding doors. The rough-hewn door was heavy and formidable and, in many ways, Veral felt safer with it separating him and his immediate line from the rest of the household. It would take considerable effort for anyone to enter uninvited.

Stepping inside, he was immediately engulfed in the sweet smell of gardna blooms that grew near the groundwater springs and the spicy bark of the lanik. Someone had picked the fragrant herb and placed it throughout the room to freshen it. A happy sound escaped his mate as she sighed and drew in a deep breath. This scent pleased him, but even more so because Terri obviously enjoyed it.

Mahame paused by the door, her vibrissae swelling with pride.

"I see that these chambers are suitable. Good. The preparations for the feast have already begun, but it is not yet time for Harahna's presentation and naming. Our gazthi will let us know when she is ready. You will be retrieved then."

Veral inclined his head in respectful agreement, herding his mate deeper into the room as the door was closed behind them. At his side, Terri let out a low whistle as she looked around. She patted Harahna's back as their daughter tugged curiously at her long, yellow hair.

"They're really going to have a full ceremony for Harahna? Why does this feel like it's more than the meet-and-greet after her birth?"

"It is different," Veral agreed as he settled into a large chair, moving his foot just in time to avoid Krono's weight sprawling over it. He opened his arms for his daughter, taking her up against his chest. She was so tiny against him, fragile and dependent on them to care for and protect her—even with the symbiont. Strong emotion rose through him as it did every time he so much as looked at her or thought of her.

He suddenly understood his mother and father very well. He would not survive being separated from either his daughter or his mate. His daughter would never be processed and have her unique identity destroyed.

Pulling free of his thoughts, he continued with his explanation. "Harahna's presentation was mostly symbolic and to welcome our daughter to the house. This time, she will be presented by the gazthi, the spirit speaker of the line. She will present our offspring to the gods and spirits of the house and conduct divination to foresee her fortunes. The feast is a symbolic one that is shared with the gods of the house, recognizing the bond between the living members of the house and those they have with the gods and ancestors," he elaborated.

"You seem to know quite a bit about it," she observed.

He grunted in agreement.

"I was present for two naming ceremonies when I was a young male, still early in my training. They are strange rituals, but important ones among my kin."

His mate hummed thoughtfully.

"You respect their beliefs even though you don't share them."

"I do not know what to believe. Belief in an unseen world is illogical and self-deceiving."

"But...?" Terri prompted.

A low hiss escaped him. He hated to admit to anything that defied logic.

"But in the Galithilan, or even among the dunes of the Quarnet'safet, it is more difficult to dismiss the possibility of such

246

beings. I am not programmed to believe. My processors struggle with it," he admitted.

Terri settled on the arm of his chair, her sweet scent surrounding Veral.

"Do you want to believe?" she asked.

He paused, considering.

Did he want to?

He thought of the joy and reverence on the faces of his far-kin when they received blessings from the gazthi, or even among other species, many of them salvagers he had met who had expressed joy from their beliefs.

He would like to know what that was like. It seemed a wholly organic experience that was out of reach for a highly modified Argurma—and a secret part of him desired it. He also recoiled from it. His world was perfectly calculable as it existed now. The possibility of feeling less control and understanding regarding his world was not a thought he enjoyed.

"I have never seen or experienced a divinity," he said instead.

His mate laughed, brushing a kiss lightly against the tip of one ear.

"I don't think it works that way," she murmured.

He leaned into his mate's touch, his heart heavy with emotion that he did not understand or know how to process or express. He felt it filling him without direction. Perhaps that was part of what belief was like, too.

"I do not know," he admitted at last.

Hours later, as they sat among his far-kin, tables of food stretched out in front of the communal benches, he still did not know if he wished to experience such a thing. No one ate. All eyes were attentively fixed on the gazthi.

The last time he had witnessed the spirit ceremony, the gazthi had been ancient, her vibrissae nearly translucent with age and her scales dull and colorless. This was not the same female. Her successor was young, her expression serene as she carried Harahna to the low altar that was a permanent fixture in the room.

Laying his daughter amid a nest of blankets, she spoke in a soothing voice. It was too soft him to make out properly, but Harahna did not cry nor struggle against the female. Instead, her little glowing eyes followed her curiously as the gazthi anointed her with fragrant oils. A bowl set up on long three long iron legs stood off to the side filled with hot coals, a cloud of sweet, white smoke erupting from it when she suddenly cast a handful of powder onto them.

The gazthi inhaled deep, her voice taking on a rolling quality, one word blending into another in a stream of indecipherable chant. Her hand twitched, and she dug into her pouch with one hand as she brought the opposite one to her mouth. Biting down on her thumb, she allowed three drops to fall onto the hot coals before her nanos were able to repair the wound.

The blood sizzled on the coals, but she took no heed of it. Her eyes rolled back in her head, her strange chanting growing louder and filling the room, drawing tension from the onlookers, as she pulled out a token from her pouch and set it on Harahna's belly. Another was set at the crown of her head and another at her feet. Tokens were then placed at either side of her shoulders.

The gazthi shuddered as she leaned over his offspring, her eyes staring unseeing at the tokens. Her words were barked in a strained rasp.

"Harahna'monushava'terri spans the worlds. The gods favor her and will see her grow strong. She will see many places unseen and will grow in wisdom and cunning. The gods will this that they send their daughter out beyond us, to not return for fifty cycles around the sun. She will not know Argurma air or sand, but she will return, and her footsteps will be known across our world. This is as the gods will that she will be a powerful warrior who will rally the world that shall break and fall in her absence. She has been marked by destiny!"

The gazthi's voice snapped through the room like the crack of lightning. The deafening silence that followed was short-lived as conversation erupted from all corners. Never had a child of their line been offered such a foreseeing. Dishes clattered, the sound joining with the chatter as food was passed around. The feast had begun, but Veral's entire focus was on his daughter as the gazthi carried her over and lay her gently in his arms.

"You will raise her well, and her brothers and sisters that come after her," the gazthi whispered, her eyes glowing unusually bright even still, her voice throatier with a rough rasp like a blade drawn over a rock. "Do not fear her fate. The gods will protect your line."

The gazthi drew back, the ornaments around her neck rattling. She did not join in with the feast but disappeared through a narrow hall at the opposite end of the room. With her body still trembling from the aftermath of the ritual, he calculated that she required time of solitude. An older offspring followed her with a platter and jug so that her needs would be seen to.

At his side, his mate drew in a deep, shuddering breath. Her lips were parted, and her eyes with awe and some undefined emotion. Sensing his gaze, she turned and looked at him and gave him a nervous smile.

"Wow," she murmured with a weak laugh. "So much for a peaceful life of adventuring among the cosmos."

"We will have that life," Veral swore.

He would not let down his mate.

$\mathcal{T}$erri grinned at the Argurma female sitting across from her. They were both seated cross-legged on the floor as their babies, only a month apart in age, sprawled on the floor at their sides. Unlike most other parts of the planet, the Galithilan Houses, while slow to breed, weren't suffering from any recent reproduction issues.

Not that they would share that with the council.

They kept to themselves, hidden deep within the sands, sending out only occasional caravans with goods to their kin on the borders. Secretive, they preferred to remain as unchanged as possible. They hadn't been able to avoid the introduction of nanos, but they rejected most other things outside of tech they specifically selected that would increase the enjoyment of their lives without bringing misery.

Although reserved, the lack of "upgrades" made a noticeable difference among their population. Children were showered with affection. Males laughed and attempted to outdo each other in stories and contests or drank pulsed and fermented vansik—something she still couldn't get her mind around, as much as she enjoyed eating the little critters fried. The females drew her into their company, showing her how to do various tasks that she demonstrated interest in. Although there were plenty of female guards, Terri found herself gravitating more and more to the males and females who were weaving and making household goods. She was terrible at it, but with all the fighting that had occupied her time, she discovered that she enjoyed it.

Veral accompanied her much of the time, conversing with his cousins or with his far-kin as he lingered nearby. When he was absent, she always had guards hovering close. It had taken time, but after a few days, he reduced her guard to one so that Malraha and Dreth could alternate shifts. It allowed them to engage in other activities in their downtime and was far less stifling to her, so she approved.

She was going to miss the place when they left. The days had passed quickly as Harahna grew by leaps and bounds. At a month old, she was able to crawl around a bit before she exhausted herself and was interacting with everything she could grab and stick in her mouth. They would be leaving any day now. Veral conferred with his people on the best way they could bring the starship down to collect them. It was going to have to be a quick exit directly from the canyon to avoid sand blowing into the engines and vulnerable points of *the Wanderer*.

Dari'samah met her eyes and smiled as they worked together, weaving knotted fibers into a large rug between them.

"You will be leaving very soon. I will miss you, Terri. When your daughter returns to our world, you must come with her. We can speak of all of our offspring and return to our weaving together... and you can tell me of all your adventures," the female added with a teasing light in

her eyes.

"And will probably bore you to death with half of them," Terri snorted with a laugh. "Salvaging and doing odd jobs isn't glamorous. It's often just dirty and boring work. I'll miss you too, and will send you comms. I know they'll take time to get to you, but I will stay in touch so you're updated on all of the dull details."

Dari chuffed.

"I am sure you will find a way to make it interesting in your duty, unlike some." She grinned, her head tipping toward Malraha, who stood stiffly a short distance away with her dorashnal standing tensely at her side.

Poor animal seemed as miserable as her bonded Argurma.

"She looks like someone has asked her to hold a galgar in her mouth," she whispered, her mandibles vibrating with amusement.

Terri bit back a laugh. A galgar was a small scorpion-looking insect, but rather than possessing a venomous sting, its tail, easily twice the size of its body, sprayed a foul liquid in self-defense. The comment wasn't nice, but not incorrect since Malraha had a tight expression that Terri was starting to identify as her put-upon expression. Even the firm press of the Malraha's lips looked sour.

Knowing that the female would have been able to hear the comment with her enhanced hearing, Terri didn't want to embarrass her further. It was bad enough that the female had embarrassed herself with bitter comments and rude observations about everything. Veral's far-kin had tolerated it, but it seemed that Dari wasn't above poking at the too-serious female.

As they finished their knots, completing the rug, Dari sighed and pushed up to her feet. She shot a narrowed look at Malraha but smiled at Terri as she folded up the rug and tucked it over one forearm before scooping her son up into her arms. Although toothy, Terri decided she enjoyed the genuine smiles of the Galithilan people.

"Come, Terri. We have finished our work. Now is time for enjoyment... if your guard knows such a thing," she said.

Malraha bristled, but Terri jumped to her defense before a fight broke out.

"Things are different beyond the Galithilan, but they do enjoy games of chance and strategy as well as gardens."

Dari's brow rose in surprised as if it never occurred to her that those beyond their territory knew how to enjoy anything at all.

"Indeed," Malraha snapped. "Just because we are controlled and civilized does not mean we do not have our enjoyments. We are not as crude as the Galithilan people. Judging by the way Veral growls and moans, rutting like a beast whenever he has the opportunity to be alone with his mate, it is clear where that comes from. This entire place stinks of beasts and is unworthy to house our Ahanvala."

Terri's jaw dropped at the vehemence in the female's voice, but Dari stiffened, her eyes slitting and heating with blue fire.

"I'm sorry, Dari," Terri said quickly. "I don't know what just came over her. I'll talk to her and join you in a moment."

Dari nodded stiffly, her expression glacial as she focused intently on the guard for several heartbeats before turning to Terri. Her expression softened.

"I will be by the lower pool," Dari said. "Once you are done, she can bring you there. Do you know the way?" she asked, directing the question to Terri's guard.

Malraha predictably stiffened

"I am aware of the route," Malraha bit out. "I have the layout recorded in my processor."

The other female's lips turned in distaste, a small shudder running through her, but she nodded.

"How fortunate that you come equipped with one," Dari replied. "Having the seat of your soul opened and experimented with benefits you at least in one way, whether your soul escapes or not."

Terri bit her lip. Having discovered that the Argurma of the Galithilan believed that the head housed the soul, she was not surprised to learn they believed that those Argurmas who were processed stood a chance of losing their souls to it. It made them even warier of interacting with those they didn't personally know to still be ensouled. The dig in response to Malraha's comment was clear. If she didn't separate them soon, a fight would break out.

Malraha might have been confident of winning but Terri wasn't so sure. There was a subtle strength to the females there, even if most lacked enhancements. Those few who did were not treated any different by the brethren but nor did they lord over the unenhanced like the guard was clearly doing, whether it was conscious or not on her part.

"We'll be along soon," she assured her friend. "Go ahead of me. I'll put our supplies away while I speak with my guard."

Dari nodded and shifted her son up higher in her arms as she adjusted the weight of the rug where it lay folded over one forearm.

"I will look for your arrival," she said, leaving the weaving room and turning down a corridor.

Terri watched the female leave and sighed as she stood and began to pick up the bits of material scattered on the floor where they were working. Glancing over at Malraha from the corner of her eye, she watched as the guard stooped and picked up Harahna.

Outside of the first time, she never touched the baby if she could avoid it. Terri never took it personally since Navesha seemed disinclined to hold Harahna as well, her entire body freezing up with terror whenever asked. Malraha just had no interest at all outside of guarding them. To see her now pick her daughter up was curious. Harahna's faced pinched immediately, her eyes narrowing with extreme displeasure. It was only a matter of time before all hell broke loose.

"Thank you," Terri mumbled as she quickly took the materials to the storage area.

Malraha grunted and handed the baby over to her as she rejoined her.

"I sense your disapproval over my behavior," the female observed. "Speaking with me is unnecessary. It will not revise my opinion. These people, this place is not worthy of the Ahanvala. We belong at the compound surrounded by the strength of our line. Not here in squalor."

Terri blinked up in surprise at the snarl.

"I personally like it here," she said slowly as she fitted Harahna into her sling.

Something flickered over the female's face that might have been disdain or arrogance... Terri wasn't sure what since it happened so fast and then was gone.

"I see that," the female replied before gesturing to the corridor. "Come. I will take you to the lower pool now."

Following Malraha through the dim corridors, Terri enjoyed the various decor. A few alcoves peeked out every now and again that hosted carvings of what appeared to be ancestors or heroes, and at other times a deity or spirits with clearly supernatural characteristics added to their features. Malraha's dorashnal trotted close to the female's side, its scaled hide shuddering every now and then with unusual anxiety but never breaking from her place at the Argurma's side.

Terri frowned as the walls became rougher, tapestries and all signs of habitation disappearing. She knew that they had lower levels of storage and natural caverns below that kept the household cool, but she had no idea where they were.

"Malraha, are you sure this the right way? I don't recall the corridors going to the lower pools looking like this."

The guard shot her an unreadable glance and snorted.

"I am the one with the layout. I know the way. I may be potentially soulless according to these people, but I can store data reliably, which is beyond your capabilities... or theirs," she added darkly.

"Okay," Terri drawled, lapsing into silence.

She didn't know what had gotten into the female. If she was having a bad day, then Terri was just going to keep her mouth shut and hope whatever snit was happening got worked out.

They walked in silence long enough that she was startled with Malraha began to speak.

"There was a time not too long ago when a mating between an Ahanvala and someone of such inferior status as the people of the Galithilan would never have happened. Harahna, Veral's mother, in fact was promised to a male of the northern boundary. Did you know that?"

"Ah, no," Terri admitted, her steps slowing a little as an inexplicable unease wafted through her.

Malraha nodded her head, her vibrissae snaking around her, rattling with agitation despite her cool expression. At her side, her dorashnal whined and glanced up at her, but she kept speaking as she turned down another corridor.

From that direction, Terri could feel a cool breeze hinting at water nearby. She relaxed. This must be another route. It was creepy, but if Malraha thought it would get them there faster, she wouldn't argue.

"No. You would not. No one would speak of the mating agreement Harahna had before she met her mate. They idealize her story. The way she delayed taking the hormone and because of that found her true mate."

"It does sound romantic," Terri replied hesitantly.

The female snorted.

"It is not romantic. She had an agreement with that male. They agreed that their alliance would strengthen our territory. She dishonored and shamed him in front of his entire household. She was vile to do that!"

"But the bond just happens that way," Terri objected despite her better sense screaming at her in warning that there was something wrong with her guard.

Malraha's vibrissae flared angrily, her head whipping around.

"Wrong! There is no excuse. And because of her mating, I am here in this horrible place. I do not belong here any more than I belonged at the northern border. All of this is her fault."

A calm fell over the Argurma, and Terri watched her, uncertain of when the female's temper would flare to life once more. Their programming against emotions seemed to feed her anger once finally released, and Terri was afraid of getting in front of it, even with the protection of her symbiont.

"We are here," Malraha said suddenly as they exited from the hall into a large pool room.

Terri froze, trepidation stirring within her. There was a pool there, but it looked different than she recalled. Even more concerning, there was no sign of Dari or any of her mother-kin.

"Malraha, what's going on? Where are we?"

"The lower pool, of course," the female replied calmly. "The others are not here yet, but they will be. Come. We will sit on this rock over here by the water and wait."

"Actually," Terri said slowly. "I think I'd rather just go back."

The Argurma's eyes turned to her, their blue depths hard and chilling.

"Are you afraid, Terri?"

"No," Terri replied in what she hoped was a convincing tone. "If no one's here, I would just rather go back to Veral."

The female's lips lifted though her expression did not otherwise shift.

"Yes, your loving mate. I am afraid you cannot do that."

"Why is that?" Terri whispered as she eased back a step.

"Because your time has ceased," she growled, springing forward.

A cry of surprise escaped Terri, and she brought up her arm, but before she could unleash her symbiont, something sticky encased her entire lower arm. Her head jerked up to face her guard.

Malraha smirked at her and dropped what looked like a mini handheld cannon to the floor. Whatever it was, it had fired a projectile that burst all over her arm. The female stalked toward her. Although Terri stumbled back, she knew damn well that she couldn't outrun an Argurma hunting her. To even try would be pointless and would put her in the dangerous position of having her back to the female.

"Did you think I would not know your weakness by now, Terri?" Malraha purred with a vicious vibration of her mandibles. "I studied you because you are the key to bringing down the Monushava House. My father tried to do it when Harahna turned her back on him. He waited, drawing out his vengeance, and the moment he recorded her emotional breakdown, he sent it to the council. He was rewarded for it, but it was not enough. One case could not declare the house corrupted. Nor could the absence of her son, who turned to salvaging. They let him go because, while not uncommon, males did leave our planet to pursue careers outside our borders, bringing credits into our economy. That henaxi, Featha… she knew, however. She killed my father with her own hand but took pity on his juvenile daughter. She allowed me to live and then accepted my request for a post at her house as if she were doing me a great favor," she spat.

Lunging again, Malraha grabbed Terri by the throat, holding her in place as she leaned forward to speak quietly into her ear. Harahna squealed fearfully, her cries echoing in the room as the prick of Malraha's claws opened tiny wounds, letting blood escape down Terri's neck into her tunic. She brushed her nose against Terri's cheek, mandibles widening to better to draw in the scent of Terri's fear, and breathed in deeply.

"When Veral returned with you, I knew it was my chance. At first, I had planned just to kill you so that Veral would suffer as his mother did. It would have been fitting since my father had alerted the council as to Harahna's plan so she could not hide her son. He drove her to grief before he in turn reported her disgrace. I would have done as he did, but nothing I tried worked. Not even attempting to get him to take me as his mate so that I would take control of the house upon his seizure and termination."

"How?" Terri wheezed around the hand, her own fingers help-lessly clawing at it.

"Who do you think suggested that Navesha take you to the market? It was easy. I overheard Featha demanding that Veral treat you properly as a mate and take you with him. He looked so close to agreeing, but I could not allow that. I reminded him of his duty and your fragility. When he left to check on our transport, I suggested that she have Navesha take you with her for errands. Setting my would-be assassin in place took only one short comm. I knew that Veral would be too busy with the sudden suspicion he met with triggered by an innocent, concerned, and very anony-mous comm message, and the Navesha's presence would make her the natural choice if anyone suspected that the attack came from within the house."

Anger stiffened her face, her hand squeezing tighter. Terri just needed to keep her talking and hope that her symbiont could slowly rip its way out of the binding.

"You did not die, and I was forced to go into the market to kill the merchant just to be safe. If only I could somehow separate you and Veral. Even better if I could supplant you and earn my rightful place as the Ahanvala upon Veral's termination. He would not allow it, but it was satisfying watching your grief and sadness grow and his own struggles to contain his need to be in your presence."

"And the droid?" Terri gasped.

Malraha chuffed.

"I excelled in robotics in my training. I did not get the

advanced training that Veral and Larth and many others of our house received, but I had a particular talent with them that I gained further programming for. Because the low-level programming I received was considered inconsequential, it was not marked on my records. I chose to keep it a secret in case I needed to. I reprogrammed the droid as I pretended to set it up for sparring. I had to deflect attention away from me, but I was certain that it would destroy you."

"You were wrong," Terri choked out a laugh around the strangling grip.

The female's eyes narrowed.

"So it seems. You are harder to kill than I gave you credit for. Not even the hathals I put into your offspring's bed succeeded. I did not have time left. The registrar had arrived, and it would only be a matter of time before you left."

"You should have just let us leave. You never would have seen us again," Terri managed through gasps for air.

"That would not secure my vengeance and the vengeance of my father. The entire house supported Harahna, and you honored her by naming your offspring after her. The house needs to die with you! It is unfortunate that Veral will not receive his deserved shame, but I will be satisfied with this."

"Malraha… what have you done?"

A grin spread over the female's face, a terrible grin that displayed all her sharp teeth.

"It had to be today, Terri. For days I have attempted to catch you alone so I could properly complete my oath. Now I am out of time. Veral is preparing to leave Argurumal tomorrow. Today is my destined day of my vengeance. They are coming!" the female chuffed happily. "I sent all my data and captured vids to the council. They know you are here, and they have evidence of the house's treason against them. I will be spared as a loyal Argurma, but they will destroy this house. But for your daughter, I think I have a different plan now. I will show her the 'mercy' that was shown me."

She dropped Terri as she pulled Harahna free of her sling. Fixing a thick, sticky patch over the tiny symbiont, she carried Terri's daughter over to the dorashnal and laid her on the floor beside the animal. Her daughter hissed, her vibrissae snapping ineffectually, but the female just smirked down at her.

"The council will find her to be an interesting specimen," she remarked.

Horror welled up Terri, and she rolled onto her belly, fingers scraping against the rock as if to crawl across the floor as she desperately tried to draw air into her starving lungs. Her nanos rushed to repair her throat, but it wouldn't be soon enough.

Malraha strode over to her again and lifted her up effortlessly, carrying her toward the pool.

"There is going to be an accident, Terri. You fell in and drowned. Veral will suffer at least that much before the council kills him. That will be good enough."

Terri struggled helplessly, her legs kicking out and arms flailing. The blows made impact but did not so much as make the Argurma flinch. The female's smile widened at her effort, and Terri knew that they had arrived at the edge of the water when she stopped walking and pressed a kiss at the top of Terri's head in painful mimicry of Veral's affections.

"Goodbye, Terri."

Water surged around her as she was plunged into the dark depths and held down. She flailed in the cool liquid; tiny bubbles swirled around her as she struggled. She felt the weakening of the binding over her symbiont, but her lungs burned.

Her breath escaped her in a sudden burst of bubbles, death staring her down through the shadowy outline of the face of the Argurma holding her under and the two burning blue eyes staring down at her with hate.

32

"*V*eral, you have a guest. A strange female who claims to be of your house who demanded entry," Mahame said serenely, though he caught the faint puzzled pull of her brow. "She arrived with Anahal to vouch for her presence with us and Hitani who came with them."

Veral glanced up at his far-grandmother in confusion from where he was looking at plans on a large data screen.

"You know Anahal?"

"Yes. My friend has kept me informed of all occurrences within the Monushava House since my Goralth went to the ancestors. I have asked her for many lunars to come to us and be safe here since it became known that you broke your programming and mated with an offworlder. I am pleased to see her, although I do not know this Navesha she brings… and one Farhal, which is curious. She insists that it is an emergency."

Veral straightened and turned toward the door, perplexed. He had expected Navesha to comm him if needed. Why would she travel all the way to the Galithilan—and with a Farhal? Did she bring Vazan with her?

"Access permitted," he replied.

"I thought you would say that," Mahame said as she turned and gestured to a male standing by the doorway.

The male nodded and disappeared, returning with two familiar females walking briskly beside him. The large Farhal at her side was not Vazan. The male was bigger, easily as tall as Veral himself, with thick ropes of muscle. Whoever he was, he was armed with blasters and kept close to Navesha's side, his eyes scanning them all with the wariness of a male who had been born to battle. Navesha's face pinched with impatience as she rushed past the Argurma escorting them.

The older female smiled but drifted off to the side to join Mahame, leaving Navesha to her purpose with the male close at her side.

"Navesha," Veral greeted her curiously as he gave a polite nod to Anahal. "I expected a comm, and why do you bring an unknown male here?"

The female's vibrissae puffed out and twisted, mandibles twitching with unease for seconds before they stiffened and narrowed her eyes at him in challenge.

"Is it fine for you to mate with an alien and not for anyone else?" she snapped. "This is Gargoluk, and he is mine. We might not have any hormonal mating bond, but we chose each other. As an ex-mercenary, he adds to our house."

Veral stared at her thoughtfully and then the male. There was certainly a ruthless quality about the male's gaze that spoke of experience. Even his tusks had a razor edge to them as if they had been carefully sharpened.

"Ex-mercenary... What is that you do now?"

"I cook in the market," the male snapped. "I have no desire to be a guard, and I know my way around a kitchen and feeding people. Is that a problem?"

Veral's vibrissae twitched in amusement. "It is admirable to have a position that requires considerable patience and skill." He

263

cocked his head once more at Navesha. "That does not answer the question of your presence here."

"I tried to comm, but I could not get through."

Larth let out a raspy sigh at his side.

"That would be a satisfactory explanation. We have only just now adequately positioned the transceivers to allow communications from long-range comms. Before that, we had faint comm abilities with the eastern border, but the increase in storm activity has dampened even those until now," the male reminded him. "If she tried to comm via the eastern channels, she would have been unsuccessful."

He hissed in concern. That was a weakness he had not accounted for. No one from the house had been able to contact him for an entire span!

"Precisely," Navesha snapped. "Gorgoluk transported us up to the eastern border to request passage. I get here, and you are wasting time quizzing me on my mate!" Her eyes frantically scanned the room, widening as they landed on Dreth. "Where is Terri?" she shouted.

The frantic yell made Veral recoil, his vibrissae snapping up in a rattling menace. Bringing up his comm unit, he attempted to connect with Terri as he debated for the hundredth time suggesting that she get a small processing chip that would allow them to open a private channel.

Nothing.

Mouth tightening, he terminated the connection and turned to address his head guard.

"Larth? Locate Terri," he snarled, before lifting his comm once more. "Dreth? Report immediately!"

"Scanning for her comm signature," the male barked from his place beside the systems relay.

While they lacked basic security and much of the luxuries, there was enough of a technical relay to allow comm access. Even in the Galithilan, Argurma enjoyed the usefulness of their comm systems. It would be a matter of minutes before they would be able triangulate her position.

Tension radiated through him, something dark settling into his gut. That feeling tightened when Dreth entered the room alone, his vibrissae twitching in puzzlement.

"Veral?"

Growling, Veral stormed over to the male, grabbing a handful of his vibrissae as worry and bloodlust sang through his blood. He would kill the male if he had done anything to his mate.

"Where is my mate?" he snarled.

Dreth jerked in his grip, unmindful of the pull on his vibrissae, his eyes widening.

"Malraha volunteered to take the shift today. Terri mentioned wanting to spend time in the weaving room today," Dreth said uneasily. "I was discussing with one of your far-kin their manner of taming and training dragnar to ride in the courtyard. I will attempt to connect with her."

"Malraha?" Navesha spat as she whirled away. "We must find her. Malraha is the betrayer!"

"What?" Veral snarled, falling in behind her. "Larth, connect with me immediately on our private channel when you have the coordinates," he ordered.

The male jerked his head in hasty agreement, eyes shifting as he peered into the digital world, going through codes to search for Terri.

Veral caught up with Navesha, and she darted a sidelong look his way.

"Are you certain?" he hissed.

She dropped her head in a nod, her expression grave as they sped through the corridors. Veral moved into the lead. Although Navesha's worry spurred her forward, she did not know the layout of the compound. She gave over the lead graciously; her expression becoming increasingly worried as they turned down one hall and then another.

"I am certain of it," she growled. "I spent days going over the security feed, trying to connect the attacks on Terri. I discovered nothing suspicious until I accidentally switched to the courtyard feed the night after Terri was attacked. Someone had tampered with the vids, but they were sloppy and did not alter it completely. I discovered this on closer inspection—something we did not notice before. I am transmitting to you on the common channel."

Veral's eyes widened as an image rose in his mind. It was blurry, as if catching movement, and undefined due the alteration to the vid. Fury rose swift and brutal within him as Malraha's profile mocked him. It was followed by another cropped and magnified image of the female's hands on Harahna's bed. Nothing unusual about that except for the hathals slipping out from where she had them tucked in the flowing sleeves of her tunic. They were blurs connecting with the edges of the bed, but he had no doubt as to what he was looking at. He never would have caught the fleeting image. To have found that, Navesha would have had to have spent hours going over every millisecond of the security feed.

"She was setting me up," Navesha grumbled. "Featha had me under surveillance when you left. She was suspected I was the traitor. Malraha had roused suspicion against me. She made certain the attention was called to my absences whenever I left the compound to meet Gargoluk. She made certain that I was with Terri when she was attacked. She even cast suspicion on my fondness for collecting and raising maripala, as far as your mate would be concerned, since she saw me pick up the egg capsules."

"Maripala," Gargoluk rasped at her side, a hint of amusement in his voice.

The female huffed in annoyance. "The winged insects are attractive, and I enjoy their colors. Do not veer off subject, anastha." She shook her head grimly and continued. "With some digging into her records, I discovered that she had programming for robotic systems. That was the last clue required to link all the events to her. Every incident staged. Even then, it took some convincing for Featha to truly look at my data and believe me."

"Why?" he growled, his voice thick with emotion.

Navesha glanced at him her expression sober.

She drew in a hard breath. "I had cause to hate you. Our mother allowed herself to be consumed by her grief after you were taken for processing, and I hated you all throughout my youth for that. Not even processing could wipe the memories away and give me the nothingness it gives others. And I hated you more for that. But when you arrived with your mate and I saw your love for her, it reminded me of our mother and father, and I could not wish harm on you. No matter how angry I was with you —unreasonably so, I know—I could not harm you or your mate. In my mind, you were their legacy, and you gave me hope for my own mating," she muttered with a glance at her mate as they rounded another bend.

He shook his head in bewilderment. He had birth-kin? How had he never known? He understood how he would have forgotten; he would not have remembered her or anyone from before his processing, and afterward there had been only Anahal in his mother's stead to care for him and his programing had accepted her lead. He rarely saw Featha then or during his training. In that first revolution, he had not even known that his mother was going through corrections until she was determined a failure and terminated. He had no memory of his mother or father. It reasoned that he had none of his sister, either.

"You are my sister…"

She shot him a cool glance.

"Do not get emotional over it, Veral. We have no bonds between us. We share blood from our mother and father. I give you my loyalty and assistance because of it. It is nothing more. That I retained memories of it after my processing is unpleasant enough. I have no interest in dwelling on it further."

He inclined his head, respecting her position. It was her choice.

"As you wish. And Malraha?"

His cousin snorted at that, her vibrissae coiling tightly and snapping with agitation.

"I asked Featha that. Although in her mind I am the angry sister who might kill your mate in cold blood, she had fostered another female under her wing far deadlier in her anger. Malraha is the daughter of a male our mother had a mating agreement with. He took another mate after she joined with our father, but he bred his hate into his daughter. He reported your mother's plans to hide you, and when her grief became great, he reported her, too, in an attempt to ruin our house, and he murdered our father when his grief at his mate's death made him vulnerable."

She trembled with repressed fury.

"Featha killed him. She admitted this to me and acknowledged that she had hoped to reverse the damage her father did on the female to give her a better life. She did not realize that she had set a predator among us. We agreed that the only logical conclusion was that Malraha was replaying that same strategy against you. We tried to comm you multiple times until we decided that I would leave with Anahal as my escort."

Veral's brow rose. "She knew?"

Navesha chuffed drily.

"Featha knows most things that go on around the compound. She may have been blind in this one matter, but she is resourceful. She is the one who introduced Anahal to Mahame."

Veral grunted, slowing as he shot around a corner. It was only by correcting his trajectory that he was barely able to avoid colliding with the female standing in the corridor, clutching her offspring. He staggered to a halt, head whipping to her, and was relieved to find that she was fine other than a slight tremor among her vibrissae. He gripped her forearm to steady her, and she sent a grateful look in his direction.

"Veral!" she breathed in relief. "My apologies, I am looking for Terri. She was supposed to meet me at the lower pools, but she never appeared. I know that Malraha said she had the layout, but I am worried that…"

Her voice was drowned out by the connection coming to life in his head.

"Veral, I have her coordinates. Sending them to you now. She is below the habitation zone heading toward the lower cooling pools. I do not think that Malraha is taking her there to swim," the male growled.

His hand tightened on Dari's arm before releasing her.

"Navesha, I have the coordinates of Terri nearing the cooling pools. We must hurry."

"The cooling pools!" Dari hissed. "No, come this way. I know another way there that I discovered as a juvenile. It is rough, but it will get us there quicker than using the main halls. This way!"

The female shot off to the left, ducking through a narrow hall.

Veral did not have time to question it. He changed course to follow the female. Anything that would get him to his anastha before Malraha carried out whatever plans she had for his mate.

Dari led him through the narrow halls, cutting into an even smaller gap. It was tight, barely leaving room for his shoulder spines to pass as he raced after the limber female, moving swiftly despite her offspring tied tightly to her by a sling crossing her torso. At the very end, the crevice narrowed and he was forced to turn sideways to push through until at last he stepped out into the deep shadows of a cavernous room.

Malraha stood there in the artificial lighting set up around the room, arm upraised as she held Terri by throat, her voice taunting.

"I sent all my data and captured vids to the council. They know you are here, and they have evidence of the house's treason against them. I will be spared as a loyal Argurma, but they will destroy this house. But for your daughter, I think I have a different plan now. I will show her the 'mercy' that was shown me."

Fury roared through Veral as the female took his offspring and set her with the dorashnal before dragging Terri into the water. He was already up and moving, nearly blinded by his rage as Malraha drove his mate's body into the water and held her down. Her eyes flicked up at him in surprise, and just when it appeared that the bubbles ceased, she dragged his mate back up from the water, holding her choking, gasping body in front of her like a shield, her blaster held against his mate's head.

Everything within him stilled as he drew to a stop, tracking every move that Malraha made as she held his precious female in her grasp. The only sounds he was truly aware of was Terri's weak, watery gasps for life and the soft hum of the fans that circulated the cool air coming off the pool.

"Drop your weapons, Veral," she hissed.

He stilled only minutely, aware that she had not addressed anyone else. He did not look around, but his vibrissae vibrated as they moved around him. There was no one near him except the deranged female holding his mate hostage. The others were still hidden by the absolute darkness around the crevice, camouflaged behind a group jagged rocks that filled that part of the cavern.

"Release my mate," he growled.

The female smirked, her vibrissae coiling about her slowly with their faint vibrations.

"I do not think so. You are not giving orders anymore," she growled as she lowered her blaster away from his mate's head. "This is my vengeance. Do I kill you first and enjoy the cries of your mate grieving for you, or allow you to watch her die?"

Extending her arm, she leveled her weapon at him thought-fully, her face a mask of cold calculation. All that mattered to her was making them suffer—and so she toyed with them.

Veral gritted his teeth. If the gods he questioned were willing, he would die first to give Navesha the opportunity to save his mate.

A shot rang out from a plasma rifle, the beam neatly slicing Malraha's hand off. A shriek of pain left her as her weapon splashed into the thigh-deep water around her legs. She stumbled as another burst, this one from an Argurma assault blaster, slammed into her shoulder. Veral grinned as he strode forward, ignoring the whistling shots that came from Navesha and Gargoluk as they emerged into the clearing, taking shots to hurt and weaken.

"Hinaxi!" Navesha snarled as she took one shot after another. "Enjoy your pain!"

Approaching the injured Argurma who still, despite her injured state, held Terri tightly in her grasp, Veral was surprised when a growl of a dorashnal took him by surprise. He had forgotten the beast!

He turned as the small female rushed him, her vibrissae fanned out erratically in desperation. A lower snarl responded, making the female draw to an uneasy stop despite Malraha's screamed commands seconds before Krono careened out of the shadows and collided with her. His mouth closing around her neck, he ignored the stinging slaps of her vibrissae as he dragged her down to the ground viciously. Drawing one leg over her back, he pressed her firmly down beneath him, muscles straining with tension as he awaited command.

Veral gave Malraha a chilling smile, his lips pulling back fully from his teeth, his mandibles spread wide. There was nothing left to save her.

Her body jerked as another blast hit it, this one taking off a chunk of her vibrissae. Blood streaked down her face from the side that had lost part of her cheek bone and her ear. She was a quivering, bloody mess as she glared defiantly at him, her claws tight around Terri's throat.

"I will still win," she snarled through blood bubbling from her lips.

"No. You will die," Veral growled as he removed a blade from his side and struck deep into her gut.

Malraha gasped in pain but only for a second. Terri's tendrils ripped through whatever had confined them and drove up, forming a long spike as they punctured the Argurma's jaw. The female's head snapped back, a rattling sound escaping her.

"When you want to kill someone, bitch, kill them. Don't talk at them about it," Terri sneered.

Never had he loved his female more.

Jerking her arm down, she released her symbiont from the female's body at the same moment that Veral released his blade and they watched the body drop into the water at their feet. His arms immediately snapped around his mate as she sagged against him.

"Harahna?" she called out as she struggled to escape his embrace.

He did not let her go but turned to where their daughter was left to see the large Farhal scroop her up off the ground. He crooned to her, bouncing her gently in his scarred arms as Navesha leaned in close, holstering her weapon with a look of profound relief on her face. Glancing up, the male nodded his head solemnly.

"She is unharmed," he assured them.

"Oh, thank fuck," Terri gasped as she crumpled back against him. A shiver stole over her, but she forced herself to stand up straight with his help as she glared down at the submerged body.

"Veral, my love," she said icily. "You know those grisly trophies you always love to gift me?"

"Yes, anastha?" he purred.

"I think I want it this time." She turned and brushed her lips just over his mandibles joint making his cheek twitch. "Make it beautiful for me to have a place of honor among our little collection. I want to be able to spit on her every time I get the urge."

Veral chuffed, a thrill of pleasure running through him. He would show his mate his adoration by providing her the finest skull once the small colony of vansik that he kept encased in the engine room finished with their job. The little insects enjoyed dining on flesh just as much as his mate enjoyed their taste.

"For you, anastha," he purred as he reached down with one arm, his other clasping Terri tightly to him, and grabbed ahold of the remaining vibrissae on the female's head.

With a savage yank, the already partially severed head snapped away from her spine and came free in his hand as he straightened.

"It's not over yet," Terri cautioned, her warm brown eyes meeting his.

"Not yet," he agreed. "But soon."

---

33

*T*erri huddled close to her mate, enjoying the feel of his arms around her as he held her, like he would never let her go. They stood together in the comm station of the compound facing the image of Featha, who stared back at them solemnly.

"Are you certain?" she asked.

"Affirmative," Veral sighed. "She tapped into our transmitters here under layers of system code to get the message out to the council. Once we were aware of what she had done, it took us little time to locate the message and verify its content. They will be arriving at the Monushava compound soon."

"I see. Never have I been so painfully mistaken about a female of our line… except maybe once," she added, regret crossing her face as she looked at Navesha, who refused to meet her foster mother's eyes. "It seems we have no choice now," she said, her spine straightening as her vibrissae puffed out regally.

"We do not," Veral agreed. "The Monushava compound and the household of the eastern border must be evacuated. Hitani has already left to alert her people. Featha, please send out on the Monushava channel that this is code evac 7892. It is a mandatory evacuation. Remain at your own peril."

Featha inclined her head, her eyes closing as she sent out the message on the access channels from the compound. When she opened her eyes again, she stared back at them sadly, her eyes turning to Dreth.

"I will not ask you to come with me, but should you choose to find me, I will be in the Iliari system. Remember we visited a planet there when you were small. I think that will be an appropriate place for me to return to. Your father is en route from his trading venture to collect me within the next five minutes and is in agreement. I hope to see you there someday."

"One day," Dreth agreed.

A sigh escaped her as she looked back to Veral.

"You are ready, then?"

"*The Wanderer* is making her descent. We will be departing immediately with our mother-kin."

She inclined her head, her eyes meeting Terri's.

"It was a true pleasure and honor to see what our species has to look forward to." Her lips twisted into a grim smile. "Change can be unpleasant, but I think I understand." She straightened; her proud bearing pronounced as she inclined her head to them. "Evacuation signal is now broadcasting." Her eyes shifted, becoming more distant as she linked to what had to be numerous other channels. "Monushava mother-line, all ships have system-wide clearance for departure. Leave immediately. Initiating countdown to release of media files Harahna from the compound in twenty minutes. To all mother-kin now facing an unknown life in space—Our line shall not perish. We will be reunited again. Be well, everyone."

The comm station's viewscreen blacked out for a moment before another signal lit it up with a scrawl of confusing symbols. With a flick of his fingers, Veral accepted the coded channel.

Azan grinned at them.

"Coming in hot! Prepare for imminent evacuation. Arrival

time… well, just hold onto your asses because we will be there quick."

The transmission cut off, but Terri grinned, cuddling Harahna close. Time to go home. Leaning her cheek into her mate's chest, she walked with him at a leisurely stroll, their family behind them as they exited the compound, their supplies and one particularly nasty trophy carried by the Larth and Dreth. The whine of the ship as it careened through the canyon blasted her ears, but she laughed aloud.

The ramp extended, and the hatch door slid open, allowing the Blaithari to pop her head out. Two of her six arms waved as she beckoned them inside.

"We need to move," she shouted. "Planetary defenses are starting to come online!"

Terri swallowed back a laugh as Veral scooped her up in his arms and raced toward the ramp. Harahna giggled into her tunic, her little fists clutching the material tightly. The pound of feet on the ramp was loud as their family ascended and made their way to their flight harnesses. The scrape of claws from the dorashnals was louder as they followed them in and dug their sharp claws into the well-padded flooring of the flight deck designed for that purpose. The skinny female that had belonged to Malraha clung to Krono's side as they settled in.

Although the male tolerated her presence, Veral had been uncertain about keeping her since Krono would never bond with a female that was not bonded with Veral's mate. Terri was stubborn enough to try to win her over, however, and the renamed female Taka was now a part of the family whether the dorashnal liked it or not.

Terri was never averse to their family growing. She grinned at the sound of Navesha giggling as Gargoluk carried her by. Not just merely chuffing, Navesha giggled like Harahna did as Gargoluk grumbled about how retirement wasn't working out for him as he secured first his mate and then himself. Larth chuffed in amusement at their banter as he tightened his harness around his impressive mass, while Dreth and Tarik took their places beside him, neither of them looking too happy to seated next to the male.

Terri hadn't been able to figure out what set the males on edge about Larth. She personally found him very likable.

Veral smirked as he slid past them and strode to the two captains' chairs. Plopping Terri in one, he secured her harness and gave Harahna's symbiont a gentle tap causing it to instantly form its safety harness around Terri's body, keeping their daughter snugly in place. A smile of satisfaction crossed her face as he settled in the chair beside her that Azan hastily evacuated and began initiating the flight sequences.

Azan secured herself next to Wendy and winked at Terri as she threw one arm around the exasperated human, who punched at her bicep. A laugh burst from Terri as *The Wanderer* lifted off from the canyon floor, zipping at a dizzying speed beyond the stratosphere of Argurumal. There, they drifted for a moment as Veral began to initiate the hyperspeed drive, and all around them Terri saw starships bearing the Monushava emblem. Veral paused and watched them, something sad flickering on his face as they winked out one by one.

A warning light blinked on as the AI voice filled the flight deck.

"Planetary defenses initiating fire in ten, nine, eight, seven..."

The light of the stars around them dragged, pressure increasing in the room until, like a rubber band, everything snapped forward and the built tension released as *The Wanderer* hurled through space.

Gazing up at her mate, Terri smiled.

"Are we onto our next adventure?"

He raised a brow and chuffed down at her.

"I think a revolution of peace... a vacation, as you say."

"Perfect," Terri murmured. "I love you, anastha."

"And I you," Veral purred. "Forever."

"Quit with the lovey shit. Let's just focus on getting to my ship," Azan huffed. "I have a crew of miscreants—lost boys, each of them—who will have no doubt gotten into trouble while we have been away."

"Oh, for fuck's sake," Wendy sighed. "Azan Petera, shut the fuck up. Let's just enjoy the rest of our vacation."

Terri choked on a laugh but grabbed her mate's nearest mandible and drew his head down. His lips claimed hers eagerly, the kiss deepening as his two tongues stroked along hers. She sighed into his mouth, happiness flooding through her.

Every adventure should end with a kiss. Or so it seemed to her.

EPILOGUE

*A*zan had played it safe. It took them two months to get out to her ship. In the time since, they had dropped off Larth and Tarik, who surprisingly decided to travel together, at a nearby space station en route, and Dreth disembarked on a quiet little planet that was a little out of the way but not so far as to make Azan complain.

As much as Terri enjoyed her friend, she couldn't feel too sympathetic when she had chosen a rendezvous point that was so far off of any travel routes that it was the outer space version of "the middle of nowhere." Or that was what Veral alleged. Navesha and Gargoluk stayed with them longest, until they eventually also went their own way, boarding a mercenary vessel commanded by Gargoluk's brother to bounce around the universe before they decided where they wanted to settle down.

Veral seemed to relax more as everyone left, but she had caught a fleeting look of unhappiness when Navesha left. They had gotten closer during their time in space, and she had even smacked his shoulder spine affectionally as she left. He would deny it until every star died in the sky, but she knew that as much as he loved his freedom, he was going to feel her absence and stay in communication with her. They had made their own private channel, and so now there was no chance of them being separated again.

Despite her mate's curmudgeonly behavior toward their guests, Terri and Harahna had been enjoying all the company. Harahna especially loved the numerous arms—especially if one counted Azan—that she could be passed off to. Even Navesha had begun to warm up to the baby and was a lot less afraid of holding her, actually seeming to enjoy it every now and then. Now everyone was leaving them, and Terri could understand Harahna's bewilderment as their crew gradually shrunk.

She missed her family.

At least winning Taka's loyalty and affection had lessened the wound a little. The female clung to Terri in ways that made her believe Malraha mistreated the animal, but she was gaining weight and confidence. Just the other day, Krono mounted her for the first time... which came as a rude interruption while Veral and Terri were making love, their whines blending in with Terri's cries and Veral's growls. She had been embarrassed, but her mate had merely chuffed and told her that was the natural way of dorashnal. Krono now had his mate because Taka had bonded to Terri.

She still found it a little odd to suddenly have synchronized matings going on, but she was happy for Krono and tried to ignore it. It was just part of their family growing, even as it was shrinking.

And now they were saying goodbye to the rest of their fellow escapees from Argurumal.

The dark pirate vessel drifted with only minimal lights on. Its size made Terri think of a monster hidden in the depths of a sea. Even Wendy seemed to stare at it quietly, whereas just a short time ago she had appeared excited to return to their ship.

Azan looked down at her as she gathered their supplies, her brows rising in question.

"Ready, Wendy?"

The female sighed and nodded her head.

"Yes, let's go."

"If you aren't ready to leave, I'm sure we can circle about here for a few days," Terri offered, ignoring her mate's dark glower.

Azan shook her head.

"I got word form one of my contacts that humans have been spotted at a famous slave port. The male who runs it is an ex-pirate who styles himself as some sort of businessman now. He owns a space station called Neverland. It's supposed to be a place unlike any other. A dream place of leisure…"

"And where paying customers can have every fantasy fulfilled, including exclusive markets for pleasure slaves," Wendy added. She shuddered, her expression turning bleak. "I thought it was possible that there might have been other women kidnapped. It would have been odd if Veral and my kidnappers were the only ones to have found what's left of our species on Earth. Neverland is probably one place out of many with human captives, but we have to start somewhere."

Azan nodded; eyes narrowed thoughtfully as if trying to puzzle out the best way to take out their enemy.

Veral growled from his station, claws digging into the armrest in a telling way as he vented his anger. Despite all their faults—and there were many—Argurma did not endorse slavery, and as far as she knew, her mate abhorred it more than any other.

He slowly released the armrest and stood as he gave a formal nod to Azan.

"I will repay your favor to us. In this venture against Never-land, if you require anything at all, comm me and I will assist you." He paused. "It is my fervent hope that you do not require my aid, but your task is noble, and I will do all that I can."

Azan grinned as she nudged the male on her way past.

"Thanks, growly, but I think we have it from here. If we get into a tight spot, we will comm, rest assured."

Wendy snorted and followed Azan as she gave Terri a wink.

"Code name can be Dark Crocodile," she suggested with a playful gesture to Veral's scales.

Azan laughed and pulled the female into several of her arms as they continued to the docking bay where a shuttle from the pirate ship awaited them.

Veral's frown didn't let up until he saw the shuttle depart the vicinity of their ship with his own two eyes. A smile curved his lips as the tension rolled off his body like drops of water sliding off his scales. Eyes brightening, he turned a heated gaze to Terri.

"Now that they are gone, I have a gift to show you. And then we will mate while Harahna sleeps."

Terri chuckled as she leaned in and kissed her mate, nipping at his bottom lip.

"Depends on how much I like the gift... and whether Krono and Taka wake her up in the middle of things," she replied.

Veral sighed deeply and muttered something uncomplimentary about the level of the noise of the dorashnal as he led her through their starship into a back display room where they kept mementos. The lights flicked on as they entered and Terri stared at the Argurma skull displayed in the center of the room, gold gilding the places where the skull took damage from their fight.

Her mate's head dropped, his lips caressing her neck, making Terri shiver against him.

"Are you pleased, anastha?"

"Oh, yes," she whispered. "A true love gift from my mate: my enemy vanquished."

A low growl vibrated against her neck as he pulled her hips back so that her bottom rested against the bulge of his civix.

"And that is how it will always be," he hissed into her ear. "I will never tire of you, never cease loving you, and never will I balk from destroying any who try to harm you. You are mine, Terri."

"And thank fuck for that," she whispered as she turned in his arms and embraced him.

No matter where they went and what adventures they had, Terri knew that he would be the one constant. For the rest of their very long lives.

AUTHOR'S NOTE

Whew so we made it through Terri and Veral's Trilogy. This was my first run doing a trilogy with the same characters and, honestly, I've been terrified of messing it up. I don't tend to read running series involving the same characters, preferring books that change with each couple and the romance packaged with a neat bow in one book, so this was a unique challenge for me to come back to their story and let readers accompany them. First to see what life in space for a new human mated to an alien, and book 3 experiencing a homecoming.

In many ways this sets up for the spin off series Argurma Chronicles which will start with Kaylar's story but will include many of the characters you've seen in this trilogy. Dreth will have a book, as will Larth and Tarak.

I am also planning on doing a novella for Azan and Wendy in the near future. So there is plenty more to come despite finishing up with this hero or heroine. I may revisit Terri and Veral from time to time with a short story of one of their adventures (I still want to tell about their first assignment together as escort guards for an alien princess heh) so these little bites will hopefully give readers fun trips with them continuing in the future.

Although house Monushava is now in the stars, I hope to return to Argurumal in some future books. I had a lot of fun building the world there and loved the sand dragnars (I want one!) I sincerely hope you have enjoyed this journey with our duo and look forward to future books from the Argurma universe.

SJ Sanders

OTHER WORKS BY S.J. SANDERS

The Unicorn's Mare (coming soon)

Sci-Fi Fairytales
Red: A Dystopian World Alien Romance
Sirein

Ragoru Beginnings Romance
White: Emala's Story
Huntress

Ragoru Romance
A Mother's Night Gift

Dark Spirits
Havoc of Souls
Forest of Spirits
Desert of the Vanished (coming soon)

Dark Spirits Fairytales
The Mirror (also part of Mischief Matchmakers)
Matchsticks

Shadowed Dreams Erotica
The Lantern
Serpent of the Abyss

The Mintars
Librarian and the Beast

The Atlavans

The Darvel Exploratory Systems
Classified Planet: Turongal

Serpents of the Abyss (coming soon)
Mist World: Asylum of Graelf (currently an ongoing serial in
reader group)

Argurma Salvager
Broken Earth
Pirate's Gold
Sands of Argurumal (out now!)

ABOUT THE AUTHOR

S.J. Sanders is a writer of Science Fiction and Fantasy Romance. With a love of all things alien and monster she is fascinated with concepts of far-off worlds, as well as the lore and legends of various cultures. When not writing, she loves reading, sculpting, painting and travel (especially to exotic destinations). Although born and raised in Alaska, she currently as a resident of Florida with her family.

Readers can follow her on Facebook https://www.facebook.com/authorsjsanders

Or join her Facebook group S.J. Sanders Unusual Playhouse
https://www.facebook.com/groups/361374411254067/

Newsletter:
https://mailchi.mp/7144ec4ca0e4/sjsandersromance

Website: https://sjsandersromance.wordpress.com/

Printed in Great Britain
by Amazon